"Neither of [...] want," Bolan said

Masozi tilted his head. "What do you mean?"

"Mubarak had a weapons stash that he was parceling out to us," Bolan stated. "We want our gear."

The Shabaab leader turned to Kamau. "Does this sound like a good idea?"

"I'm just in this to get some payback. Those were my men murdered by the sneaky bastard."

Bolan realized that something bigger had just replaced his mission to destroy the Shabaab militia under Masozi. Something dark and ominous threatened more than just the shipping lanes around the Horn of Africa.

The incinerated remains of jars full of ricin seed, buried in the collapsed storeroom, were the portent of an apocalyptic threat....

Don Pendleton's Mack Bolan®

Desert Fallout

A GOLD EAGLE BOOK FROM

WORLDWIDE®

TORONTO • NEW YORK • LONDON
AMSTERDAM • PARIS • SYDNEY • HAMBURG
STOCKHOLM • ATHENS • TOKYO • MILAN
MADRID • WARSAW • BUDAPEST • AUCKLAND

Recycling programs
for this product may
not exist in your area.

First edition September 2010

ISBN-13: 978-0-373-61539-1

Special thanks and acknowledgment to
Douglas P. Wojtowicz for his contribution to this work.

DESERT FALLOUT

Printed in U.S.A.

Asclepius, why do you weep? Egypt herself will be persuaded to deeds much wickeder than these, and she will be steeped in evils far worse. A land once holy, most loving of divinity, by reason of her reverence the only land on earth where the neteru (gods) settled, she who taught holiness and fidelity will be an example of utter [un]belief.

—*Hermetica,*
Asclepius III : 25

No nation is immune to the tragedy of being fooled into wicked deeds. But it is for the sake of those who still believe in justice that I never rest. My fidelity to them will never waver, and I shall defend their faith.
—Mack Bolan

To Fe. Patience, compassion and wisdom are gifts
that grow the more you give them away.
Thank you, sir.

CHAPTER ONE

The southern coast of Somalia

This was Africa.

That phrase popped into Mack Bolan's mind as his lean, powerful frame sliced through the air over the hood of a rusty automobile, only moments ahead of the rattle of an AK-47 firing on full automatic. The fender and engine block stopped the swarm of rifle rounds looking to rend the Executioner's flesh. He wouldn't have more than a moment's respite, but he made the most of it, reloading his Beretta 93-R and closing the slide on a fresh round.

The phrase was a cynical response to the violence that stalked through the continent, a place where life was cheap, and the forces of Animal Man reigned supremely. A child, starving despite tons of food in a nearby port? This was Africa. A family chopped to pieces by machete-wielding sociopaths? This was Africa. One violent government replaced by scum just as murderous? It often happened.

Bolan didn't believe that any place in the world was more doomed than any other, that innocent people couldn't be saved from the forces of greed and misery.

The Somali gunmen who had targeted him were fast and ferocious, already flanking the automobile to get a line of fire on the big American who had infiltrated their stronghold. One of the gunmen pivoted his AK to take out Bolan, but the Beretta machine pistol snarled, ripping a line of 9 mm bullets into the man from sternum to throat. The pirate stopped as if he hit an invisible wall, and the rifleman behind him staggered wildly, tumbling as he collided with the still-standing corpse. Bolan whirled and with one smooth movement pulled a knife from its sheath on his battle harness. The wicked, double-bladed, spear-point weapon gleamed in the sunlight, the only warning that another of the Somali killers had before the six inches of merciless steel plunged through the fragile bone triangle between the eyes.

Lobotomized by the razor-sharp blade, the pirate lost his grip on the FN FAL battle rifle he carried. Bolan released the handle on his knife and caught the big gun before it could clatter on the ground.

The Somali pirates skidded to a halt, gawking now that their opponent was suddenly in possession of a full-powered automatic weapon. Bolan let the partially spent Beretta fall to the ground, his trigger finger caressing the assault rifle to life. A volley of 7.62 mm NATO thunderbolts tore into the distracted rifleman who had been stopped by a collision with his dead partner. At over 2500 feet per second, the 165-grain rounds plowed aside bone and flesh like bulldozers.

"Get back! Get back!" another rifleman shouted in warning. Bolan swung the assault rifle around and took off the gunner's head with a single bullet through the chin.

Retreating gunmen poured fire from their AKs into the car, but the fender and engine block proved sufficient to stop the much lighter 7.62 mm COMBLOC rounds that they fired. Knowing that their enemy was implacable and now much more heavily armed than he was when he'd whittled down their numbers with only a pistol, the Somali raiders retreated toward their compound.

Bolan gave them a few seconds' lead, retrieving his Beretta, his knife and a bandolier of ammunition for the FN rifle he'd acquired.

Bolan checked his Beretta for any damage from its sudden meeting with the dirt. It was in perfect working order, so he slipped it back into its shoulder holster, keeping in mind that it had a few rounds missing from its magazine. The FAL was given a reload, simply because he had the luxury of seven full boxes for the rifle. The partially spent magazine went into the empty pouch on the bandolier. Fully armed, the big American scanned for signs that one of the Somali gunmen had hung back, ready to take a shot at him.

No snipers were in evidence, and Bolan took off on the trail that the remaining compound guards had left behind them. As the only white man in the streets, Bolan knew he'd draw a lot of attention. He'd lost track of a shipment of diamonds illegally mined across the continent in Liberia. Actually, it wasn't a matter of losing the shipment. He had determined where the bloodstones were going—the port city of Kismayo to be exact. However, Bolan fell behind in pursuit of the diamonds in order to free the slaves who had been sent to hard labor by Liberian militiamen who were still sympathetic to al Qaeda, the Hizbul Shabaab. The precious gems were going to Kismayo as part of a plan to reinforce the finances for their pirates operating out of the hard-line Islamist-controlled southwestern coast of Somalia. Both the Ethiopian army and the Islamic Courts Union had tried to tame the port city, but there was still violent lawlessness.

Unfortunately, the ICU was standing by its claim of Kismayo, even after being pushed into retreat by the Ethiopians and Somalia's Transitional Federal Government, and were reluctant to act against the renegade Shabaab militia, which had worked so diligently as an impromptu special forces assisting the Islamic Courts' military units against the Ethiopians.

It didn't bode well for the country that the authorities turned a blind eye to Shabaabist activities that included kidnapping Western journalists and murdering unarmed and wounded enemy soldiers in their hospital beds.

Bolan wasn't in Kismayo to determine the legitimacy of the ICU and the Taliban-like enforcement methods of their youth wing. He was here to make sure the murderous thugs who collaborated with slavers wouldn't profit from the blood and sweat of Liberians kidnapped and abused on the other side of the continent.

So, walking in public, his general description known by the smugglers, was simply the best way to home in on the profiteers. The trail of wounded or frightened Shabaab militiamen was clear as they rushed back to their home base.

"Thank you, gentlemen," Bolan whispered softly.

He continued his pursuit, knowing that every moment he delayed, the longer the Shabaab gunmen would have to prepare against his assault.

ORIF MASOZI FROWNED as Ibrahim Mubarak patted the crate. Masozi's briefcase full of diamonds was supposed to go toward buying rocket launchers for his fellow pirates. The crate, however, didn't look as if it contained top-of-the-line Egyptian-issue 84 mm Carl Gustav recoilless rifles and the big, powerful rounds of ammunition they fired.

"What the hell is this?" Masozi asked. They shared the Arabic language, but the dialects were far enough removed from each other, and Masozi's native Arabic was flavored with Somali phrases and dialects. They were forced to converse in English.

The Egyptian smiled to his Somali trading partner. "A little something extra for the Shabaab."

Masozi's frown deepened, and he was tempted to brush his fingertips over the 9 mm MAB pistol under his untucked white shirt. "The dimensions on that crate are all wrong for military armor-piercing shells and their launchers."

"You've got your recoilless rifles," Mubarak returned. He pointed at a pair of containers.

Masozi did some quick mental math, and realized that there was only room in the two standard crates for three-quarters of the shipment he'd needed. "Son of a bitch! You shorted me on the firepower, and now you're making up for it with what?"

Mubarak pried open the crate with a crowbar. "Good stuff."

Masozi looked and saw there were two Egyptian jars. "Artifacts? Who are we going to sell secondhand Egyptian treasure to?"

"You could throw the jars away for all I care," Mubarak said. "They're only replicas."

Masozi took a deep breath, his patience starting to fade. "Give me a good reason not to open up your idiot skull, Mubarak."

"Seeds of the castor oil plant, Orif," Mubarak explained. "*Ricinus communis,* in Latin."

Masozi's eyes widened as he looked in the open-topped jar. "Ricin."

Mubarak smiled. "The plants originated on this continent, my friend. And I'm a little off in the actual botanical title of this particular strain."

Masozi raised an eyebrow. "But you can process this stuff into ricin."

Mubarak nodded. "A particularly powerful strain. Just the thing your people would need to push back against the Ethiopians and the TFG."

Masozi looked at the seeds, temptation tugging at him for a brief moment, then his frown returned.

"Weapons of mass destruction bring down some serious heat," Masozi said.

"This is Somalia. The Americans went after North Korea, and lost. North Korea developed nuclear weapons, and all those cowards could do is negotiate. They were murdered up the coast in Mogadishu, and they will never come back. The sentiment among those who would have the courage to go against the Islamic revolution here is that Africa isn't worth the effort. You don't see them landing in the Sudan, or invading Libya. They'll turn a blind eye, and you can poison all the Christians and Ethiopians you want," Mubarak said.

Masozi ran his fingers over the case full of diamonds. "Why not sell this to someone with some real backing?"

"Because Syria already has those markets filled," Mubarak replied.

"Don't try to screw with me, Ibrahim," Masozi snarled. "If your group had real, viable weapons of mass destruction, you wouldn't be fucking around with a bunch of people who can barely afford rubber rafts and recoilless rifles and ammunition."

Mubarak squeezed the skin between his eyebrows, his eyes clenched shut as he fought off a wave of frustration. "Fine, you don't want it, keep the third of the diamonds that would have gone to the missiles I didn't bring."

"Don't get testy with me. I wanted that firepower so that we could make damn sure that we could deal with the gunboats sent to escort freighters rolling past the Horn," Masozi said. "Even if we have ricin on our side, how is that going to help against a twenty- or thirty-foot craft bristling with cannon?"

"It's for whatever ground forces the TFG and Ethiopian government send after you," Mubarak replied.

Masozi looked at the seeds in the jar. "Are they safe to touch?"

Mubarak nodded. "They haven't been processed."

"And if we do process them?" Masozi asked.

"Twice the yield of standard ricin," Mubarak told him.

Masozi let the seeds sift through his fingers. "Twice the yield? Where did you get this shit? Syria?"

"Egypt," Mubarak said.

Masozi frowned. "Not a lot of arable land to plant

this stuff. Whatever there is, it's all dedicated and you can't mix it with other crops."

"They were grown in a hydroponics laboratory," Mubarak said.

"How'd you develop that?" Masozi asked.

"Are you buying it, or what?" Mubarak countered.

Masozi's frown turned into a grimace. "I—"

There was commotion at the storehouse door. Masozi sighed and went to it.

"Sir, there's an intruder in the compound," his security chief, Kamau, announced. The Somali guard was well over six feet tall, and Masozi often imagined that there had to have been the blood of giants in his background.

"How long has he been here?" Masozi asked. He pulled his French MAB-15, flicking off its safety.

"We had a group encounter with a white man out on the docks. Two had gunshot wounds, and the other four were scared witless," Kamau said. The muscles on the big African's forearms swelled as he clenched his huge fists. "They arrived about fifteen minutes ago, and we've been securing the compound."

"A white man," Masozi said with a grunt. His brow furrowed at the thought of the stranger who had hit the mining camp in Liberia. "How did they describe him?"

"They said he was big, almost tall as me. Black hair, blue eyes."

"It can't be a coincidence," Masozi replied. "That's the one I told you about."

Kamau nodded.

"What one?" Mubarak asked.

"An American agent was harassing the diamond mine we have in Liberia," Masozi explained. "More than six feet tall, approximately two hundred pounds, all lean muscle. Fights like twenty men."

Mubarak's caramel-colored features paled. "Oh, hell."

"You look as if you've seen a ghost," Masozi said.

"It's the man they call the soldier," Mubarak whispered breathlessly.

"That's a myth. A story spread to make us afraid of Americans now that they're too lazy to send their Marines and Army," Kamau replied.

"He's real," Mubarak said. "He's been active in Egypt."

"And there were rumors that this bogeyman took out another faction of pirates a little farther up the coast a while back," Masozi said. "So what?"

Mubarak looked at the crate and its two jars of seed. His hands trembled. "You said your soldiers returned fifteen minutes ago?"

"I've heard the stories," Kamau said. "The man is a ghost, and he could hide, even among black men, as one of their own."

"Why did you come to me just now?" Masozi asked.

"We found one man, his neck broken, but positioned as if he were still on guard duty," Kamau explained. "This was about two minutes ago, and he hasn't been dead longer than ten minutes."

Mubarak licked his lips and fumbled a pistol out of his belt. "Damn it, damn it, damn it."

Masozi turned to see what had panicked the Egyptian

so badly, when something metallic clattered onto the floor under a side window of the storehouse. He couldn't get a clear look at what was on the ground as Kamau picked him up as if he were a rag doll. The Somali giant carried him several feet, behind the cover of a stack of crates, instants before a fragmentation grenade detonated with a roar of doom. The Shabaab leader's ears rang in the aftermath of the detonation. Kamau shook his shoulder, mouthing words that didn't penetrate the sonic haze of aching eardrums.

Mubarak, or more precisely what was left of him, was a ragged floor mat of bloody, crushed flesh.

"We've got to move!" Masozi bellowed.

Kamau rolled his eyes at the Shabaab commander's statement, and Masozi realized that was probably what the security chief was saying. The Uzi submachine gun in the big man's fist looked as if it were a mere toy as he poked it over the top of the crates and raked the area around the window.

Masozi didn't need to hear to know that Kamau was going to cover his exit from the storehouse. Fortunately, the hand grenade hadn't damaged or detonated the crated rocket launchers, otherwise the explosion would have caused far more than temporary deafness.

Everything was going to hell.

MACK BOLAN WAS disappointed when he saw that his grenade had blown the panicky Egyptian into chopped meat. It wasn't a total disappointment, since Mubarak's face was intact and he could get the answers he needed from other sources, but it would have been easier to interrogate the Egyptian to get the lowdown on exactly

how the man had gotten his hands on jars full of seed
that could be turned into a powerful toxin. Now, he
would just have to rely on established intelligence databases to identify Mubarak and the faction of terrorists
he worked for.

Masozi would likely provide those answers, if Bolan
weren't forced to kill him. Either way, he had recorded
the men's conversation on an MP3 file thanks to the
compact PDA, and a wire-thin high-audio-definition
microphone built by Hermann "Gadgets" Schwarz of
Stony Man Farm's domestic antiterrorism squad called
Able Team. Bolan would be able to transmit the conversation back to the Farm, and the computer staff would
run through analysis on what was being said.

Bolan's efforts at delaying the compound's hard force
from finding him, leaving a trail on the far side of the
complex, had given him the opportunity to spy on the
two men and their meeting. Normally the Executioner
would have immediately begun dismantling the terrorist
headquarters, but the sight of the vehicles parked inside
the compound had tipped him off to the possibility of a
larger conspiracy. This was confirmed when he identified a trio of Arab men armed with compact machine
pistols, obviously bodyguards for a visitor from far to
the north.

The big American dropped to the floor and moved
to the ragged corpse. A few quick snapshots with his
digital camera recorded Mubarak's features for future
identification. Another moment was spared to get the
man's fingerprints on a strip of plastic-topped adhesive
that the warrior had kept in his war gear for such identification processes.

It wouldn't take long for Kamau to arrange a counterattack, sending sentries into the storehouse to clear it out. Bolan scooped up the dead Egyptian's pistol and spare magazines, adding them to his web belt. The soldier hadn't been able to bring his customary Desert Eagle with him across various borders. Its ammunition had been depleted and he couldn't get more .44 Magnum rounds to feed it here on the Horn of Africa. Mubarak had been armed with an Egyptian army–issue Beretta 92-F. The spare magazines would feed Bolan's own machine pistol easily.

He also had the FAL rifle slung across his shoulders, but after listening to Masozi and Mubarak's brief argument, he knew that he'd need something to give him equal footing with dozens of heavily armed pirates.

A solid kick snapped open the container for the stolen Carl Gustav rocket launcher. The meter-long weapon was heavy, but still remarkably handy. He took the time to stuff a variety of 84 mm shells into a bandolier provided for them, and went back to the window he'd entered through. The front of the storehouse suddenly erupted as AK-47 rounds tore through the front door and wall.

Bolan didn't bother to slither through the window. He leaped, the butt of the rocket launcher leading the way, crashing through the glass. The chatter of a dozen rifles covered the noise, and his sudden appearance stunned the two guards sent around the back. The Executioner had seen them through the window, and laden with nearly seventy pounds of extra weaponry, his weight was enough to plow through the two Somali pirates, shoving them to the ground hard enough to stun them.

Bolan jammed his elbow into the throat of one of the gunmen, collapsing his windpipe. He reached out with his other hand to sink his fingers into the nostrils and eye sockets of the other guard. With the clenching of his fist, he blinded the Somali thug as fingernails popped eyeballs and tore bloody rifts through flesh. With a powerful wrench of his arm, Bolan snapped the stunned pirate's neck using the holes in the man's face as leverage. The death shriek that issued forth was drowned out by the thumps of two grenades thrown through the doors of the storehouse.

The pirates were so frightened of the intrusion by the Executioner that they were willing to risk their delivery of antiarmor rockets by using the minibombs on the storehouse. Bolan fished out another of his hand grenades and aimed the bomb at the crate of illicit firepower. Dropping the fragger in the midst of the 84 mm ammunition, Bolan whirled and ran from the building. The hand grenade would set off the armor-smashing shells, and the explosion could bring the building crashing down atop him if he didn't gain some distance from the structure.

Thunder split the night, and the storehouse seemed to swell, heaving with a gigantic sigh. Chunks of masonry and other shrapnel flew from the front of the building, the roof collapsing under its own weight. The two bodies that Bolan had left behind the storehouse were crushed as the wall collapsed on them. The guards were already dead, but Bolan's suspicion that he would have been pulverized was proved correct. He set down the Carl Gustav and its bandolier. It was too heavy, too much to move quickly with, but he still tucked it beside a vehicle for future usage.

Bringing the FAL to bear, he spotted Kamau and Masozi barking out orders, directing traffic as Shabaab pirates and militiamen scrambled, dealing with their wounded and searching for signs of their escaped opponent. Bolan announced his presence with a rapid-fire string of single shots into the crowd, the 7.62 mm NATO rounds piercing bodies, popping internal organs like balloons and sending gunmen on the fast track to oblivion. The 20-round string collapsed thirteen of the Somali compound guards, but Bolan left the men actually tending to the wounded alone.

The Executioner often struck ruthlessly, but he was no cold-blooded murderer. As long as the men acting as medics sought to save lives, and the wounded men appeared incapable of putting up a fight, he would allow them to live. Helpless and nonhostile people weren't Bolan's enemy. There were still plenty of riled Shabaab killers to keep the warrior busy, however.

After a quick magazine change for the FAL, Bolan scurried to another position as rifles snarled in the darkness, dumping bullets toward where the blaze of muzzle-flashes had issued. Though he was only moving from one end of a pickup truck to another, the change in location gave Bolan a new angle on the enemy forces.

The Shabaab militiamen took the lull in return fire as an invitation to break from cover and stalk toward the vehicle that they'd hosed with their automatic weapons. Bolan let them get to within two yards of the Peugeot's rear bumper before he cut loose with the big Belgian rifle. The leader of the security detail stared down at the smashed crater in his chest where his heart had once been. Blood sneezed from his nostrils, soaking his shirt with even more crimson before his legs folded beneath him. The second and third gunmen didn't have time to register the death of their partner, Bolan's next rounds spearing through their skulls.

The remainder of the squad spun and retreated, so the Executioner turned his attention toward Somali riflemen who had stayed back to provide cover. He took down the two snipers after he flicked the selector switch to full-auto. Most people wouldn't have been able to handle a 7.62 mm NATO rifle at 600 rpm, but Bolan's 220 pounds of finely tuned muscle and sinew, as well as years of experience, allowed him to drill tri-bursts into the Shabaab gunners who had opened up on him.

Pivoting, Bolan turned his fire toward the enemy troopers who had halted their retreat and turned their AKs toward him. The soldier had good cover, and better aim than the Islamist fanatics, but there were enough of them, spread out, that he wouldn't be able to take them all down in one burst before they threw a wave of deadly steel-cored torment at him.

Moments later the Somalis jerked violently under gunfire from some unknown source. Bolan almost took it as a sign that a new player had entered the fight on his side.

The pickup truck Bolan crouched behind suddenly heaved as the unmistakable bulk of a .50-caliber rifle round smashed into its fender, seeking the Executioner's flesh.

The death raining down on the Shabaab pirates came for Mack Bolan, as well.

CHAPTER TWO

Bolan leaped from behind the Peugeot's fender as a second .50-caliber antimatériel round sliced through the vehicle as if it were made of paper. Had he not moved, he would have been caught in the path of the metal-crushing round and churned into froth by the passage of the irresistible bullet. He swept up his FAL, looking for the shooter who was concentrating on him, but couldn't see a thing in the darkness.

The Shabaab gunmen were in a panic as they swept their AKs in all directions, opening fire on every shadow and flicker that caught their eyes. They had gone from warring with a one-man army to being surrounded and gunned down mercilessly. Bolan could see Kamau tuck Masozi under one arm and take flight once more, just as he'd done when he threw the first grenade through the storehouse window. Bolan was tempted to cut the two men down, but he needed answers. Everything had gone wrong, and the only way to salvage the situation was to get some inside information. That meant that suddenly, Bolan was on Masozi's side.

Without a target, the Executioner was going to have to apply his razor-sharp intellect to determining where the new enemy was firing from. He couldn't use muzzle-flashes, since whoever was firing utilized suppressed weaponry. It was disconcerting that the .50-caliber antimatériel rifle was also wearing a can, dampening its dragon's-breath belch of flame down to a dull red glow that wouldn't carry far in the night. However, there was no way for the riflemen to hide the angle at which their bullets impacted the ground, or the dust kicked up when they hit. The rounds impacted the dirt at an acute angle, meaning that the elevation of the enemy gunners had been between eight and twenty feet off the ground. That ruled out warehouses neighboring the Shabaab compound, which were thirty to forty feet tall with no windows.

Bolan swung back to the Peugeot and ducked below the fender. He put his eye to the cavernous tunnel that the enemy Fifty had torn through the metal, and saw shadowy figures crouched atop one of the small barracks buildings inside the complex. The enemy was dressed in black, making them almost impossible to see if they remained still, but because the Shabaab scattered under the onslaught of stealth weaponry, they had to change positions.

Bolan popped up over the pickup's hood and triggered his FAL at the rooftop, raking the night sky. Drawing on his limited, halting Arabic, he shouted, "Over there!"

The big American pointed at the rooftop. Four Somali gunmen turned and saw what the Executioner had indicated. The young radicals hoisted their Kalashnikov rifles and opened up on the rooftop, as well.

The soldier sidestepped and sought new cover, this time behind the bed of the Peugeot. He'd moved just in time as the front of the pickup truck was clawed by a storm of automatic fire punctuated by the muffled thunderbolt of the enemy heavy antiarmor rifle. Bolan grimaced and knew that the Shabaab pirates who were aware of the mysterious marauders wouldn't last long, and any hopes of additional forces following their cue were slim because of the death toll and terror inflicted upon the Somali militiamen by both Bolan and the hidden squad of killers.

The 84 mm rocket launcher and its bandolier sat at the wheel well of a Mercedes four-wheel drive, just where he'd left them. A mad dash across open ground drew the snipers' attention, but Bolan was too swift, his own dark form flowing through the shadows, keeping ahead of the lines of bullets chasing him. He skidded to a halt, snatched up the launcher and swung behind the bulk of the jeep. Bullets hammered into the Mercedes's frame as Bolan swung open the launch tube and stuffed a black, serrated warhead into the breech. Closing the action, he now had a weapon capable of evening the odds against the hidden gunmen. Rather than aim across the hood of the Mercedes, Bolan swung around the front fender, locked onto a spot at the top of the wall and triggered the Carl Gustav. The range was a mere twenty meters, but it was enough for the warhead to arm itself, and when it struck just below the roof, the explosive impact split the building, carving out a terrible furrow. Screams resounded from the marauders' vantage point, at least two of the enemy shrieking as shrapnel reduced their limbs to bloody stumps.

The sniper fire had died out immediately, but Bolan swung back behind cover anyway. He took the lull to feed the FAL rifle another magazine, and just for good measure, he popped a fresh 84 mm warhead into the Carl Gustav. He'd come to stop the flow of illicit diamonds into Somalia, and he had been determined to give another crew of pirates a crippling blow.

The discovery of a batch of raw materials for processing a particularly toxic strain of ricin and the intrusion of a mysterious party of well-equipped and stealthy commandos had altered the mission. It didn't take much imagination for Bolan to realize that Mubarak had gone rogue, taking a secret supply of deadly biological poisons to the black market in exchange for a suitcase full of illicit diamonds. The dark-clad assassins had all the earmarks of a retrieval team.

At least, that was the hope Bolan harbored. The gunmen had opened fire so quickly on the Shabaab militiamen and Bolan, that it had to be a shock-and-awe strike.

The suppressed antiarmor rifle was the thing that gave Bolan the most consternation.

"White man!" someone called.

Bolan turned at the sound of the voice. He spotted Masozi and Kamau, crouched behind the corner of a building. They were armed, but they hadn't leveled their weapons at him.

Yet.

"What?" Bolan asked.

"Who was that shooting at us?" Masozi asked.

Bolan settled quickly into the role of lone mercenary. "Not a damn clue. I was just here to get the Egyptian back for shorting me."

Masozi's eyes narrowed.

Bolan patted the Carl Gustav launcher. "I was supposed to get six of these."

"He promised me four," Masozi answered. "You made a mess of my people."

"I just came for the cheater," Bolan said. "I may have fired on a couple of your boys in self-defense, but I nearly got flattened when they blew up half your storehouse."

Kamau glared. "That so?"

"You might have bought his story about magic beans," Bolan began.

"What's your name?" Kamau cut him off.

"Matt Cooper," Bolan replied. "You?"

"Orif Masozi," the Somali answered. "This is Kamau, my chief of security."

Bolan stepped into the open, keeping the launcher at low ready. There was the chance that there was a second squad of sharpshooters among the rooftops, but there hadn't been a shot fired in the minute that Bolan was conversing with the Shabaab. "I think it's clear."

"What the hell was that?" Kamau asked. "And never mind the name, who are you?"

Bolan didn't lie with his answer. "I'm a free agent who needs a lot of firepower. What say we grab the diamonds and get the hell out of this place."

Masozi pointed at the storehouse. "If you can sweep them up and sift them from the ashes, they're all yours."

Bolan grimaced looking at the gouts of smoke pouring out of the shattered warehouse.

"So much for that plan," Bolan grumbled. "Let's get a closer look at the guys who shot at us then."

Kamau frowned, but after a moment of consideration, he nodded in agreement. Leading he way, Uzi locked in his massive fist, he approached the half-wrecked barracks. Through the shattered wall, Bolan and his companions could see the bullet-riddled bodies of Shabaab militiamen, slumped on their cots or strewed across the floor. It was a complete slaughter, and Bolan felt better.

The kind of commandos that Bolan could consider soldiers of the same side wouldn't engage in wholesale execution of unarmed opponents. The corpses were evidence of bottomless ruthlessness that trained U.S. special operations forces wouldn't resort to. None of the Shabaab gunmen had even gotten close to a sidearm. It was one thing to end the life of an armed sentry on patrol, even after knocking him out, but shooting unarmed, half-naked, half-awake men as they lay in their berths was a sign of brutal, cold-blooded murder.

Kamau sneered as he looked at the carnage. "Bastards. What kind of coward shoots a sleeping man?"

Bolan looked at the tall Somali and held his tongue. He had to remember that the Shabaab had declared that they would execute any American sailors they encountered after the United States Navy executed several pirates who'd held a U.S. merchant captain hostage. Looking back at the littered corpses in the barracks, he remembered that these sleeping men could easily have taken another ship and gunned down unarmed crew members.

Their loss wasn't one that the Executioner would mourn, even if he would have waited until they were awake, dressed and armed to put bullets into them.

"Give me a boost to the roof," Bolan said. "I'll help you up then."

The Somali giant nodded and laced his fingers together, lifting Bolan to the top of the building. It was empty except for a couple of fallen weapons and a stripped-off load-bearing vest. Bolan reached down and gripped Kamau's massive paw. Had not the Executioner's muscles been honed by countless hours of exercise and almost daily combat, the three-hundred-pound bulk of the Somali giant would have proved a strain. Even so, Bolan was glad that Kamau dug the waffle tread of his boots into the wall to assist in getting to the roof.

"They grabbed their wounded and dead and ran," Bolan noted. "They left behind a vest and a couple of weapons, though."

Kamau pulled a flashlight from his belt, and Bolan did the same. It was to examine the evidence left behind by the mysterious marauders, but it was also to look for weakened sections of roof. Neither man relished the potential of crashing to the ground if he took a misstep.

Bolan crouched by the vest and saw that it had been sliced off. Blood soaked into the ballistic nylon of the shell showed that one of the commandos had shorn off the garment in order to reach a chest or neck injury. Kamau, on the other part of the roof, prodded an assault rifle with the tip of his machete, just in case the weapons left behind were rigged with booby traps.

"They were too busy trying to escape to leave us a surprise," Bolan said.

"Not that you're taking chances by pawing that assault vest," Kamau noted.

Bolan nodded. "Whoever it was unsnapped the pouches of spare ammunition and took them with when they bugged out."

"That's very odd," Kamau said. "No spent casings."

Bolan frowned. "They probably had brass catchers hooked up to their guns."

Kamau squinted at the circle of light as he ran it across the rifle. Bolan recognized the gun as a Steyr-AUG, an A-3 model, from the rails mounted on it. The compact bullpup allowed a full-length barrel on a short, handy rifle. The weapon was the size of a submachine gun yet had the punch of a rifle. Bolan had used the Steyr quite a few times in the past. Its plastic furniture was dull, dark slate gray, in variance with the usual olive-drab shell that the AUG was adorned with. Kamau flipped over the rifle, and in the glow of the flashlight beam, Bolan could see frayed fabric hooked to a collar around the ejection port.

"They took their brass with them," Kamau noted. "Probably will ditch it off a pier."

"Those are paranoid levels of operational security," Bolan said. He picked up the Steyr and worked the spring-loaded bolt handle. The chamber was empty. Whoever had sanitized the weapon had thought to take the round in the breech, as well as the remainder of its magazine. "We won't get fingerprints off this, nor do we have serial numbers on this thing."

"Fingerprints," Kamau noted. "You have your own crime lab or something, Cooper?"

"I've got a few friends who can look through Interpol databases for relevant information."

"How do we know you're not a policeman?" Kamau asked.

"Would a policeman drop a grenade in a suspect's lap?" Bolan countered.

"This is Somalia, Cooper. We chop off thieves' hands and hurl rocks at the heads of women who won't let their husbands have their way with them," Kamau answered. There was a hint of a sneer on the big Somali's lips, a hint of disgust at the behavior of the men who claimed to be the law. "Blowing the hell out of a man with a grenade would make you a saintly police officer, because you at least give a quick death."

"I'm as much of a cop as you are, Kamau," Bolan said. In all likelihood, the Executioner figured he hadn't told the man a lie. Bolan was no officer of the law. He wasn't some civil servant with a .44 Magnum. The Executioner was his own man, a warrior who haunted the shadows of the world, seeking out the criminals and psychopaths who haunted decent citizens of every country. Kamau, with his hint of moral indignation at the abuses of the Shabaab and the Islamic Courts Union in Kismayo, was someone who was more likely a policeman, working undercover. If he wasn't working for a government law-enforcement agency, then he was likely a lone crusader, much like Bolan himself.

Kamau looked at Bolan under a heavily hooded beetle brow, suspicion dancing in his eyes like reflected firelight. It was a moment that the Executioner had experienced many times before, facing down a man who could have been either friend or foe. Though Kamau could easily have been mistaken for a muscle-bound brute, he had a sharp awareness in his gaze. The Somali strongman buried his glimmer of curiosity and extended a hand. "You mess with Masozi, I'll tear you apart."

Bolan nodded. "I don't doubt that. The Egyptian…"

"Mubarak," Kamau interjected.

"Mubarak cheated me. I only came to show him my displeasure," Bolan said.

Kamau looked around at the spatter of blood. "You were displeased by these people?"

"Yeah," Bolan answered.

"Then let's file our complaint together," Kamau suggested, a grin forming on his lips.

Bolan nodded. That Kamau offered Mubarak's name indicated that there was a foundation of conspiratorial trust between the two men. Cop or crusader, the big man was offering a shred of cooperation.

"You two done up there?" Masozi asked.

"Cooper's rocket launcher sent the bastards packing," Kamau called down from the roof. The pair hopped off and landed on the ground, crouching deep enough to absorb the impact of their fall.

"Whoever they were, though, they were interested more in Mubarak than they were you," Bolan told Masozi.

"Perhaps," the Somali said, derision dripping from the term. "They brought a fight to my doorstep."

Bolan looked at the storehouse. "And whatever they did, they were done with this place. They could have stuck around, but since the storehouse and Mubarak's magic beans were destroyed, they bugged out."

Masozi sneered. "Mubarak was pretty convincing about the potency of those seeds."

Bolan shrugged. "Neither of us have what we wanted, and it's not like this remaining rocket launcher is going to satisfy the both of us."

Masozi tilted his head. "What do you mean?"

"Mubarak had a stash that he was parceling out to us," Bolan answered. "We want our gear."

"So we head to Egypt and grab Mubarak's weapons?" Masozi asked. "With what army? My Shabaab has been decimated. Did you find *anything* at all?"

"They left nothing. No casings, and a completely empty rifle that we won't be able to trace," Kamau told his boss. "But since they had lots of firepower, and came here after Mubarak, if we find out where the guns came from, we will not only get that for ourselves, but hit back against the scum who hurt our operation."

Masozi looked around. "We don't have a lot of resources."

"I could help," Bolan offered. "I generally operate solo, but I'm not going to be able to haul a lot of stuff by myself."

"What makes you think we'd let you take anything?" Masozi asked.

"What makes you think Mubarak's people don't have more than all of your people could carry, and then some?" Bolan asked. "We go there, we hit the mother lode."

Masozi looked to Kamau. "This sound like a good idea?"

"I'm just in this to get some payback," Kamau replied. "Those were my men murdered by these sneaky bastards. Can't hurt to get some free weapons in the trade-off."

Masozi nodded. "All right. Let's get some order back in this compound. We'll need whatever boats we can scrounge to transport the men to retrieve the guns, and to bring them back here."

Kamau and Bolan looked at each other.

Something bigger had just replaced the destruction of the Shabaab militiamen under Masozi. Something dark and ominous that threatened more than just the shipping lanes around the Horn of Africa.

The incinerated remains of jars full of ricin seed, buried in the collapsed storeroom, were the portent of an apocalyptic threat.

CHAPTER THREE

Egypt, the Sinai Peninsula, two days later

Blunt fingers clamped around Rashida Metit's upper arm as she was hauled out of the tent where the women of the archaeological expedition had been held hostage. She struggled to break free of the ham-handed grasp, but her captor slammed a handgun slide across her cheek. Metit could feel a trickle of blood dribble from the cut on her face.

When the man tugged again, she went along without further resistance. Metit recovered enough of her senses to do no more than put one foot in front of the other, and when her captor shoved her into another tent, she stumbled headfirst through the flaps, crashing to the sandy floor.

The structure she was in had become the official "rape tent." It stunk of sweat, sex, blood and vomit. Metit and all the other female archaeological students on this dig had been on this floor at least twice in the past four days, dragged there by bored and angry terrorists who had grown tired of waiting for Ibrahim Mubarak's return from Somalia.

Metit clawed at the sand and scurried a few feet deeper into the tent. Her tormentor chuckled at the sight of her desperate attempt at escape, and walked

over to the trunk. The heavy lid and combination lock
would prevent the hostages from getting to their captors'
weapons when the rapist dozed off in postcoital exhaus-
tion. He spun the dial on the lock, rolling through the
tumblers in order to open it, then dropped his AK-47
and Glock 17 into the trunk. The two simple guns and
their ammunition would prove problematic if they fell
into the hands of even a novice like the pretty twenty-
three-year-old Rashida Metit. The Glock had no thumb
safety, and was always ready to fire, while the AK-47
had been designed so that even untrained irregular militiamen from Angola to Zimbabwe could use them.

Her captor took one stride toward her, and Metit
kicked out. Barefoot, she didn't have much of a chance
of causing him harm, even if he hadn't danced lithely
out of the path of her driving foot.

"Still have some fight, eh, bitch?" the rapist asked,
chuckling as he unbuckled his belt.

"Get away from me," she growled.

His chuckle turned into a deep guffaw as he slipped
the belt out of its pant loops. He wound the leather
around one fist, the cured hide creaking as it was drawn
tight into an improvised fist weapon, the buckle hanging
across the top of his knuckles once he was done. Metit
knew what punches from that felt like. "Get undressed,
girl. It's fun time."

Metit gritted her teeth, showing no intention of following his orders. He was going to have to work for what
he wanted, and she lashed her foot out again. Only the
rapist's reflexes had protected his testicles from being
smashed, her kick instead landing on his muscular thigh.
The belt-wrapped fist came down hard on her shin and

pain seared from ankle to hip, the leg gone numb from the brutal, jarring impact.

She grabbed at the side of the tent, her splintered fingernails clawing for a handhold, and her tormentor stepped in closer to her. Her fingers ached from the days of abuse as a prisoner, the nails cracked and worn down to the quick as she and the other women had scratched at the ground in order to dig an escape tunnel from their prison tent. It was when the terrorists had discovered their efforts that the rape tent had been initiated.

The wound belt bounced off Metit's jaw, and her brain spun helplessly inside her skull. The impact hurled her against the canvas, which was taut enough to hold her hundred-and-five-pound weight without tearing. Then she crumpled to the ground.

Moments later, a rough hand squeezed her chin, holding her limply bobbing head still for a moment, and a second later, blessed unconsciousness descended upon her.

REALITY BROKE THROUGH her fever dreams of unconsciousness, and Metit managed to rise to her elbows before her stomach contracted violently. Bile coughed out between her blood-caked lips, and the acid in it burned the puckered wound on her inner cheek. Tears flowed down her cheeks as she rolled onto her side, instantly regretting the decision as she put her weight on her injured leg. Metit righted herself, lying on her back to alleviate her injuries.

Numbly, she reached down to take inventory of herself with her fingers. Her T-shirt was still intact, only having been shoved up and out of the way to bare her breasts. Her shorts and panties were gone from her hips, however. The sob she released transformed into a pained cough from a dry, blood- and bile-clotted throat and she turned her head to spit out the choking glob.

She took several deep breaths. Her leg ached badly, but gently flexing her foot and toes, she knew that no bones had been broken. It was a small mercy. Metit grimaced and saw that her shorts and underwear were still wrapped around one ankle. Stiffly, she slid her hurt leg through them, and pulled them up.

Getting dressed took on a new level of discomfort, every movement aggravating aching muscles, spearing her pain receptors mercilessly.

Her rapist was still in the tent, lying not far from her, his pants open and his genitals exposed. Metit was tempted to jam her thumbs into his closed eyes, gouging them out and blinding him for the horrors he'd inflicted on her, but as she had trouble even tugging her shorts over her hips, such aggression wasn't in the cards for now.

Something was wrong. The way the terrorist lay was unusual. Her pain and nausea had been so distracting that she had missed the fact that he wasn't breathing. A closer examination in the dim light of the rape tent showed that his throat had been slashed from ear to ear. Metit bit her lower lip and she crawled away from the corpse of her tormentor.

Emotions conflicted in her. She felt nothing but disappointment that she didn't get to see the actual execution of her rapist, but if she had been rescued, then why were there no medics around to tend to her injuries? She closed her eyes in an effort to focus on her hearing.

Even with the normal day-to-day routine of the Sinai archaeological dig disrupted by the presence of hostile riflemen, there had been sound, from chatting guards to sobbing hostages, as well as the smell of cigarettes and coffee percolating on the fire.

Silence and old, stale odors were all that answered her reaching senses. Metit's stomach turned, but there was nothing down there to come up. Filled with a bottomless well of dread, she struggled to her feet and took a tentative step to the flap of the rape tent. Peering through the slit, she couldn't see anyone, and the silence was thick and ominous. Her rapist had dragged her to the tent around noon, and she could see that the sun had dropped considerably in the sky. Since the terrorists had taken her watch, and she didn't know the exact time of sunset by memory, all she could guess was that she'd been out for at least half the afternoon.

Metit was hesitant to leave the tent alone and unarmed. She also didn't want to make a lot of racket smashing open the trunk that the hostage-taker had stashed his weapons in. The eerie silence may have sounded empty, but it all could have been a trick.

Maybe, she thought, the rapist had his throat slashed because the other terrorists thought he'd killed her, ruining the fun for the rest of the group. It was a grim, morbid thought, and she was acutely aware of the foul taste of her bile still in her mouth, as if it was punctuating the realization that she had been counted among the dead.

It would probably explain the inactivity of the camp. With one of their own having killed off a valuable hostage, there would have been enough of a panic to evacuate the dig site, moving to another area so as not to be associated with her murder. Metit rubbed her cheek, and looked at her hand, watching the dried flakes of blood and vomit tumble like dust off her skin. She didn't have a mirror available, but she could easily imagine that she appeared like death warmed over.

The belt had been discarded by her rapist, tossed casually aside after Metit had been battered into unconsciousness. She picked it up and wrapped the strap around her fist just as her rapist had. She could only get half the belt around her hand, as it was smaller than his, and the buckle dangled like the ball of a flail. Metit nodded. It was a better weapon than a glorified fist load. She weighed a little over a hundred pounds, so her punches wouldn't have the same benefit as a full-grown man's fist and body mass. However, centripetal force would amplify the strength of her swing, enabling her to cave in a cheek or gash an eyeball from a socket easily. She felt a moment of uncertainty, shocked by how swiftly she had descended into a kill-or-be-killed state of mind, determining the lethality of one form of weapon over the other.

She remembered what an anthropologist once told her. The will to survive was universal human nature, but what needed to be done to achieve that survival often seemed to go beyond what most people called civilization. Every animal engaged in brutal conflict to survive, and combat was hardwired into each and every human. Going into a murderous state of mind was natural.

Metit pushed the tent flap aside and stepped into the open, the buckle of the belt dangling heavily from the end of its leather strap. She couldn't decide if the wobbly tremors of her knees were weakness and pain from the abuse she'd suffered at the rapist's hands, or if it was from the adrenaline overdrive of fear. It helped to concentrate on walking, every movement of her battered right leg sending a spike up the length of her side as she took a step.

"Keep going," she whispered to herself. She closed the prison tent, a breeze whipping across the camp. The rush of air flipped up the unfastened opening, and she saw glimpses of shadows within, just enough to see bodies strewed across the floor. Metit froze, her heart hammering inside her ribs.

More slow, tortuous steps, a few more yards before she could hook the tent flap with her free hand and tug it aside. As she did so, the light spilled over her shoulder, illuminating the scene she'd only briefly glimpsed moments before. Hostage and terrorist alike lay in crumpled heaps on the floor, bodies twisted and mutilated by bullets. Flies buzzed around the open, sticky wounds on the corpses, crawling over faces stretched out in fear and surprise. Her best friend, Rani, had died with her eyes open, and the sight of insects walking across the white surface of her orbs would have brought up a torrent of sickness had Metit not emptied her stomach earlier.

Her knees gave out at the sight of Rani. Metit curled forward, her forearms crossed in front of her face, trying to block out the sight. Her heart felt as if it wanted to explode with the horror of the atrocity before her. Unarmed, bound women, all of them shot to death. Metit could understand if someone had just killed the thugs holding them all hostage, but there was no reason to kill a bunch of archaeology students on a field study.

Metit tried to hold in the sobs, but she didn't have the will or strength. Her body had been denied its impulse to vomit, so it took its solace elsewhere. Deep, ragged breaths were sucked in between the torrent of tears and wailing over the brutal murders. She called upon God, begged for all of this just to be a nightmare that she would awaken from. She wanted the hell she was stuck in to melt away, evaporate like spilled water on hot sands. Metit asked what she had done to warrant such torment. The rapes were survivable, even if they had left wounds on her heart and soul that would never heal. But Rani, her face spattered with the blood of another woman, her chest riddled with bullets, was something that she couldn't bear.

She looked around the tent and saw that one of the terrorists had gotten his handgun out. It had fallen from his lifeless fingers before he could pull the trigger, his existence ended with as much violence as those of Metit's friends. She reached for the pistol's butt, fingertips running along the Glock's plastic handle.

This is too much, she thought as she curled her grasp around the gun. Suicide may be a sin, but hell cannot be worse than this…

Metit tilted the muzzle up to her chin, and her thumbs felt for any levers on the weapon. She pressed a small tab she'd found, hoping it was the safety.

Rough hands suddenly grabbed her, prying the pistol out of her hands. Reflexively, Metit pulled the trigger and the 9 mm round exploded past her face, hot gases and powder burning her cheek, striking her deaf in one ear, but she was still alive.

Strong arms wrapped around her shoulders as tears

flowed, and she clawed at the man who'd grabbed her. One squeeze and her arms were pinned against her chest, between them. Metit thrashed her head, her one good leg kicking at the ground in an effort to get leverage. That's when she heard the whispered words in her good ear.

"Relax. Relax," he said in English. "You're safe now."

"Safe," she repeated. She let out an anguished shriek, and through tear-blotted eyes, she could see the tanned face of a white man, American by his accent. Cool blue eyes looked into hers, and her rage subsided.

This man wasn't like the thugs who had taken to rape when they'd gotten bored. He held her not to dominate her, but to prevent her from hurting herself, to console her. Muscles in her shoulders bunched, trying to push away from him, but slowly, she was more aware that this was a helper, not a murderer. Metit also noticed that they had moved away from the carnage of the prison tent, both of them standing in the middle of the camp.

"I know it's hard, but you're safe," he told her in a deep voice.

"Everyone's dead," she whispered.

Those blue eyes softened with empathic sadness. "I know."

Metit let herself relax, resting her head against his broad, muscular chest. "Why?"

"That is what we're here to find out," Mack Bolan told her softly. He caressed her reddish-brown hair, a gentle touch that soothed her nerves. She wanted to sleep again, but Bolan cupped her chin and looked into her eyes.

"Sit down. You look like hell," Bolan told her. "You might have a bad head injury."

"I just want to sleep," Metit replied.

"Not yet," Bolan said. He pulled a pencil flashlight from a pouch on his belt and shone it in her eyes. He looked relieved as her pupils dilated under the glare. "No concussion."

He ran his fingers through her hair, and Metit could tell that he was examining her scalp. When he reached the bruise that her rapist had inflicted on her to knock her out, she winced, shoulders trembling at the touch.

"The skin's not broken, your eyes dilate and there's no sign of blood from your ears or nose," Bolan said.

"Does that mean no concussion?" Metit asked weakly.

Bolan nodded. He gave a low whistle and called, "Kamau!"

Metit noticed Bolan's companion for the first time. He was a black African, well over six and a half feet tall, with powerful arms jutting from the sleeves of a khaki shirt that stretched tautly across a barrel of a chest. Kamau's head was shaved bald, but he wore a bushy mustache and a scruff of chin growth. The African was laden with weaponry, much as her savior was, but she still hadn't gotten a feeling of menace off either of the men.

"Not another living soul in sight," Kamau reported as he reached into his pack for a medical kit. "How's she doing?"

"She's beat to hell and back," Bolan replied, "but she doesn't have a concussion or any other signs of a skull fracture."

"Small mercies," Kamau said grimly, looking around.

"Who are you?" Metit asked as Bolan put a wet compress to her forehead. He also slipped some painkillers between her dry lips and gave her a sip from the straw attached to the hydration bladder on his backpack. The straw kept her from gulping the water, but she suckled for a minute before her thirst was sated. Her stomach was no longer empty, but water and pain pills wouldn't make her heave more. Metit's nausea had dissipated.

"Matt Cooper," Bolan answered.

"Kamau," the big African added.

"Names don't explain why you're here," Metit said.

"No, they don't," Bolan told her. "This looked like an archaeological dig. Who were the goons with the rifles?"

"Terrorists who hit us a few days ago," Metit answered. "We were looking for the hidden tomb of a fabled Egyptian sorcerer."

Kamau looked at her, then to Bolan. "That explains where Mubarak got the seeds."

Metit blinked, her brain starting to clear. "They were waiting for Mubarak to come back."

Bolan's lips drew into a tight line. "He's the reason we came here. Someone followed Mubarak to Somalia and tried to kill us."

Metit wrinkled her brow. "Are you…"

She looked at some of the murdered riflemen.

"No," Kamau said. "I'm an undercover agent. Cooper, he hasn't said. But we are here with the support of people Mubarak wanted to sell the sorcerer's seeds to."

"Undercover agent?" Metit asked.

"I'm Ethiopian," Kamau confessed. "Our country is not thrilled to have a bunch of radical fundamentalists controlling a large part of a neighboring nation."

"And I'm not thrilled to see any terrorists trading diamonds for military weapons," Bolan told her.

Metit shook her head numbly. The clarity she'd felt when she'd recognized Mubarak's name was fading. "Is it all right for me to lie down? My name, by the way, is Rashida Metit."

Bolan nodded in acknowledgment of her introduction.

"Kamau?" he said.

"I'll check the perimeter again," Kamau replied. "Whoever did this left to get into the catacombs your people were exploring. They could be on their way back any moment and they have guards at the cave entrance who could have heard you."

Metit shuddered. "I'll stay awake. And quiet."

Kamau gave her a warm, reassuring smile, then stalked toward the entrance to the catacombs that had been built into the side of a mountain.

Bolan rested a calming hand on Metit's shoulder. "I'll see what medical attention I can provide, and you fill me in on this sorcerer."

"Set Akhon," Metit explained. "He was a master of death according to the few hieroglyphic references to him in the prepyramidal tombs."

"Prepyramidal era?" Bolan asked. "It makes sense. More than a couple of ancient peoples had developed poison sprayers and chemical flame projectors around that time."

"You know your ancient history," Metit answered.

Bolan looked toward the catacombs, then to the bodies strewed around the camp and sighed. "Only because some people don't see humankind's greatest mistakes as anything other than inspiration for more madness and carnage."

The Executioner tended to the young woman's injuries. The psychotics who had wrought this destruction in the name of an ancient weapon were bound to return to camp sooner or later. Bolan needed Metit in peak health and able to fend for herself.

Then, Bolan would be free to deliver justice to a ruthless squad of murderers.

CHAPTER FOUR

Isoba Kamau thought about the twisting journey that had brought him from his youth as the child of ethnic Somali parents in Addis Ababa to the Sinai Peninsula, specifically the most recent stretch. The Ethiopian army Intelligence Division had sent Kamau undercover into Somalia, since his physical features and the Somali and Arabic taught to him by his parents enabled him to blend in, despite his great size and strength. Working his way through the ranks of infighting among the radical Islamists who had dissolved into competing factions with the defeat of the Islamic Courts Union in 2006, Kamau had risen to a position of trust under one small unit leader of the Shabaab. With his strength and fighting ability, he had proved himself to Masozi, and managed to limit his violence to rivals of the Shabaab splinter. Uncovering the pipeline of illegal Liberian diamonds that helped the young militia commander had been Kamau's goal.

That was when the American, Matt Cooper, arrived and the Shabaab splinter was hammered mercilessly. Cooper admitted that he had been behind some of the damage wrought among the renegade Islamists, but the major issue had been where the Egyptian Mubarak had gotten his hands on potential weapons of mass destruction like *ricinus* seeds. Whoever the American really

was, he had seen through Kamau's position as Shabaab
security chief.

It was probably Kamau's polylinguistic ability, as well
as the reaction to the deaths of his supposed comrades.
Cooper had a sharp eye, and had betrayed that he was
on his own mission of justice in the war-torn Somalia. Kamau was glad to finally drop the act of fanatic.
Though he was familiar with Islam as practiced by his
mother, the zero-tolerance xenophobic variety practiced
by the hordes swarming southern Somalia was a heavy
weight on Kamau's broad, powerful shoulders.

He whispered the Lord's Prayer, the Somali-Orthodox
version of it in Amharic, thanking God for the relief of
breaking away from the Shabaab on a scouting mission
to seek Mubarak's stash of deadly arms and poisons.

Masozi had whispered, before he and Cooper left for
Egypt, to keep a close eye on the American. Masozi was
paranoid and utterly bigoted. A white man was a devil
in disguise, and Cooper's guise as a mercenary only
reinforced the Shabaab leader's anxiety that he would
betray them. Kamau, being a fellow African who knelt
to Mecca five times a day, was utterly trustworthy.

Kamau smiled at the irony as he knelt behind a rock,
observing the guards at the entrance to the catacombs
of Set Akhon. The AK-47 gripped in his massive hands
felt like a toy, but anything larger would be impracti-
cal. He noticed movement at the entrance, and in the
late-afternoon sun, he was able to finally see what the
enemy looked like.

Each was dressed in a black Nomex flight suit, the
de rigueur uniform of special operations teams in the
field. The suits had multiple pockets and were made of

environmentally resistant materials that protected the
wearer from anything from fire to ice. They allowed
easy, unrestrained movement, and could be kept as warm
or cold as necessary, thanks to the use of chemical-pack
inserts. Under the jumpsuits, the men likely had on body
armor, or they had incorporated it into the load-bearing
vests that held their ammunition. The mystery killers
were packing modern, twenty-first-century weaponry.
Their black rifles were compact bullpup weapons with
rail sights. Kamau wasn't quite certain what they were,
but they bore enough resemblance to the Israeli Tavor
assault rifle that he had to wonder exactly whom the
commandos worked for.

The Tavor had been around long enough that some
models had been found on the black market, and undoubtedly, there were knockoff producers who had reverse engineered the guns to make their own versions. It
was also entirely possible that these were some form of
gun produced in Brazil or China, Kamau thought. The
"Uzi" pistol that rode on his hip was actually a Brazilian
look-alike, and the Beretta he wore in a shoulder holster
had been built in South America.

Cooper was similarly rearmed, since both men had
had to dispose of their weaponry to avoid undue attention by customs officials in Egypt. Unlike in southern
Somalia, Egyptian law enforcement was on its toes,
alert and ready for trouble at all times, being a target
of extremists who thought that the rightful, democrati-
cally elected government in Cairo didn't adhere strictly
enough to the principles of Islam.

Men had appeared at the mouth of the cave, pushing
a small cart loaded with crates. Kamau knew that the

mystery commandos had retrieved some of their deadly cargo from within the catacombs. It was likely that more of the raiders were following with their own containers. Kamau gritted his teeth, knowing that he and Cooper were outgunned as well as outnumbered.

He turned and raced on quiet feet back to the camp. The woman student was on her feet, her long, reddish-brown hair pulled out of her face in a ponytail so that a damp bandage could be wrapped around her head. She didn't look as if she could fight, but Bolan had given her a handgun in a belt holster that had been cinched around her hips.

Bolan nodded as he saw Kamau and turned to Metit. "They're on their way back here. They'll notice that you're gone, so we need to move."

Metit's eyes at least looked as if they could focus. She rested her shaky hand on the grip of her pistol. "We're going to let them get away with this?"

"No," Bolan answered. "Kamau?"

"I saw four, but four people couldn't take down this camp that fast. There's at least another squad of four," he answered.

Bolan turned to Metit. "Go with him, Rashida. I'll make certain they don't follow us."

"Alone?" Metit and Kamau asked in unison.

"I'm used to long odds, and I won't take any action until I'm certain they're moving on us, and you haven't gotten to a safe distance," Bolan replied. "Inside those parameters, I won't even have to take any action if you get moving quickly."

"You heard the man," Kamau said, gently taking Metit by the arm. "I'm just going to help you along."

Metit nodded. "I know."

Kamau shot a look to Bolan.

"She'll be fine. Move it," he ordered.

Kamau gave the American a small salute and led Metit toward a gully off to the side of the camp.

MACK BOLAN WAS no stranger to this situation, alone in the desert, unarmed and outnumbered, providing a firebreak in defense of allies. Luckily, the enemy hadn't become aware of their presence yet, but once they returned to the camp, and if they happened into the tent where Metit had lain, they'd discover that the woman they thought was dead was very much alive.

The team had been sent to ruthlessly eliminate anyone involved in the archaeological dig and who knew about the discovery that was made. Mubarak had gotten away by a couple of days, so the arrival of the enemy in Egypt meant that this may have been the same group that had struck in Kismayo, and had a better means of transportation available to them than Bolan and Kamau.

Judging by the state of the corpses strewed about the camp, Bolan calculated that the students and their kidnappers had been dead for only a couple of hours. The Executioner bit off his anger and the accompanying recriminations that had delayed his arrival. Even if he had gotten here in time, there was no indication that he and Kamau could have taken down the murderers before innocents were harmed, especially if they'd stumbled onto the situation with Mubarak's allies still holding unarmed, frightened people hostage. Two men rescuing dozens of frightened people from itchy, panicky terrorists would have been a prescription for mayhem, especially since the pair hadn't thought to bring along secure communications. It had been a risk that they had taken, the illicit arms dealer only having weapons, ammunition and desert-survival gear.

Bolan remained hidden, crouched as he watched the mystery men as they brought out five containers from the cavern that concealed Set Akhon's tomb. Thirteen men were in this group, and they were outfitted with all manner of equipment. Safety goggles and head wraps made determining their nationality difficult, and the way they handled their weapons indicated that they were well-trained professionals. With their index fingers straight and off the trigger, muzzles pointed to the ground, never sweeping their allies, they betrayed themselves as skilled warriors.

One of the group brought a hand unit with an antenna to his mouth. It was somewhat bulky, so that meant the man was in contact with someone far away. Cellular phones could be made tiny due to the fact that they were in contact with local broadcast networks. The bulk of the commando's comm unit indicated that it was high-powered, able to transmit to satellites and communicate with people as far as the other side of the planet. His use of the satellite phone also indicated that he was in a position of leadership among the fighters at the tomb's entrance. Commanders were the ones who tended to report back to whoever had financed and assigned the death squad.

Bolan knew that if he could get his hands on the mercenary's sat phone, it was likely he'd have a handle on who was running this operation. Outnumbered, however, Bolan wasn't certain that he could take the enemy by force. It would have to be by stealth. Luckily, the Executioner's combat PDA had a series of universal connectors, and generally sat phones had their own ports for communication with computers, allowing the download of encryption and important information to secure transmissions. The software and hardwire links built into the Personal Data Assistant built for Bolan by Hermann Schwarz might be able to give him an edge in finding out who the enemy was.

Bolan reined in his speculative plans on intercepting the enemy's communications. There was too much at risk with one hostage still alive, but in no condition to survive an intense fight. While the mission was important, the life of a noncombatant was too precious to endanger. There would be ways to pursue the opposition without getting hold of that sat phone. They'd be less efficient, increasing the risk that the deadly poison could be utilized before he caught up with it again, but Bolan knew that if the enemy was willing to backtrack and kill anyone aware of the ricin, they had to have had a plan that was running on its own timetable.

It was a gamble, and Bolan didn't like it, but he decided to bide his time.

To avoid combat unless absolutely necessary was the strategy he'd plotted for now.

A conspiracy whose perpetrators were paranoid enough to pounce on Mubarak as he bartered the biological toxin in Somalia might have enough contingencies to frustrate the Executioner and his cybernetic allies back at Stony Man Farm. Protective software, dense encryption and even a simple self-destruct mechanism in the sat phone could be in place to cover the plotters.

He swept the approaching commandos with his binoculars. He'd shaded the lenses with a collar of PVC pipe duct-taped in place, preventing the glasses from creating a glare of reflected sunlight. As an experienced former Army sniper-scout, it was second nature for the Executioner to disappear, even in plain sight. Stealth was more than merely camouflage, though the soldier had unfurled a desert-pattern lightweight blanket and had fashioned it into a cloak that not only blended him in with the terrain at the edge of the archaeological camp, but also shielded him from the sun's burning rays. His head scarf was in place to keep his head from getting too hot, absorbing any sweat he did give off, and to keep his jet-black hair from providing stark contrast, which would have betrayed his position.

As a sniper, Bolan had learned about human perception and how to avoid being noticed in the field. He could observe the commando team with relative impunity. Still, the big American knew that he could find himself in trouble if his own observational skills had failed him.

The leader of the group spoke to his men in Arabic, directing them to store the containers out of sight. Bolan didn't speak much of the language, and he wasn't capable of determining the dialect that they spoke, pinning down their nation of origin, but he could make out what was happening with the assistance of the commander's hand movements and phrases he did recognize. He also heard the word *helicopter* and knew that there wasn't going to be much time to spy upon this group. Depending on the tent where the commandos stored their ancient prize, it was also possible that they would discover Metit's disappearance.

Just to be certain, Bolan readied his Egyptian Beretta to buy a few more moments of time. He screwed a sound suppressor onto the pistol's threaded barrel. He would rob the hardball ammunition of some of its velocity as the silencer baffles would trap propelling gases as well as their resistance against the bullet. Fortunately, Bolan and Kamau had picked up a supply of military-grade ammunition, loaded to much higher levels than civilian rounds. Again, experience had taught the warrior that 9 mm full-metal-jacket bullets would do the job he needed them to do, if only his accuracy was dead-on.

With Bolan's lifetime of shooting experience, as well as his training and familiarity with the Beretta 92 platform, he didn't think the slightly lower velocity and lack of frangibility would hinder him from making swift, decisive kills. He slithered toward the rape tent, his senses reaching out not only for conspirators heading toward the enclosure, but for indications that the enemy had noticed his presence. Luckily, the Executioner's stealth had kept him in the shadows, just outside their awareness.

He shadowed one of the teams that had been given the task of stowing the containers that the whole group had brought with them. They rolled one toward a tent next to where they had found Metit. It was a small bit of fortune on a mission that already seemed so wrought with troubles. Bolan had only two advantages so far, one of them being Kamau, an assistant who was luckily a man of the same moral caliber as the Executioner, and who had the skills to assist him. Kamau's knowledge of Arabic dialects as well as African languages was worth the Somali's weight in gold. The other advantage was that his enemy was unaware that Bolan was pursuing them. It wouldn't last long, though. His luck couldn't hold out forever.

Bolan glanced toward the gully and saw that Kamau and Metit were long gone from sight, but he wasn't willing to risk that the gunmen couldn't track the pair even on the hard rocky ground. An added problem was that the small gash in the earth was the most blatant route that an escaping woman would take. If the mystery soldiers headed out to capture Metit, they'd know that Bolan and Kamau were present. He turned his attention back to the two men who were retrieving one more of the containers, the last one that was out in the open.

There was some brief conversation as the two men spoke with their commander. They pointed at the storage tent, then over to the one that Metit had been in. The leader nodded and waved them toward the rape tent. Bolan grimaced and circled to the front, the hammer on the Beretta drawn back to give him an effortless pull of the trigger if necessary. From his new angle, he saw only one of the men push the container on its trolley through the flaps of the tent. He left, leaving the trolley just inside the entrance, then turned back to his leader.

It was a moment of laziness, a lapse in judgment that gave Bolan's allies a reprieve. He allowed himself a brief smile when the clatter of a falling crate sounded just inside the flaps. The trolley had to have been on uneven ground, or worse, it had been shoved against the corpse of Metit's rapist, an act of happenstance that blew things for Bolan.

The flap had been pushed aside by the dolly's back. There was a moment of grumbling as the guy bent to pick it up. He stood, his head tilted at a quizzical angle. Bolan rested the Beretta's front sight on the commando's goggles. The beginning of a question escaped the soldier's lips, and Bolan applied just over three pounds of pressure. The Beretta 92 wasn't a gun that kicked much, and with the suppressor weighing down its muzzle, the recoil impulse was nonexistent. Plexiglas imploded as the 115-grain FMJ round speared through it, driving deep through facial bones. Splinters of shattered skull exploded through the soldier's brain and his head snapped back violently.

The sudden, violent death of one of their own froze two of the mercenaries in their tracks as they watched their comrade collapse to the dirt in a lifeless pile. Their confusion gave the Executioner a couple more targets while the rest of the group sprang into motion. The commandos' training and experience was readily apparent as most of them broke for cover at the first sign of violence.

Bolan took one of the stunned gunmen with a second Beretta round to the throat. The sneeze of the 9 mm's passage was discreet, but he knew that even that gentle sound would betray his position. He didn't wait to see the effects of his shot on the second of the marauders, sidestepping to the shelter of a slab of sandstone before he rose from the ground, his camouflaging cloak fluttering behind him. The burp of 5.56 mm rifles popped through the air, and Bolan slid around the other side of the flat stone he'd swung behind. In the transition from one side of the rock to the other, Bolan had holstered the sidearm and gripped the AK on its sling. Two of the Arab-speaking gunmen were visible to the Executioner from his new vantage point, firing their bullpup assault rifles in profile to him. He shouldered his AK and triggered his own autoweapon.

The first of the enemy gunners jerked violently, his skull smashed under the hammering force of 7.62 mm steel-cored slugs. A grisly, thick soup of brains and blood slashed from the remains of his head, smearing across the goggles of his compatriot. With a curse, the other rifleman wiped his bloodied lenses and spun. Bolan triggered a second triburst from the AK, this blast of autofire crashing through the man's shoulder and upper chest. The gunner's arm flopped limply at his side, but his body armor had prevented serious trauma to his torso. All that mattered was that the second gunman was temporarily out of the fight.

The Executioner scanned for fresh targets as he began a short retreat to a man-size column of stone. It was a calculated move that allowed Bolan to draw the attention of the marauders away from Kamau and Metit. The chatter of gunfire would hopefully give Metit a little more pep in her step, but Bolan was concerned that Kamau might double back and assist him. Bullets smashed clouds of pulverized stone off the column, and the big American knew he had to make certain that this engagement ended quickly. Four men were out of action, but nine trained fighters were still operating, and the torrent of gunfire that they threw at him was consistent. It wasn't panic fire, it was concentrated autofire that would pin down any lesser man.

Bolan realized that the covering fire would only

have been provided by a few of his opponents, alternating their bursts in order to keep up the pace while they reloaded. He reached under his cloak, grabbing a hand grenade hooked onto his harness. He jammed his thumb through the cotter pin's ring, then flicked the safety out of the minibomb. Once the pin was pulled, the grenade was no longer a friend to anyone on the battlefield. Bolan loosened his fingers on the fragger so that its spoon lever would pop free, beginning the countdown on its fuse. It was a process called cooking the grenade, burning off a fraction of the bomb's timer to make it less likely that the recipients could throw it away from them. With a powerful lob, Bolan sailed the grenade high over his cover.

Bolan had heard the cry of "Grenade!" in dozens of languages over his years of combat, so he knew that the enemy saw death drop from above. The concentrated autofire that held Bolan in place sputtered and died out. The subsequent detonation of several ounces of military-grade high explosives shook the ground and filled the air with thousands of pieces of notched wire and the grenade's broken steel shell.

Bolan kicked into the open and charged toward the next position he'd picked to take cover behind. To his right, an assault rifle opened up, chewing at the ground and plucking at the camo-pattern blanket that had given the Executioner his concealment. The flowing cloak no longer provided a stealth function now that the enemy was aware of his presence, but the cloth obscured Bolan's body. The enemy gunners had been trained to fire at center of mass, and the concealing cape altered that target, moving it away from Bolan's body and saving his life by a matter of inches.

With a wild dive, the Executioner returned to the column he'd previously evacuated. Bullets slammed into the ground, chasing him.

The enemy was smart and fast. The gunners didn't have a good angle on the Executioner yet, but it would only be a matter of moments before they could get him in their sights.

The doomsday numbers tumbled as Bolan looked for a way out of this trap.

CHAPTER FIVE

Bullets slammed into the stone column Bolan crouched behind. The mystery commandos surrounded the veteran warrior. Alone and outnumbered, he scanned for an angle where the enemy's rifles hadn't filled the air with blazing-hot steel-cored slugs.

During his career, the Executioner had found himself backed into many corners by overwhelming enemy forces, so much so that one part of his mind always sought escape routes from any location or situation. Countless hours of practical experience had ingrained a situational awareness that would give him the means of evasion once an emergency presented itself.

The eruption of bullets against the face of one stone showed Bolan that there was a two-foot gap, close to the ground. Thought was action for the lone soldier, and he tucked his rifle flat to his chest. In another heartbeat, his long, muscular legs propelled him into that gap, his tattered cloak flapping behind him and jerking as rifle rounds tore through its fabric. Nothing struck Bolan's back or lower limbs, and with serpentine agility and speed, he slithered along the ground and out of the path of enemy gunfire. He could hear shouts of communication among his Arabic-speaking opponents. They knew he'd moved out of the pocket they'd tried to sew him into with full-auto fire as their needle and thread.

Bolan didn't spare their consternation another thought, seeing another furrow in the earth that would allow him to run while maintaining cover. He somersaulted into the crease and got his feet beneath him. After two long strides, he felt the air shake as a hand grenade detonated behind him. His improvised camouflage cape shuddered as it absorbed a wave of shrapnel that would have been deadly had Bolan not gotten enough distance between himself and the explosion. It was an uncomfortable set of factors that spared the soldier's life for a few moments more, but he charged on, unhooking one of his own explosive eggs from his harness.

With a deft turn and a hard throw, Bolan sailed his grenade at the torso of an enemy gunman who scrambled into view. The baseball-size knot of steel and RDX crunched against the man's goggles, cracking them and knocking him onto his back. Moments later, the fuse ticked down to zero and detonated. Arms and legs were thrown into the air in a grisly display of carnage. Shreds of human tissue vomited upward in a column of debris that would rain down once gravity overcame their initial acceleration.

Bolan knew he'd taken down one more of the enemy, but given the skills of the group, he wasn't going to take that as a major victory. They were simply too good to take for granted. He skidded to a halt and dropped prone while facing the direction he'd just come from. The collapse to the dirt was swift, and his tattered blanket settled over his flat form. The crunch of racing boots sounded in the distance, and Bolan swung the barrel of his AK toward the noise. He had his weapon aimed, and one eye on the front sight, but his ears were open and his peripheral vision was peeled in order to keep from being flanked. He was still outnumbered and outgunned.

A crunch off to Bolan's left spurred him to roll onto his side, transitioning from the rifle to one of his sidearms. Aside from the AK and the Beretta, Bolan liked to have a handgun with considerable penetration and power. Normally, that was the .44 Magnum Desert Eagle, but the rapid trip to the Sinai had left him needing a locally acquired alternative. His substitute was a Smith & Wesson .45 Military and Police with a 10-shot magazine. A hooded, goggle-wearing commando head appeared where Bolan had aimed the hand cannon, and he pulled the trigger, spearing a 230-grain round-nosed slug through his pursuer's face. The goggles vaporized, along with the man's eyes, and he flopped backward out of sight.

The bellow of the polymer handgun's discharge slowed the approaching boot stomps. Unfortunately for the pair of mercenaries, their forward advance hadn't halted soon enough to save both of them. Bolan had kept his AK trained on the spot he'd expected them to appear, and now that the enemy was in sight, he held down the trigger on the Kalashnikov. A snarl of full-auto fire raked across the upper thighs and groin of one of the mystery gunmen. Heavy, steel-cored slugs shattered the rifleman's femurs and pelvis while other rounds tore through femoral arteries. The sputtering roar of the AK was a death sentence for the gunner, and he toppled into a thrashing heap.

The second of the killers managed to throw himself back toward cover. His reflexes had helped him to avoid the relentless, merciless slash of bullets that had taken down his partner. Bolan would have been tempted to go after the escaping gunman, but a hand grenade clanked on the stone furrow he was in, thrown by a third mercenary who hadn't jolted out into the open. With his own reactions honed by countless battles, the Executioner hurled himself out of the gully, rolling on the flat ground as the fragger went off. In his tumble to escape the shrapnel and shock wave, the AK was torn from his grasp.

Bolan didn't bother to retrieve the assault rifle, both hands clasping around the grip of the Smith & Wesson .45. He rolled to one knee, maintaining a low profile out in the open. Two more grenades sailed from the crack, and Bolan scrambled to the cover of a low mount of stone. Thunderous booms resounded from the double blast, jarring the soldier's ears, but the concussive energy wasn't strong enough to do more than momentarily disorient him. With practiced wisdom, Bolan lay still behind the mound, allowing the plumes of dust and smoke from the explosions to obscure his presence.

He heard the enemy conversing, wishing he had enough of a grasp of Arabic to pinpoint the style of speech. They could have been emissaries of any of a half-dozen governments, from Syria to Pakistan, and only their cold-blooded execution of hostages had dispelled any qualms Bolan would have had for gunning them down. Even if they were a "friendly" government's death squad, Egypt or Saudi Arabia, they were heartless murderers, and as such had earned the cleansing flames of his wrath.

Bolan noticed the man he'd shot in the face, sprawled on the ground not far from him. To replace his fallen rifle, he made a crablike scurry on all fours toward the fallen assault weapon. With a quick scoop, he retrieved it, a Steyr AUG A-3. He tore the pouch holder off the dead man's thigh. It felt half-empty, but it was still more ammunition than none at all. With the straps clattering on the stone, he made enough noise to draw the attention of the enemy riflemen, but by the time they focused on the sound, Bolan had reached the cover of the outcropping he'd initially hidden behind. Bullets speared into the ground where he'd been only seconds earlier.

The Executioner shouldered the rifle and tapped the trigger lightly. Unfortunately, the assault rifle he'd acquired had no selector switch; only the position of his finger on the trigger shifted the cyclic rate from semi-auto to full-auto. His tap on the trigger was to release a 5.56 mm round on a single shot. He needed to conserve ammunition, and at this close range, he was able to kill an opponent with a single shot, though he wasn't going to stick around for long. He popped a round toward a standing figure, causing him to retreat. Another pair of quick taps induced a salvo of enemy rifles to erupt, spraying the area where they had seen his muzzle-flash.

Bolan faked an agonized cry. It was a convincing ploy, and the warrior slithered along the ground. The enemy commandos had unintentionally kicked up new, thicker clouds of debris and dust that concealed Bolan as he slithered back into the gully. The sun had descended lower in the sky, and the long shadows cast by the ridge to the west had given the battleground between the Executioner and his enemy plenty of places for Bolan to conceal himself. The patches of darkness and the obfuscating clouds worked both ways, unfortunately. He needed to keep his senses sharp in order to continue his retreat.

Bolan needed some information, which meant one more retrieval. He stayed low and rushed toward where he'd seen a specific part of a grenade-blasted corpse drop. While the enemy was busy making certain that the Executioner was down for the count, Bolan decided to give himself a hand. Specifically, he grabbed up the severed forearm of the commando he'd taken out with a high-explosive blast. The tattered remnant would give him some fingerprints in order to identify at least the origins of this enemy force. He didn't need the whole limb, but for now, he'd carry it.

It was time to get back to Kamau and Metit, before the Somali giant's sense of duty brought him back to pitch in on this fight. Bolan wasn't a moment too soon as he spotted the tall, powerful form of Kamau crouched in the shadows, AK at the ready. The two men made eye contact, and Bolan hand-signaled his colleague to remain concealed. Kamau nodded.

Behind him, Bolan could hear the commandos as they conversed with one another. They had halted their advance on Bolan's former position. The clouds had dissipated, and he could see them clearly, despite his presence in the shadows providing his own concealment. It wouldn't last long.

Kamau looked anxious, but he held his ground. This was going to be a stealth extraction. Rotors thumped in the distance, indicating that the mystery commandos were about to extract. They had to make a choice between finishing off Bolan, or grabbing the weapon they had killed dozens for.

The enemy began an orderly retreat back to the camp, making their decision quickly apparent. From the shape of the helicopters in the sky, Bolan could tell that there was at least a transport as well as a smaller, more agile craft with lethal armament providing escort. The presence of the escort bird or birds would mean trouble for Bolan and Kamau if they had infrared optics on board, but it wasn't an insurmountable problem.

Bolan rushed to Kamau's side, holding his grisly prize. "Where's Metit?"

"I dropped her off in a cave fifty yards that way," Kamau said. "Those helicopters convinced me that I made the right choice."

"Is it big enough for the three of us?" Bolan asked.

"And then some," Kamau answered.

"Then let's get out of sight of any eyes in the sky," Bolan offered.

The two men didn't have to debate it further. Already, both Bolan and Kamau could see the dark, bug-like forms of the enemy helicopters in the distance. The Executioner had been tempted to pull out his binoculars to get a better glimpse of the three aircraft, but to do so would be to court death. Even without advanced optics, the helicopters would be able to see him once they advanced, getting closer to the two men on the ground. Right now, their only saving grace was that they were out of naked eyesight range and in the shadows of the swift-flying specks in the sky.

What he did see, however, was disheartening. There was one transport helicopter and two smaller escorts.

The smaller craft were undoubtedly armed or packing more commandos to replace the several that Bolan had eliminated. If they were of the same caliber as the ones the Executioner had battled, then there was no doubt that he would be pushed harder, especially with eyes in the sky assisting in tracking down the warrior and those he'd sworn to protect.

The difficulty of dealing with enemy aircraft was just too much to surmount with the firepower and numbers he had on his side. Right now, all he could do was hide, and hope that he could catch up with the opposition later. He had the hand and the fingerprints, which hopefully would give him an indication of who the enemy was.

Bolan and Kamau scurried into the cave, Metit watching them wide-eyed in shock as the two were in full retreat. She bit her upper lip and looked at Bolan.

"I hear helicopters," she whispered.

"We're staying out of sight," Bolan said. "It doesn't look as if we've got to worry about too much trouble sticking around."

"The gunfight?" Metit asked.

"It was touch-and-go for a while. I did enough to convince them to evacuate as soon as possible," Bolan explained.

Outside, the unmistakable thunder of a heavy machine-gun salvo slashed down from the sky. A storm of lead tore at the ground, eventually a line of bullets clawing up the ground in front of their cave. Bolan and Kamau shielded Metit from the flying debris kicked up by the bursts of heavy slugs striking the earth. Bolan gritted his teeth as rocks and pebbles bounced off his back, pelting him relentlessly. Kamau grimaced as the leaden rain ceased. "Fifties."

"Something in that range," Bolan agreed. He looked at the roof of the cave, and gave a silent thank-you to the cliff that had shielded them. "If they swing around and go on a second strafing run, we don't have enough cave to get out of its way."

Metit's lips had drawn tight into a bloodless line. She was getting close to the breaking point. This was going to be too much for the young woman, so close on the heels of her torturous captivity and the murders of so many of her friends. Bolan reached out and squeezed her hand, giving her an emotional anchor. Her smoldering, beautiful eyes glinted in the shadows of the cave, and he nodded to her. He'd shield her against the nightmares swarming outside on the plateau.

He allowed the young woman to bury her face in the crook of his neck, his strong, muscular arm wrapped around her shoulders like a cape, providing warmth and comfort against the maelstrom of horror that plucked at her nerves. The rumbling thud of helicopter rotors made the shadows vibrate, and he could feel Metit whimper.

Though it was just an arm, muscle stretched tautly over bone, sheathed in tough, rip-proof nylon, Bolan's embrace was a spiritual fortress for Metit. The shudder of her sobs had disappeared, and even the clawlike grasp she had dug into Bolan's sides had loosened.

It was several long, nerve-racking minutes that finally faded with the retreat of the helicopters' rotors.

Kamau looked toward Bolan. "Stay with her. I'll take a look outside."

Bolan made a face at the suggestion, but the big Ethiopian held up his hand. "She's practically glued to you, Cooper. I'll be careful."

"All right," Bolan replied. His jaw set as he waited. Metit finally pried her face from where she'd buried it against his chest.

"You can go if you want to," she whispered.

Bolan shook his head. "Too many scouts can betray our presence here. I'll let Kamau do his recon."

"I'm sorry," Metit offered.

"For what?" Bolan asked. "You did fine."

"I'm a wreck," she explained.

"You're human," Bolan told her, cupping her chin gently. "It's normal to be scared, especially with all of that racket going on."

Metit's teary eyes glistened as she looked at Bolan.

Kamau returned, kneeling at the mouth of the cave. "The helicopters are gone, but they shot up our wheels."

Bolan sighed. "How badly?"

"They saw through the little bit of concealment we tossed over the vehicle," Kamau explained. "We'll have to hike it, because I'm sure they didn't leave any of the archaeological crew's vehicles in any condition to use."

"I'll double-check," Bolan said. "Look for supplies just in case we do have to go. We leave as soon as the sun sets, regardless of how we have to leave."

"One more thing, Cooper. While the one helicopter was hosing down the area around our cave, the other one fired rockets into the opening of the tomb that Metit's people had discovered," Kamau added.

"Totally caved in?" Bolan asked.

"There's no way the two of us could dig into there to see what's left," Kamau replied.

Bolan frowned. "Meanwhile, if they did need more of their ricin, they could bring in digging equipment by helicopter."

"And enough men to make the job worthwhile," Kamau said. "That is if they'd left anything behind."

"It's unlikely they could have taken all that'd been stored in there," Bolan replied.

"Very," Metit spoke up, her voice brittle. "We found an entire cavern lined with pots like the ones they removed, loaded with an unusual-looking form of castor bean. We had only just begun to catalog the contents when the terrorists attacked. Ricin?"

"Yes," Bolan answered.

"That's a deadly poison, isn't it?" Metit asked numbly.

"It can be, but it takes a lot of processing," Bolan explained. "Even the best military minds of the twentieth century couldn't weaponize it."

Metit's brow wrinkled. "The ancient Egyptians had over a thousand years to think of something. And there are indications that they did use poisons as defenses of their tombs."

"That kind of chemistry would have been lost to antiquity," Kamau interjected.

"Maybe," Bolan said, cutting off the conversation. "Kamau, we don't have time to talk now. We'll discuss this later."

Kamau noted that the American's attention was focused on the sky where the helicopters had originally approached from. The implication of his urgency was unmistakable. As soon as the transport helicopter had returned to base with its precious payload, the escort craft would race back to the camp and scour the desert in order to hunt down the lone stranger who had somehow stumbled onto their operation.

Three humans, hiking in the desert at night, would be like beacons to eyes in the sky equipped with night-vision goggles. That, plus the firepower mounted on the small, swift gunships, would outmatch even a warrior of Bolan's skill.

Kamau realized that he'd have to work quickly in gathering gear while Cooper sought to salvage whatever transportation that they could find. Flight across the desert would have to be taken as fast as conceivably possible.

"Rashida, what kind of transportation did you have?" Bolan asked her.

"We had two large military surplus trucks to haul gear out here and whatever we found back to the university," she answered. "The rest of us traveled by SUV."

"All one style?" Bolan asked as Kamau busied himself searching through the camp for leftover water. Hydration was just as important as speed of escape. In the desert, especially with the kind of stress Metit had endured, the human body couldn't maintain its performance without a fresh drink every few hours. Food wouldn't be an issue for over a week, and Bolan and Kamau didn't intend to take that long to get back to Alexandria.

While Kamau filled canteens for the upcoming journey, Bolan had Metit lead him toward the SUVs and the truck. The vehicles had been stored at the bottom of a cliff, but the stench of burning fuel and metal assaulted Bolan's nostrils. The commandos had crippled the vehicles at the back of the canyon, saving their ammunition. A two-and-a-half-ton truck blocked most of the passage, nearly impossible to squeeze past. The other vehicles were in running condition, but nearly three tons of slag formed an impassable dam for them to pass. Bolan sighed and looked through the pouches in his gear.

He had several grenades, but they wouldn't be enough to move the deuce and a half. It would take at least twenty-five pounds of C-4 to shove the truck, or at least break it down into small enough pieces to drive around. Just to be certain, Bolan examined the other two-and-a-half-ton, grimacing as his flashlight revealed damage to the truck's electrical system. It wouldn't start, and it was the only thing strong enough to plow past the wrecked hulk blocking their swift exit.

Kamau came down to join them, laden with three rucksacks. "We've got five gallons of potable water."

Bolan nodded. "We don't have a way out of this canyon with this junk blocking the way."

"How about we drive over it?" Metit asked. "We've got wood and planks back at the camp. Just make an improvised ramp."

Bolan and Kamau shared a grin at the simplicity of the woman's suggestion. "We don't have time to tell you that you're brilliant, Rashida. Just know that you are."

The two big men ran back to the camp after they made certain that there was at least one well-fueled vehicle that could start. Secure in the knowledge that they had a working set of replacement wheels, Bolan and his partner checked the two trucks. They managed to find four sturdy planks of wood used as loading and unloading ramps for the transports. Kamau tested one of them with his weight, knowing that if it flexed under only three hundred pounds of human, it'd be useless for the Peugeot jeep they'd chosen as their escape vehicle.

"Did it bend?" Kamau asked.

"Just a shade," Bolan said. "But we can brace it if we move quickly. We'll also lash two of the planks together for one wheel."

"Good idea," Kamau replied. "How long do you think we have before the helicopters return?"

Bolan frowned. "Judging by the rigor of the victims, the commandos struck about three hours before the other craft showed up, but we could simply be dealing with perhaps a two-hour lead time so that they could do their job."

"They may have been dropped off by the same helicopters. Call it twenty minutes to a staging area?" Kamau asked.

"Most likely," Bolan said. He tipped over a drum, then placed one plank atop it. Kamau immediately set to work wrapping cable around it and a second plank sandwiched to it. Bolan walked up the ramp, feeling how solid it was beneath his feet. "Looks solid enough."

"A forty-minute round trip, and we've burned about twelve minutes so far," Kamau replied. "Give us another eight to work up the next ramp?"

"Add in refueling time," Bolan said. "No way the escort birds are going out on a sortie to gun us down without enough fuel for a wide-ranging patrol. We may have more than a half hour to get moving."

"And out of range, but this isn't a paved road," Kamau mentioned.

Bolan and Kamau planted a second drum, taking two minutes to brace it in place with dirt before they struggled their other ramp into position. "Whatever the case, we'll have wheels. I'll drive."

"You'll drive, but what could I shoot at a helicopter on our tail?" Kamau asked.

"If it gets to shooting, we're as good as dead, but I've got the captured Steyr and you have your AK," Bolan offered. "It'll be nothing compared to the range of the helicopters' guns, so we need to get far away."

"So you drive like a madman," Kamau returned.

Bolan frowned. The Somali didn't seem convinced. He didn't want to risk Metit's life, even if he were callous enough to be cavalier with Kamau's safety. "Think these will last for three SUVs over them?"

"What are you thinking?" Kamau asked.

"The aircraft will be flying the same route back to this camp, so they'll be coming from the north," Bolan explained. "You get a head start, and I'll lag behind, playing lame duck."

"You'll be bait," Kamau stated.

"You need to get Rashida to safety. I'll meet with you in Alexandria."

"You're not coming with us?" Metit asked, walking up on their conversation.

"You'll be in good hands," Bolan told her.

"I don't like it either, but I'm not going to change his mind," Kamau told the woman. "We don't have time to debate this."

Metit looked to Bolan, then threw her arms around his neck, hugging him. "Be careful."

"You too, kiddo," Bolan answered. "Godspeed, Kamau."

He turned to prepare his SUV for the coming trial.

CHAPTER SIX

Isu Nahyan flew his helicopter nap of the earth as he raced back toward the archaeological camp. The Hughes 500 zipped over the darkening terrain at over 120 mph, but he felt as if he were racing behind the curve. His initial run on the perimeter of the camp had found the vehicle of the lone opponent who had harried his allies. It was amazing that a single man had been able to match the skills of over a dozen trained commandos and take down five of them without sustaining an injury.

Nahyan had taken some pleasure in turning the Mercedes SUV into a pile of bullet-riddled trash in the desert at the behest of his ground-pounding allies. The team leader, Brahim Khaldun, rode in the chopper with him now, and it had been a rare instance when Nahyan had seen the man disconcerted. Khaldun had boarded Nahyan's chopper for the return to the camp, and the soldier's face was a grim mask.

It had been at Khaldun's suggestion that there be four gunships sent after the lone enemy. Nahyan thought it might be overkill, but the man had disappeared, evading the choppers easily.

"Is he really that good?" Nahyan asked.

Khaldun turned to look at the pilot, as if roused from a trance. "You know the caliber of my men. He killed several of them. On his own, outnumbered and surrounded."

"So this isn't overkill," Nahyan said.

"There is no such thing as overkill. There is only re-loading when your weapon is empty," Khaldun returned grimly. "We will rain hell upon him."

Nahyan chewed his lower lip, then glanced to the commando. "He couldn't come up with something that could take on our gunships, could he?"

Khaldun remained silent. He was back hidden behind the curtains of his mind, lost in thought. The conflict with the solitary opponent had driven him to distraction, and Nahyan could see the gears turning in his comrade's mind.

The pilot frowned at the implications of his ally's concerns. The Ancient Masters had chosen Khaldun as the leader of his strike force simply because he was the ultimate example of combat skill and experience and augmented by the best equipment in the world. The Spear of Destiny, if it had been known by anyone outside the small circle directly involved with it, would have been considered the finest special operations unit in the world. Fortunately for the Eternal Pharaoh, Khaldun and his force were so good that no one had ever survived an encounter with them. The elimination squad had a perfect record, until now.

The end of this streak wouldn't be just a onetime fail-ure. If the lone enemy had survived this fight, he might be able to figure out who they were, and in discover-ing the Spear of Destiny, then he would get an inkling of who the Eternal Pharaoh was. The discovery of the Eternal Pharaoh would be a catastrophe, the undoing

of centuries of plotting to guide the world to where it
needed to be. Nahyan felt a lump of unnerving dread
deep within his gut. One of the most terrifying commandos that the pilot had ever seen was himself frightened
by an opponent. Such did not bode well, and Nahyan
no longer felt invulnerable, even with the machine gun
and rocket pods bristling off the landing rails of his
helicopter.

THE RAILS HAD WORKED, and Bolan saw Kamau and
Metit off immediately. The Ethiopian driver put the
hammer down and had driven off at top speed. Bolan
trusted Kamau to protect the Egyptian woman, but the
Executioner knew that they would both be safe only
for as long as they had a distraction from whichever
air force had been dispatched to scorch the earth in
an attempt to eliminate any trace of them. Somehow,
Bolan had uncovered an enemy that had been off the
world's radar.

He was glad that he had been prescient enough to
give the severed arm to Kamau for transportation, but
Bolan had taken an extra moment to make a copy of fingerprints, just in case they remained separated. Kamau
might be able to use his own government's resources
to track down the identity of the murderer who had
lost the limb in case Bolan were killed, and Bolan had
prints to send to Stony Man Farm in the instance of
his death, capture or the opportunity to trail the conspiracy away from Alexandria. The folded paper was
snug inside the big American's money-and-document
belt, tucked around his hips and hidden by his BDUs
and load-bearing vest.

Knowing he didn't have much time for preparations, Bolan had gotten his SUV past the jammed two-and-a-half-ton truck, then gone back to the camp, searching for supplies. It had taken him only four minutes to scavenge a thousand rounds of ammunition, twenty grenades and two spare AK-47 assault rifles to replace the one he'd lost. He kept the AUG from the enemy commandos, as well. Bolan felt fortunate that one of the terrorists who had initially taken the archaeological camp had a Russian variant of the M-203 grenade launcher mounted under his rifle, but the ammunition the kidnapper had brought wouldn't be suitable for knocking a helicopter out of the sky.

The mystery commandos who had slaughtered kidnapper and prisoner alike had taken the time to remove high-explosive shells from the loops on the dead terrorist's chest pack. While the Executioner had been skilled at modifying weapons and crafting ammunition to feed his more esoteric firearms, there was little he could do in the brief minutes before the arrival of the helicopters to turn simple smoke and tear-gas shells he'd retrieved from the corpse into antiaircraft rounds. He had also assembled the pieces to make a smoke pot, which he hooked onto the Peugeot SUV he'd chosen as his transportation and distraction. As soon as he heard the distant thud of rotors, he'd light up the pot and begin to drive. The trail of inky smoke would be a beacon in the dark pointing to the SUV.

Bolan's plan had been to make his vehicle seem as if it were damaged as well as to make it more noticeable from the air. The sun had disappeared beneath the horizon, meaning that the tracks left behind by Kamau's truck would be difficult to see. Every bit of distraction, every opportunity Bolan could give the big man, was another step toward safety for the Ethiopian and the shell-shocked Egyptian woman.

Bolan checked his watch. The speedy effort to equip for his ploy against the enemy aircraft may have distracted him enough to lose a minute or two here and there. He saw that he'd finished everything in just over thirty-five minutes since the commandos had made off with their poisonous cargo. He took the Kalashnikov with the grenade launcher and checked the round in its tube. His best bet with the weapon would be to fire a smoke round into the cockpit of the Hughes, either through a side door left open for commandos in gunnery positions, or through the pilot's window. The aircraft safety glass was strong enough that it would take a concentrated stream of steel-cored rifle bullets to penetrate, and given the superior speed and agility of the 500 series of helicopters, Bolan wasn't going to get that kind of opportunity, even if they were flying nap of the earth.

Bolan paused at that thought. If the enemy birds were flying at that altitude, whatever advance warning he would get from their sound would be negligible. By the time the roar of the aircraft reached his ears, it would be too late. Rather than be forced immediately into a reactionary role, Bolan estimated that he had another five minutes. Further preparation was going to be necessary to get an advantage over the enemy helicopters.

The top of the canyon suddenly shook under the concentrated thunder of four gunships, rocks shattering under the monstrous torrent of eight 50-caliber machine guns. Bolan lunged behind the driver's seat. The enemy had gotten back quickly, probably having been much closer than the Executioner had anticipated. With a curse, he slid behind the wheel and gunned the engine. A half-dozen weapons and countless magazines of ammunition for them had been stored in the passenger-side seat well.

Bolan knew that those rifles were no match for the range and penetration of the helicopters' Fifties, and the rain of doom that had crashed down left its toll on the hood and roof of the Peugeot. Dents were everywhere, and one dagger-shaped shard of stone had embedded itself in the hood, like an assassin's dagger through the heart of a victim. Bolan gave a breath of relief as the engine turned over—his wheels hadn't been killed by the fallen rock, but he knew that he wouldn't have much more luck.

Ramming the gearshift through the stages to third gear, Bolan accelerated through the canyon. His smoke pot clanked on the rear bumper, unlit, and that was going to be trouble. Night had fallen enough to make it hard for the enemy to see into the passenger section of the SUV, but there was going to be some suspicions if only one man was firing. Bolan knew it was a long shot, but he gambled that the commando force had reported only one opponent.

His only saving grace was that Kamau had done as the warrior had ordered—stayed out of action, thus remaining a hidden asset. As long as the enemy was only looking at a lone warrior, Bolan didn't have to worry about helicopters breaking ranks and heading south across the desert, looking for another escaping vehicle. Bolan had placed two corpses in the backseat, one small man, and one approximating his size, to duplicate the remains of two escapees when Bolan put his next bit of planning into place. He was going to have to ditch the SUV shortly, and he had counted on them wrecking the vehicle.

Bolan dropped the hammer and the engine roared violently to life, the rock sticking from the hood a mere flesh wound, not hindering the engine as it shoved the SUV along at full speed. The rear kicked up rooster tails of dust, prompting another spray of autofire from one of the orbiting helicopters. They knew that their initial attack hadn't done anything to Bolan or his Peugeot, but the warrior didn't think such thorough opponents would be that naive to believe that they had finished him off in one strafing run.

Bolan poked one folded-stock AK out of the driver's window. He was nearly as good with his left hand as his right, and his years of combat had granted his arms remarkable strength. Coupled with the tension of the Kalashnikov's sling, he had a solid base for the assault rifle as he triggered it. It was blind shooting, but he wanted to give the enemy a show before he got to the end of the line for this particular vehicle. Short taps delivered rifle shots through the gap in the canyon above his head, the helicopters above swerving. Bolan had been rewarded by the flare of sparks against the belly of one gunship, but those sparks meant that the steel-cored .30 rounds had been stopped cold by the aircraft's armor.

This wasn't a movie where a triggered burst turned an aircraft into a roiling fireball. If someone had gone to the trouble of mounting weaponry on a helicopter, they also spent some time armoring the belly and vitals of the craft. Still, Bolan knew that they were low enough to hit. He slid the partially depleted AK back into the SUV, laying it in his lap. A hollow thump filled the air and a rock face shook with an explosion. Dust and pulverized chunks of stone blew out, raining messily onto the canyon floor, but Bolan's forward momentum kept him ahead of the punishing rain. With a hard twist of the wheel, he spiraled out of the mouth of the canyon, the hand brake providing an extra bit of resistance to turn the vehicle into a spinning mass of dust and smoke. Bolan turned his rifle toward the back corner of the Peugeot and opened fire, putting two bullets through his smoke pot. The steel-cored rounds ignited the concoction, thick ropelike clouds spiraling out of the top.

Heavy machine guns hammered above and behind him. Bolan released the hand brake, tromping on the gas to shoot immediately out of the path of slugs raining down from the helicopters. Rotors slapped the air, mixing up dust and smoke, pulling trailing tendrils out behind them as if the clouds were made of cotton fiber. The conspiracy pilots were doing their best to increase the level of obfuscation that Bolan had initiated.

Picking up the AK with the grenade launcher, the Executioner stood on the brakes. As soon as the Peugeot was a stable platform, he swung up the 40 mm tube and triggered the first round at a hovering body. Spotlights shone from beneath the aircraft, making it a perfect target, and Bolan aimed high. The canister round kicked hard, shaking the AK in his hands, but his aim felt true. He couldn't see through the swirling mass of dust and chemical fog, nor could he hear the shell strike any part of the aircraft, but years of operating with the launcher's

American counterparts gave him an indication of their arcs of travel.

The spotlight, a gleaming fire point in the choking cloud, provided the feedback that the Executioner needed. The aircraft jerked violently as the pilot reacted to something crashing into his domed windshield. Bolan triggered the rifle toward the aircraft, letting the AK rock and roll on full automatic. The safety glass would have been up-armored like the rest of the ship, so he doubted that he was going to do more than cosmetic damage to the gunship. Still, it was a good show, the firefly glares of the other three helicopters swerving wide of their out-of-control formation mate.

Bolan left off the brake, wrenching the gearshift through its paces and blazing out of the bulk of the cloud before a thunderstorm erupted from the three stable gunships. Machine guns and rocket pods belched out their deadly messages, turning Bolan's former position into a turgid mass of blasted rock and sand.

Outside the cloud, Bolan could see the enemy ships a little more clearly. He kept his headlights off, while the spotlights of the birds sought to spear through the mess they had created. One of the pilots got a clue and cranked back on the stick, gaining altitude in order to provide himself a better bird's-eye view. The helicopter pilot also had the presence of mind to kill the spotlight that had made his compatriot a hovering target. Bolan swerved and cut into the fog of war that he'd orchestrated.

One-handed, the warrior popped the breech of his grenade launcher and thumbed a fresh shell into the heavy weapon. His opening salvo with the launcher had been a tear-gas round, the burning chemical mist likely ineffective against men inside an aircraft. There was still a possibility that the thick white clouds vomited out of the shell would have made it harder for the pilots and crew to see clearly. The rotor wash would have whipped any of the tear gas aside. Still, any extra smoke screen that Bolan could provide for himself could only help.

Bolan triggered the launcher, the smoke round detonating and belching out its contents. Heavy rounds speared the ground too close for comfort, and Bolan whipped the muzzle toward a spotlight. Rifle fire knifed through the fog of war, the spotlight winking out as 7.62 mm rounds smashed its lamp. Bolan let the rifle drop so that he could twist the wheel with both hands. His hard steer to the left saved his life, a pair of artillery rockets detonating a dozen yards to his right, exactly where he would have been had he stayed the course.

Leaning over, he looped an arm through the straps on his spare ammunition bag, then shrugged it over his shoulder. Still weaving and keeping the SUV in tight circles, he stayed within the radius of the concealing dust cloud. Bolan grabbed the larger of the corpses in the backseat and hauled him between the two front seats of the Peugeot. It wouldn't be perfect, but if the helicopters cut loose with all the firepower they had remaining, all that would be left were charred bones anyway. The machine guns' roar was relentless in their quest to burn the Executioner and his ride.

Bolan plucked out the shovel handle he'd measured for the job and jammed it between the driver's seat and onto the gas, and with a surge, he launched himself into the sand. Still under the blanketing darkness of the swirling clouds, Bolan lay flat as the SUV rocketed out into the open.

The unmistakable hiss of rocket pods loosing their lethal missiles hit Bolan's ears just before their warheads detonated violently. The ground shuddered under the high-explosive impacts, and Bolan knew that he'd guessed correctly. He got to his feet and moved through the cloud until he felt where machine guns and rockets had loosened the earth with their power. Immediately, he plucked out a small folding shovel from his ammunition bag and quickly set to burrowing into the softer ground. He didn't need much, and as soon as he'd clawed a furrow deep enough for himself, he lay flat in it and scooped dirt and sand over himself, making certain that the soil caked to his wet hair and face. His sweat had made it easier for the dust to cling to his exposed flesh, and Bolan disappeared, like a crocodile posing as a log in the water.

Bolan tapped his old sniper's stillness, becoming one with the ground he'd dug himself into. The whine of helicopter engines powered down as one alit several yards away. The whirling rotors continued to spin, the pilot intending to let the oversize fan clear out the cloud just in case the enemy had evacuated from the vehicle as a fake-out ploy. Some of the dirt shifted off Bolan, but as he'd settled at the bottom of a crater gouged by an artillery rocket, a lip of earth kept all his concealing dust from flying away.

Bolan kept his Smith & Wesson .45 pistol at the ready, his finger resting on the trigger guard so a flinch wouldn't discharge the pistol, but he could work the smooth six-pound trigger instantly. Under an inch of dirt, he blended into the terrain, but if the enemy commandos were thorough, then it was likely he'd be discovered.

The .45 would give the Executioner a few moments of surprise to survive the revelation, but eventually, he'd be back to square one, except this time he'd be trapped on foot.

A second helicopter landed, disgorging a second squad of commandos to search the blasted ground for a sign of their opponent. The third bird had landed near the burning remains of his Peugeot.

Bolan had enough water to survive for a whole day if the commandos remained on station to search the desert for him, and while there was a surge of impatience, he stifled it. Kamau and Metit would be fine. It might take until the next night to get to Alexandria, but once Bolan did, the hunt for the conspiracy would begin in earnest.

A third still-operable SUV had been stashed near the entrance of the canyon, far enough in to be invisible, but far enough from the blockage and Bolan's initial starting point to have been spared the rain of firepower meant to snuff him out.

Boots crunched in the sand near him. A less skilled man would have shifted in reaction to the enemy's nearness, but under the loose dirt, Bolan remained still. No physical reaction or sound betrayed him, his breath light and shallow, giving him just enough oxygen to continue remaining conscious. Any more than that, and he would make noise that would draw the searcher to him.

Another set of boots met up with the ones that had stood so near. Through heavy-lidded eyes, Bolan observed the pair as they spoke in hushed whispers. Sighs of frustration escaped one of the men, but the other delivered an admonishment in quick, clipped Arabic.

Bolan didn't understand what was being said, but the tone was unmistakable, as was the sudden tensing of the recipient's stance.

As a sergeant, Bolan had delivered a similar "belay that tone" message on countless occasions, before and since his military days.

There was a shout, and the two men stalked away.

The bodies had likely been discovered in the wreckage of the Peugeot. Bolan didn't move.

High in the sky, the fourth helicopter orbited, its spotlight slashing across the darkened desert. Luckily, the ground was still warm, recently roasted by the impact of an artillery rocket. Any infrared imaging would only see the glow of heated ground. Bolan blended into the radius thanks to the dirt he'd covered himself in.

The Executioner remained motionless for an hour as the enemy commandos satisfied themselves over his fate. Still and invisible, he observed the teams board their aircraft and the helicopters rise into the night sky. It took another ten minutes for the sound of their rotors to disappear, and Bolan allowed himself another hour to make certain that the pilots didn't turn back in an effort to catch an impatient survivor.

Now, truly alone in the darkened desert, Bolan rose from his shallow grave and marched toward his reserve vehicle. It would take a few hours to reach Alexandria, but he was in the clear now.

The Executioner had fooled his enemy. Now, he had to find out who they were and track them down, and with a set of fingerprints from a dead man, he had a sliver of hope.

CHAPTER SEVEN

The deep rumble of Kamau's breathing awoke Rashida Metit from her slumber, at least she thought it was that sound. It was the only thing she could hear, and she lifted her head from the pillow, squinting through the darkness at the bulk of the Somali giant as he sat in a chair not far from the bed. She had fallen asleep while Kamau worked at a laptop. The screen was blanked except for a rotating, multicolored cube spinning on a blackened expanse. The notebook computer had gone to screen saver, and it illuminated him softly, the only source of light save for a small crack between the curtains.

She crawled off the bed, tossing aside covers she'd tugged across her fully dressed body in her sleep, and reached for the curtains.

"Don't touch them," a familiar voice whispered, causing her to hop and yelp in surprise as she reached out. Kamau's eyes opened and he sat up straight, but lowered his handgun, the click of a safety being applied reaching the woman's ears. She calmed from the sudden startle, recognizing the speaker as Matt Cooper, the man who had rescued her from the camp.

Bolan turned on the light, and she saw that he was crusted in dirt and sweat from his journey. "Sorry. Didn't mean to frighten you."

"It's all right," Metit answered.

Bolan tilted his head. "Did you have a chance to get her clean clothes?"

Kamau shook his head. "I did manage to use some liquid soap, the sink and the hair dryer as an improvised laundry while she showered."

Metit blushed. "He was a perfect gentleman."

Bolan smiled. "I know."

Kamau pinched a knot of skin between his eyebrows and sighed. "I was doing research on castor beans and ricin as a poison while we waited for you."

He tapped a key on the laptop, bringing up a Web browser on the screen. In one corner, a molecular diagram showed, while black text on a white background filled the rest of the page. "From what I've read, conventional ricin is difficult to weaponize without a fairly high-tech laboratory. Still, it is a powerful poison."

"It takes only five hundred micrograins to kill a full-grown man," Bolan said. "From what I've read in the past, a bit the size of a single grain of salt could end your life. It's fortunate that it's tough to disperse with cluster bombs, though that hasn't stopped scientists across two world wars and the KGB from working on perfecting it."

"So what the hell was Mubarak saying about an extra-potent form of bean?" Kamau asked.

"Normally, the ricin content in a castor bean prevents its digestion by birds and small animals that eat them. This way, their bodies pass them through in a condition where they can drop in soil and grow new plants," Bolan explained. "That five-hundred-micrograin sample that can kill a person requires considerable distillation from a number of beans."

"But this new plant has a stronger concentration?" Metit interjected.

"Apparently," Bolan said. "I'm going to take a shower now that everyone's awake."

"Good plan, Cooper," Kamau replied.

Bolan peeled out of his BDU shirt, and Metit watched as his muscles flexed and shifted under his skin like pools of liquid power. In the weak light of the bulb, she could see that he had several scars, but nothing that hindered his mobility. He glided through the bathroom door, moving with grace and precision. There was no hint of clumsiness, even though his face appeared tired.

Metit looked over to Kamau. "How old do you think he is?"

"Maybe early forties," the Ethiopian answered. "At least, that's how he looks."

"So, you don't know?" Metit asked.

"Not a clue," Kamau replied. "I just know he's the finest combatant I've ever worked alongside, and he managed to figure out I was on his side from just a few minutes of observation."

Metit quirked an eyebrow. "Whose side you were on?"

"I am undercover for my government against Somali pirates," Kamau confessed.

"You came from Somalia, which is where Mubarak went, right?" Metit inquired.

Kamau nodded. "Cooper became interested in the pirates when they were using conflict diamonds from Liberia to buy weapons from Mubarak. Things went crazy when someone came after Mubarak. Cooper was instrumental in fighting the team who attacked the pirates."

"I've heard about the Somali pirates in the news," Metit said.

Kamau remained silent, his eyes cast down to the pistol in his lap. His index finger rested on the trigger guard of the weapon, and its muzzle was aimed at a spot on the floor, even though the safety lever was on. His lips turned down into a frown, and he released a soft sigh. "They are not the nicest people in the world, and I had to prove myself to them."

Metit bit her lower lip. "I'm sorry."

"It had to be done," Kamau said numbly. "I've managed to save a few lives, and with this, I'll have the potential of protecting a lot more people."

"To balance out your karma?" Metit asked.

Kamau looked up to her face. "I don't know if it works like that. It would be nice, though."

Metit managed a smile for him. "Someone once said, if you do evil in the cause of good, you can pay the devil his tax and be allowed into heaven."

Kamau sighed. "I'm iffy about the presence of a universal embodiment of evil, even though I am Christian."

Metit raised an eyebrow. "Somali Orthodox?"

Kamau nodded. "How'd you guess?"

"First, your accent, the one you primarily use, is more Somali, though you could have gotten into that rut from being undercover. Also, if you're working undercover in IOC-held territory, you better be recognizably Somalian," Metit said. "Ethiopia has a large ethnic-Somali population, and Ethiopia is generally more tolerant of Christianity than the Shabaab."

Kamau smiled. "Who knew that anthropology would come in so useful?"

Metit frowned. "Didn't give me a lot of damn help. Even less to my friends."

Kamau set the Beretta on the table and walked over to take Metit's hand in a gesture of comfort. "We'll do what we can. I promise."

Metit's eyebrows wrinkled at the thought. "I hate this. More violence and killing isn't going to make me feel better, or it shouldn't."

She blinked, a tear forming in the corner of one eye. "But I want it. And I want to come along with you."

"It's going to be dangerous, and Cooper doesn't look like the sort of person to drag an untrained person into a conflict," Kamau said.

"So, what, you're going to leave me in this hotel room until the money runs out?" Metit asked. "You're fairly good at Arabic, but your real strength lies with continental African languages. I'm not asking to have a gun put into my hand, but I do want to help."

Kamau frowned, then cupped her cheek gently. "Talk it over with Cooper."

Metit nodded.

The big man returned to his chair, his fingers wrapping around the handle of his Beretta.

THE HOT WATER hissed as it sprayed through the shower nozzle. Bolan let the near-scalding liquid envelope him, allowing its soothing warmth to sink through his skin to his tired, aching muscles. The conflict on the Sinai

Peninsula and the frenetic drive back to Alexandria had taken its toll on him physically, but he knew how to alleviate those pains. The hot shower would do much of the work, and his daily regimen of exercise included a suite of isometric routines that kept his physique limber and agile.

As he stood in the stall, he tensed and released groups of muscles, rotating joints and listening to his tendons pop as their knotted lengths loosened. The healing heat crept throughout his physique, his stressed body given to relaxation under the cleansing spray. The warm soak all along his tall form and the muscle-relaxation techniques provided the relief he required. As a younger man, Bolan had balked at the concept of yoga training being so effective a form of self-healing, but across the bloody miles of his War Everlasting, the Executioner had seen the worth of such training. Had he not discovered isometrics long ago, he would have considered the Eastern philosophy as voodoo, rather than a valid application of anatomical knowledge.

Bolan rested his damp forehead against the tile wall of the shower and took a few deep, cleansing breaths, then soaped up to scrub away the layer of grime that had built up on his skin and in his hair. At least he could clean his body, if not his spirit. Before he had entered the shower, he heard the start of Metit and Kamau's conversation, and his instincts had kicked in. He knew that the young woman would want to be a part of the operation to take down the conspiracy that was responsible for the murders of her classmates and friends. Bolan had been through too many missions with too many people not to recognize the sudden surge of courage and sense of duty in someone to see a problem all the way to its solution.

His War Everlasting, unfortunately, wasn't the sort of thing that Bolan would wish on anyone else.

Metit was in a different sort of class from the warriors who had taken up arms against oppressors and predators of humankind. She was a young woman who had been thrown into a life-altering crisis, and right now she was in a world of emotional turmoil. Bolan had chosen the path of war and vengeance at first, when he'd fired those five rounds that had killed the men who'd driven his father to madness. It was a moment of anger, a response to the agony that had seared his soul, allowing him to give in to a brief moment of insanity. When the bodies hit the pavement, Bolan had regained his senses, and knew that his life had changed forever.

Bolan couldn't deny her a chance at settling her heartache, or at least to dispel the knowledge that she had been utterly useless.

He turned off the shower, toweled himself dry and slipped into some clean pants and a shirt. His hair was short enough that it didn't need combing. It was a bonus side effect of keeping it trimmed sufficiently to keep it from becoming an easy handhold in close hand-to-hand combat. He stepped out of the bathroom and joined Metit and Kamau.

"Rashida, you can come with us. You won't get directly involved in anything dangerous, but you can help."

"You heard?" Metit asked.

Bolan nodded.

"Thank you," she whispered.

"You know what you're doing," Kamau said.

"And I know what I would be doing if I sidelined her," Bolan stated. "I've been in this situation before, and it's not easy, it's not safe. And I don't like to involve civilians. Just listen to me, and do what I say."

"All right," Metit replied.

"Try to get a little more rest," Bolan told his companions.

"You take the bed. You've been through much more," Kamau replied.

The Executioner looked at the comfort of the mattress. Kamau made a show of being fully awake as he checked on the computer. "Wake me as soon as my people get back to us about the fingerprints."

Kamau nodded and tapped the scanner hooked up to the laptop's USB port. "We'll also dispose of the arm once we have confirmation. I wouldn't want to traumatize the housekeeping staff."

Bolan tried to suppress a smile at the look on a maid's face when she pulled a severed arm from the trash. It was a symptom of how much he required a catnap that the corners of his mouth turned up and he felt a soft chuckle rumble just above his stomach. "Yeah, it's about time I took a nap."

Kamau winked. "Pleasant dreams."

Bolan didn't answer that he rarely had such dreams, but it was only because he was fast asleep as soon as his head touched the pillow.

KHALDUN TURNED ON the Web camera attached to his laptop so that his master could look upon him. He bowed his head in deference.

"Redjedef, Enduring Son of Ra, in the midst of your fifth millennium of dominion over Egypt, whose guidance reaches from Abu Rawash to Memphis, your humble servant wishes to deliver the news of his mission at the Eternal Pharaoh's behest," Khaldun stated ritually, with the religious fervor as demanded by the living embodiment of a god.

Khaldun knew that the Redjedef he spoke to wasn't the original Pharaoh Djedefre, son of Khofu. He had died nearly 4600 years earlier. Djedefre was the man who had first taken the title the Son of Ra, who had begun the legend of the mightiest of Egyptian dynasties that spawned the age of kings and pyramids and made it known to his people that the pharaohs were the children of the divine. However, the bloodline was so powerful, and there was no doubt that Redjedef was of that bloodline. That genetic mandate, the power of a god passed through four and a half millennia, was irresistible. Redjedef's commands were immutable law.

"Speak to me, Immortal Champion," came the deep-toned voice from the laptop's speakers. Khaldun's code name. It was a vote of confidence from Redjedef that Khaldun would be ever victorious and ever in his service. Khaldun hoped to live up to the Eternal Pharaoh's confidence.

"The discovery of the treasures you had placed in the Sinai has been covered. The Vault of Ages is once more hidden, its entrance collapsed," Khaldun replied. "A single rocket closed it off."

There was a deep rumble as Redjedef grumbled at the thought. "A single rocket."

"The vault will still be accessible, with the appropriate manpower," Khaldun explained.

"I understand. What of those who have defiled my treasures and weapons?"

"By all appearance, they have been eliminated," Khaldun replied.

"What?"

Khaldun cleared his throat. "There was one man who came upon the defilers and recovered one person. He battled the warriors of the Spear of Destiny, felling five of them. We returned with a full force of gunships to eliminate him, and it seems as if we killed him."

"This is disturbing," Redjedef replied. "You have no confirmation."

"Merely charred corpses, which could have been planted, culled from the dead within the camp," Khaldun speculated.

"You didn't double-check?" Redjedef asked.

Khaldun sighed. "Upon our extraction, we scoured the archaeological camp with the weaponry on the escort helicopters."

Redjedef sighed. "So even if you performed a head count, there would have been no certainty. What do you feel in your heart, my warrior? You have been chosen for your skills and knowledge, and for the blood link you share with my personal champions over the centuries."

Khaldun clenched his eyes shut. His stomach churned at the thought of the disappointment to which he'd subjected his holy leader. "I feel that the man we battled is still alive. He was too skilled, defeating professional warriors with forty years of experience between them all. The corpses we discovered in the vehicle were a diversion I am sure, something to allay our fears so that we would continue with no enhanced caution."

The face on the laptop screen smiled through the shadows that disguised his features. "That is why you are my chosen warrior, placed above all others in my Spear of Destiny."

"What shall be my course, Eternal Master?" Khaldun asked.

There was silence as the figure on the monitor steepled his fingers in contemplation. "Continue with the plan. If this enemy is aware of the Spear of Destiny, he will show his hand. Once that happens, we will know where to counterattack. This time, you will be prepared to deal with his skill and tactics. Whichever additional resources you require shall be delivered into your hands."

Khaldun bowed his head deferentially. "As you have said, so shall it be law."

"We do not have much room for interference, Khaldun. Make certain that this stranger is eliminated as soon as possible," Redjedef said. "Your pharaoh has spoken."

The Web conference cut out and Khaldun turned off the laptop.

The additional resources would come in the form of money, equipment and men, but Khaldun wondered if that would be enough to take care of the stranger he'd battled in the Sinai Desert. The mystery warrior had only been seen in sparse glimpses, but the devastation he'd wrought on a superior force was remarkable.

Egypt had been rocked on several occasions by such a wraith.

Khaldun sighed. The enemy he was thinking of officially didn't exist, but his actions were unmistakable. Entire armies of some of Egypt's best shadow warriors had disappeared with his passage. And now, he was aware of the Eternal Pharaoh. The man known as the soldier was a nightmare to all manner of men that Khaldun had been in touch with on both sides of Egypt's war on terror.

Redjedef and his predecessors had sown the seeds of their control for thousands of years, but one simple mistake had left them open to discovery by a relentless, implacable hunter. Khaldun had to brace for a war like he had never seen before, on the eve of the Pharaoh's greatest victory.

There would be no room for error.

Any who failed would be snatched up by death's swift wings.

CHAPTER EIGHT

The laptop had called up notes that Metit had kept in a flash drive that was in the pocket of her shorts, undamaged despite the roughness of the hands that had clawed them down her hips. She had set up the computer to inform Bolan and Kamau of why a university had sent dozens of people to a forsaken plateau in the Sinai Peninsula.

"The archaeological dig was of a secret temple and storage facility for the pharaoh Djedefre built around 2560 B.C., during the height of his reign," Metit explained to her companions.

"More likely a forward observer base," Bolan said, looking at the map. "The position we were at was a good place to overlook the bottleneck of passages through the more mountainous regions of the Sinai Desert. This way the pharaoh could provide for defense of his northern frontier with a minimum of effort."

"Which explains why Djedefre would have stored poisons there," Kamau added.

Metit nodded. "It makes sense militarily, doesn't it? That's the trouble with academic archaeology these days. Too often, a lot of information that doesn't make sense in terms of how professors see science becomes clear when you realize that ancient governments had savage enemies that they needed to protect themselves from. Though, all that we found were castor beans."

"Were there lower chambers within this temple?" Bolan asked.

"Yes, but we proceeded carefully, and shored up the corridors to guard against potential collapse," Metit answered. "As such, we only had the first hall secured."

"Taking your time and being careful." Kamau sighed. "Doesn't sound like the archaeologists I've seen in movies."

Metit smirked. "Never was too interested in bull-whips. Seriously, after yesterday, I wouldn't mind a sidearm."

"We'll arrange something for you," Bolan said. "Djedefre…was he one of the first pharaohs?"

Metit nodded. "The successor of Khofu, the very first pharaoh, entombed in the Great Pyramid of Giza."

"But Djedefre was discredited, wasn't he? His pyramid was destroyed?" Bolan asked.

Metit shook her head. "That's an apocryphal explanation for Egyptian recycling."

Kamau nodded. "It started with the Romans. Why mine tons and tons of marble when you can just pull it off a bunch of relics no one is using anymore?"

"I was aware that the Great Pyramids had been adorned with all manner of material that made them stunning in their era, but I wasn't aware that so much had been taken," Bolan said.

"They were breaking down pyramids and temples as late as the 1800s, and they're still selling artifacts from tombs on the black market," Metit replied. "The illicit trade in artifacts is serious business. AK-47 serious."

"I was aware of Egyptian groups using archaeological contraband to fund their operations," Bolan said. "It's popped up on my situational reports over the years. I hadn't encountered it personally in Egypt, but I'd run into a similar bunch in Peru who did the same thing with *their* pyramids."

"Abu Rawash was built so that its tip would be level with his father Khofu's tomb, forming the northern border of the rest of the tombs that would be built over the centuries. However, since it was built on a mountainside, it was considerably smaller than his father's," Metit replied. "Djedefre was careful not to make his pyramid grander than his father's in any way as an act of love and respect for Khofu."

"So since it was smaller, it had less stone to be stripped off to be put to use in building surrounding towns and cities," Bolan surmised.

"Exactly. When American scientists came to study the tombs, the locals didn't want to look bad by saying, 'Oh, yes, twenty-five years ago, we took most of that wall to provide roofs for the southwest side of the city,'" Metit said, dropping her voice an octave to mimic a guide.

Bolan chuckled. "And since it'd been over four thousand years since Djedefre left town, they didn't think that he'd mind."

Metit shook her head. "It's all around the world. Sure, there might be a few crusaders here and there making noise about saving historically important buildings, and America does a good job in that regard. But when America gets to be about three thousand years old, and in a bad economic situation, probably annexed by a younger, more vigorous empire, they'll be carving up the Alamo and Lincoln's log cabin for...whatever."

Bolan nodded. "I'm hoping America sees its three-hundredth year, let alone its three-*thousandth*."

"That worried about the weapons that those bastards stole?" Metit asked.

"Not just those men," Bolan admitted. "There's a hell of a lot of good people in the world, but the bad ones seem to keep fooling everyone, pushing hot buttons across the globe."

Metit frowned. "And ricin can be used to set off a war, can't it?"

"The Soviets had learned how to weaponize it, and succeeded in one assassination that the public knows about," Bolan answered.

"But you know about more?" Kamau asked.

"Too many more," Bolan told them. "I have my people working on former KGB scientists who are in the wind and capable of processing castor beans into ricin for use as a weapon of mass destruction. I don't know if we'll find much, but we'll burn that bridge when we get to it. Anything else interesting about Djedefre?"

"Due to the cannibalization of his tomb and accompanying funerary temple, there haven't been many historical records regarding Djedefre's activities," Metit replied. "That's why, when the university learned that there was an untouched temple for him discovered in Sinai, an expedition was arranged."

"Which drew the attention of Mubarak and his friends," Bolan added.

"You think Mubarak worked for the men who slaughtered everyone?" Kamau asked.

Bolan nodded. "They came down on him in Kismayo with more than sufficient force to send a message to the world. And it was a message that only members of the organization would understand fully. Mubarak died to keep those castor beans secret."

"And my friends were murdered to close off the loop," Metit said quietly. She looked as if she was going to tear up, but she clenched her fists, her knuckles gone white with tension.

"The people we're dealing with don't care who they hurt," Bolan told her, resting a hand on her shoulder. "But they will be stopped."

Metit looked up at the Executioner, and her fists unclenched. Bolan could see where her cracked and stubby nails had dug into the skin of her palm. Only her chosen vocation of digging in the dirt had toughened them enough to prevent her from making her hands bleed. "We will get them, won't we?"

"We will," Bolan answered.

Silence reigned in the hotel room with that pronouncement. Metit realized that she had joined a war, and her life would never be the same again.

BOLAN AND KAMAU waited in an SUV borrowed from the archaeological camp as Metit checked out of the hotel for the three of them. It was a moment when the two men could have a quiet discussion, away from the young woman.

"Do you think it'll be wise to bring her with us to the university?" Kamau asked. "It could bring up some bad memories for her."

"It sounds cruel, but she has to deal with it. Otherwise

she'll never be able to return to campus, or even travel anywhere that would remind her of her dead friends," Bolan answered. "Right now, she's dealing with some spiritual wounds."

"And doing something about their deaths is a salve on that," Kamau concluded.

"Right," Bolan said. "I wasn't certain if we were on the same page with that or not."

"We are," Kamau answered. "I also hoped to keep an eye on her. She survived, and that makes her a target the moment we interfere with these bastards."

"With us, she has more of a chance."

"So what are we dealing with?" Kamau asked. "They can track their poison down to Somalia, and then they seal off a dig in the Sinai Desert. I've been covering the news, and no one knows a thing about the kidnapping of the archaeological students, let alone the massacre."

"My people gathered that much as well, and they've been burning up the Internet looking for that data," Bolan said. "My communication was the first they'd heard of it."

"The only handles we have are Mubarak and perhaps the university," Kamau said.

"Someone in this conspiracy has some eyes on the Archaeology Department," Bolan agreed. "If we show up with Metit, while she's doing more research on what is known about Djedefre, we can draw some attention."

"Using her as bait," Kamau replied.

"She agreed to it," Bolan told him.

Kamau nodded, then frowned. "I'm more worried

about what will happen if the conspiracy hits us at the campus. It could get messy."

"We'll only stay long enough to draw some attention," Bolan said. "By the time the enemy can assemble a strike force, we'll head to a safe house I've arranged with some of my friends."

"How good will this safe house be?" Kamau asked.

"It belongs to the Egyptian counterterrorism agency," Bolan admitted. "I've made a few friends over the years."

"I'd say," Kamau responded. "Will we get anything to replace the rifles we had to ditch before coming into town?"

"Yes," Bolan answered. "I've even arranged a Glock 19 for Metit."

"Good choice. Not too big, not too powerful, very simple and more than enough firepower for self-defense," Kamau returned. "But large as I am, the Beretta fills my hand better."

"Same here," Bolan answered. "I've made certain that the new safe house is near the docks. It's a storage facility, so we can avoid dealing with bystanders caught in the cross fire."

"So we'll have clear fields of fire?" Kamau asked.

Bolan nodded. "I've used this particular location a couple of times in the past few years. I know the area, and it's sparsely populated. We'll be good dealing with attackers."

Kamau looked toward the hotel entrance. Egyptian soldiers sat beside the building's front doors under a canopy in the carport. They had a table to look over the comings and goings of tourists, a few of them casting lascivious glances toward more attractive Western women as they sipped cold lemon water decanted into glasses. Egypt was a country that lived by its tourist trade, so having a good military presence by every hotel was a sign to visitors that they were safe from terrorism. The country had been struggling with internal and external enemies for decades.

Bolan frowned. On the docks, they would be far from bystanders, including possible tourists. There would be one civilian in harm's way, Metit, but Bolan and Kamau would take care of her. One of the things that Bolan had requested from his Unit 777 allies was a set of bomb-squad armor and a helmet. The extra-heavy flak vest would protect Metit from grenades and high-powered rifle rounds, combining both Kevlar armor and trauma plates to stop any projectiles thrown against her. She'd also be kept in a secure corner of the warehouse.

There would still be windows of vulnerability for her, especially now, and later, when she would be at the university. Bolan had no guarantee that someone wouldn't be on campus, in a position to attack her with a knife or gun.

METIT WAS ALERT for signs that anyone would recognize her and be surprised at her presence. She was also paranoid, looking for signs that she was being followed. She didn't think that she'd spot anyone. Bolan and Kamau were trailing her, and they were huge men, Bolan at six foot three and Kamau five inches taller and a hundred pounds heavier. She couldn't spot either of those warriors, and she knew them by sight.

She was dealing with people who had the skills to disappear in plain sight, as well as take on forces far outnumbering and outgunning them. Metit had to get ahold of herself, though. These men were skilled, but this wasn't a comic book, where skilled men seemed to have magical powers, able to appear and disappear on a whim.

This was the real world, and no amount of stealth and reaction time was defense against a stream of bullets. She'd only avoided death because her face had been caked with blood and she'd appeared dead, the victim of rape by a deranged terrorist.

Luck and the skills of Matt Cooper and Kamau were the only things that had kept her alive. Sure, Cooper had tried to make her feel better by giving her a handgun, something he called a Glock 19. It was small, and it fit inside her purse, but she had no training with firearms. The gun would be noisy and distracting, she assumed, and she'd have to hold on with a death grip to keep the pistol from flying out of control. If anything, her lack of skill and professionalism would make her more of a menace to people, perhaps even her protectors, than anything. The pistol was simply a pacifier, something to soothe her nerves.

Not that it was doing a good job. If only she'd been given an opportunity to test the weapon, maybe she'd have some confidence in herself. Cooper had informed her that it was unlikely that there would be a conflict on campus. There might be agents of the conspiracy present, but they wouldn't be armed, and they would be present only in a passive, observational status. This didn't make her feel any better.

"Metit? You're back from the dig?" a voice spoke up. It was the secretary at the reception desk in the Archaeology Department. She smiled at Metit, though she appeared a little confused.

"We rolled in earlier today," Metit answered. "Just me and a couple of others, making a supply run."

"I thought you were going to call before that," the woman said.

"You mean Professor Qam didn't call in?" Metit asked.

The secretary looked over her message book. "He might have while I was on lunch. What are you doing here at the office?"

"I'm going to look in on the professor's e-mail. Our wireless conked out," Metit said.

This part of the story wasn't a lie, something Cooper had made certain to drill into her. The kidnappers had shot the router as soon as they had arrived at the camp. Having as many threads of truth running through her explanation would make the rest of her performance much more convincing.

"You'll have to buy a new one, then give the receipt to the Finance Department," the secretary said. "They'll see if it's worth the university's budget to buy a new wireless, long-distance Internet hub."

"And if we discover something to boost tourism into the Sinai?" Metit asked. "Like an underground cavern?"

"Tourist money helps the penny-pinchers forgive lots," the secretary answered.

Metit smiled.

She went to the professor's office, and using a lock

gun provided by Kamau, opened his door easily. *This* she was able to get a little training on in their hotel room.

Once inside the office, Metit could see that the professor's desk was a shambles. His computer had been dismantled, and she could see where the case of the hard drive had been removed. She stepped away from the desk, a little shocked, but considering that someone had gone to the dig site to close off that mess, there was very little mystery about why Professor Qam's computer would have been dismantled. She fumbled in her pocket for her cell phone and almost started to call Cooper directly, when she remembered that they should only communicate through texts, and even then, there was a list of code words necessary to maintain their operational security.

She fired off her message to Cooper and Kamau, indicating that she'd just entered a rifled office.

Be there in a second, Bolan texted.

"Don't let that be hyperbole," Metit whispered to herself. She waited at the door, looking around at the emptied shelves and filing cabinets with their drawers spilled onto the floor. The office felt claustrophobic, but she fought to maintain a steady, regular breathing rate.

Sure, it would be okay to be afraid later, when she was in relative safety. Losing her nerves and cool right now would only be detrimental to the mission and leave her wide open to a surprise attack.

When Bolan's knuckles rapped at the door behind her, she nearly jumped out of her skin, but she turned and opened it. He slipped in so swiftly, it was as if he'd poured through the crack she'd made in the door. He closed the door firmly but quietly behind him. His eyes never stopped surveying the wreckage of the office.

"What now?" Metit asked. "You obviously expected something like this, otherwise you wouldn't have given me that code to send to you."

"I want to run a few double checks on things before we leave," Bolan said. He slipped a slim, six-by-nine-inch black box out from under his vest. He opened it up, revealing a small screen and keyboard, then withdrew a CAT-5 cord to slip into a wall socket, replacing the Ethernet cable from the stripped computer.

"Tiny laptop," Metit whispered. "But they took the hard drive."

"They might have taken any data on the professor's own computer, but there's still going to be information within the school's server," Bolan answered. He tapped a few keys, and a moment later, there was a new window on the laptop's screen. He typed a sentence into a chat box.

"You hacking it yourself?" Metit asked.

Bolan shook his head. "I'm not that good. But, this laptop has a remote link from anywhere across the globe that has an Internet hookup."

"And your contacts can look through the server?" Metit asked.

"Through the interface loaded into this laptop," Bolan said. "It figures it out, and has translation programs. I just need to secure the link until they can access it on their own."

Metit nodded. "Where's Kamau?"

"He's outside the office building," Bolan answered,

observing the progress bar's growth. "He'd be notice-able inside."

Metit frowned. "I thought you two were magical ghosts."

"No," Bolan answered curtly. "Though it helps to be able to pick a lock and come up the back stairs, so the staff wouldn't see me."

"That's another thing. The secretary saw me come in here. She'll wonder why I didn't report this," Metit said.

"You didn't touch anything in here," Bolan replied. "You won't be a suspect in this break-in."

Metit took a deep breath. "And you?"

"I've taken care of my fingerprints," Bolan told her. "This isn't my first foray into an office."

"What would the professor have had that wouldn't be on his hard drive but be in the server system?" Metit asked.

"E-mails, which would have been intercepted and informed Mubarak's bosses about the expedition," Bolan said. "Or a log of his research, which could lead us to the clue that tipped him off to the location in Sinai."

"You're backtracking to see if there was another location related to Djedefre's outpost?" Metit asked. "Have your people look to see if his syllabus is still in the system. It has information about the origins of the expedition."

Bolan nodded. "Good thinking."

He typed Metit's suggestion onto the keyboard. "Even if someone managed to purge information out of the server, there might still be echoes and leftover data."

"Fragments, like what slows everything down on your computer after a while," Metit replied.

"Those fragments of data can be reassembled and made into something useful," Bolan replied. He lifted his head, hearing a noise out in the hall.

"What's…" she began, but Bolan put his hand over her mouth.

He pointed for her to hide behind the desk, then drew his Smith & Wesson .45. "That was the sound of a silenced autopistol."

Metit curled up into a ball behind the desk.

Hell was going to break loose again, and the big warrior and his big pistol were all that stood between her and death.

CHAPTER NINE

The Executioner's combat senses kicked into gear when he heard the throaty thump of air being shoved violently through the tube of a suppressor. He'd called it a silencer so that Metit would understand what he was talking about, but the proper term was sound suppressor. While the young woman had hidden herself behind the desk, Bolan opened the door a crack and slid out into the hall, moving low and quick to avoid drawing attention to himself. Having already come up the back way, he knew what was visible from the front and what wasn't. Keeping to the shadows and out of line of sight, he was practically invisible, a condition that wasn't going to last long once the armed murderers moved to the professor's office to close down the office for good.

Bolan's assumptions were dismissed immediately when he saw the suppressed pistol lying on the ground, a gunshot burn on a closed door. The Executioner heard the sounds of a scuffle, and two women's voices snarling at each other. A large man stepped into view, his gaze and pistol locked on something out of Bolan's line of sight, and he seemed to be hesitant to shoot. Bolan put his Smith & Wesson .45 back in its hip leather and decided to intervene in this fight. With a lunge, he barreled down the hall and shoulder-blocked the gunman off his feet.

The man's pistol fell from stunned hands, and the Executioner stepped between him and the gun. Glancing back, he saw a native Egyptian woman in casual business garb wrestling with a European woman wearing khakis. Rather than deal with the confusion between who was attacker and defender, Bolan made the choice to safely neutralize the big gunman before he caused anyone harm. The shooter was an Egyptian as well, as tall as Bolan with arms as thick and muscular as pythons. The muscular opponent lurched from the floor, forcing the Executioner to jump back, barely avoiding having his legs swept out from under him by a thick, quickly swung limb.

The Egyptian's flailing action had bought him some time to get to both feet, ready to meet Bolan on equal standing. A low curse in Egyptian Arabic escaped from under the man's bushy black mustache, and he reached behind himself. Bolan took the moment to surge forward, but the Egyptian's free hand swung around, stopping Bolan's advance with a black binder, heavy with forms, striking him in one shoulder. The blow, enhanced by the weight and power of the Egyptian, deflected the Executioner's charge, but luckily his reflexes had kept the massive notebook from striking his head. The binder tumbled away and the Egyptian pistoned a punch hard toward Bolan's breastbone.

With an open-hand deflection, the big American turned a breath-stopping blow into a glancing impact. Bolan snaked his arm around the Egyptian's wrist and locked the limb into place. The Executioner's other hand lashed out, fingertips sinking into the Egyptian's shoulder. Having anchored his opponent's arm in two places, Bolan pivoted on one foot and dragged the man to the ground. To keep the big former gunman on the ground, Bolan came down with his knee, driving it into the thick-armed attacker's ribs.

It wasn't a lethal maneuver; it was only meant to drive the breath out of his foe. For all the Executioner knew, this man could have been a cop. The pistol he'd held was standard issue, and no can was mounted on the muzzle, like the weapon of the assassin, whichever of the two women she could have been. With a yank, Bolan clamped his other knee around the Egyptian's captive shoulder.

There was nothing that the big man could do with his left hand, Bolan's leverage keeping that limb pinned beneath the weight of two men, the other arm snared in an unbreakable grasp.

"He's a killer!" the white woman snapped as she wrestled with the secretary. It sounded as if she had stopped herself. "Break his neck!"

Bolan wasn't going to do that, but with a free fist and a clear shot at the Egyptian's kidney, he fired off a measured punch that wouldn't cause permanent damage, but leave the big man curled up in paralyzing pain. He connected, effectively removing the Egyptian as a threat for the next several minutes, strangled gurgles escaping his throat. Bolan broke his grasp on his opponent, and the man rolled on his side, curling both his hands around his gut, knees folding up to shield his agonized torso. It was a cheap shot, but the stranger would survive it. Bolan hated inflicting pain for pain's sake, but the maneuver was the surest way to stun him without killing him.

The Englishwoman and her Egyptian counterpart were distracted by the hard thump and reaction of the large gunman on the floor. Bolan took that opportunity to step forward, his hands spearing like a wedge between the two combatants. They popped apart, tossed back by Bolan's superior strength.

"Enough!" he growled at the pair.

The British woman's fist balled up tightly and sought Bolan's chin. He easily batted the punch aside and looked for the secretary's response. Her first instinct was to crawl toward the fallen pistol. It wasn't an indication that she was part of the conspiracy, but it did make her a threat. Bolan pivoted and kicked her in the ribs before her slender, delicate fingers could wrap around the handgun's handle. The Egyptian woman tumbled away from the gun, coughing.

The Englishwoman continued to make trouble for the Executioner. Her punch had been a distraction, and she had a stapler in her hand. Bolan brought up his forearm to block being stapled in the face, and he felt the tiny bite of metal sinking into his arm. Bolan grimaced in frustration and reached around with his other hand, clamping his hand over the woman's wrist. He twisted, trying to wrench the office tool from her grip, but saw a knee speeding up toward his crotch. Bolan twisted to take the impact on his muscular thigh, and as the woman had made contact, he knew that her crotch shot would have left him at her mercy.

"I said, enough!" Bolan bellowed. He swung her onto the counter in front of the reception desk. Her body was lithe and muscular as it twisted in midair. Using all her weight and stored momentum, she popped out of the Executioner's grasp, but thankfully, she had lost the stapler.

The two Egyptians on the ground scrambled toward the man's handgun. Bolan whirled and kicked the fallen pistol, spinning it down the hallway. He turned back and cracked his heel against the man's cheek, stopping him cold. Another pump of his foot, and he caught the secretary on her shoulder, spilling her onto her back.

"I'm starting to lose my patience," the Executioner growled. "Next one who goes after a weapon or attacks me gets a bullet."

The Egyptians on the floor coughed and wheezed, still stunned by the injuries Bolan had inflicted upon them. The Englishwoman stood up, and Bolan could see that she'd found something that she'd tucked behind her curvaceous hip.

"Drop it, lady," Bolan snarled.

"You're obviously not bloodthirsty, otherwise you would have shot him immediately," the woman said.

Bolan leveled the Smith & Wesson at her face. "Try me. Drop whatever you picked up."

The graveyard cold clinging to his words were enough for the woman. Something metal, either a ruler or a letter opener, clattered on the tile behind her.

"Metit!" Bolan bellowed. "Come on out and see if you know these people!"

"That scurvy tramp aimed her gun at me first," the Englishwoman snarled.

The man groaned as he tried to stretch an arm toward Bolan's pant leg. Bolan pulled it out of his reach, then brought the sole of his boot down on his wrist. Swiftly and smoothly, he brought out his Beretta with his other hand, thumbing back the hammer and aiming it at the secretary.

"Everyone keep your hands where I can see them," Bolan ordered. The secretary raised her palms, and Bolan could see that she had gotten out a pen. Across his years battling spies and assassins, Bolan had encountered more than a few poison pens, their tips filled with lethal venom or toxins that could kill a person in seconds. Even conventional ballpoint pens had been used by the Executioner as an improvised stabbing weapon against foes. A good hard point could punch through skin easily. Aimed at his crotch, the ballpoint in her hands could have been a serious distraction and lead to infection and blood loss if the man with her still didn't manage to kill him.

"Throw it away," Bolan ordered.

She did so. Metit came down the hall, Glock 19 pointed at the floor. Out of the corner of his eye, he could see the nervousness in her features, but she handled the pistol with admirable safety and control.

"That man," Bolan said.

"Never saw him before," Metit answered.

"Her?" Bolan nodded toward the secretary.

"That's Parma," Metit told him. "She's been with the archaeological office since the start of this semester."

"And her?" Bolan asked, gesturing with the Smith & Wesson at his third prisoner.

"That's Professor Holt. She came to the university to continue her studies for the British Museum," Metit said.

Bolan took a deep breath. "You two, lay on your stomachs and cross your wrists behind your back."

Parma followed Bolan's instructions, but the Egyptian man, as soon as Bolan released his wrist, tried to lunge at the Executioner. Bolan backhanded him across the head with the butt of his Beretta. He could feel the crunch of bone through the metal handle of his handgun, and blood sprayed from a gash on the big man's forehead. He collapsed into a boneless lump on the floor. Bolan returned the front sight of the Baretta on Parma, who hadn't moved.

"Is he dead?" Metit asked.

"We'll find out once you bind Parma and the professor," Bolan answered. "I'm not taking chances."

"I'm a British citizen," Holt growled. "You can't treat me like a criminal."

Bolan glared at her over the sights of his Smith & Wesson. "Yes, I can."

Holt sighed. She was athletic and somewhere between her late twenties and early forties. When he'd thought of her as a white woman, it was because of her features. She had tried to tan, but it had only made her freckles darker and more apparent on her pale skin. The sun had burned reddish-blond streaks in her long brown hair that had almost been tamed by a tie in the back. Her wrestling match with Parma had knocked it loose, almost. Brilliant green eyes burned as they glared at him, and her full lips had been drawn tight into an angry pout. Bolan was put on alert that she felt inconvenienced, not terrified, at the sight of a big, powerful man aiming a big, powerful handgun at her head. This was a woman who had been hardened by long journeys into the desert, and she'd seen the muzzles of many weapons aimed at her.

Parma, on the other hand, looked like a typical young woman working on campus. She dressed well, at least she had before clutching hands had torn at her blouse and jacket. She looked innocent and fresh, almost harmless by design. She also hadn't shown absolute terror at being held at gunpoint, something rare for the relatively civilized Alexandria. Both women had an element of danger that set off Bolan's instincts.

It took only a few moments for Metit to find a set of cable ties on the desk, something that deepened Bolan's concerns. The cable ties had regular use, closing off bags or shoring up planks, but they were also utilized by special-weapons teams to restrain prisoners. Metit cinched the professor first, since she was closer to the cable ties. Once Holt was bound, Metit went around the desk and did the same for Parma.

Bolan holstered his weapons and checked on the bloody-headed Egyptian man. He still had a strong pulse, despite the blood that flowed from the ragged laceration across his forehead. Bolan eased the Egyptian out of his jacket and tore its sleeve, the cloth sputtering like distant machine-gun fire as he created an improvised head dressing for the captive. He also took out a small flashlight and checked his irises. They were unfocused, meaning that Bolan had given him a concussion with the pistol-whipping.

The man had a holster, but he didn't have any form of identification in his wallet, only loose cash. He also had a simple electronic room-key card, which Bolan pocketed for later examination.

"Is he dead?" Professor Holt asked.

"He's alive," Bolan answered. "What concern is it of yours? You told me to break his neck."

"I was in the middle of a fight, if you don't remember," Holt replied.

Bolan raised an eyebrow, then leveled his PDA at her face and at Parma's, clicking pictures with the built-in eight megapixel digital camera. He set the phone to transmit the JPEGs. "So what happened?"

"I came in as this bird was talking to her friend. There was a gun on the desk beside her, and she'd gotten out the cable ties," Holt answered. "Probably for your friend."

Bolan nodded. "You're more than an archaeologist, Professor. But whether it's a liar or an undercover agent…"

Parma grimaced and cut loose with a string of Arabic curse words.

"She says it's only natural for you to trust another infidel," Metit said. "You whites all stick together."

Bolan snorted. "She doesn't know me very well. Ask her why there were cable ties on her desk where she was able to reach them, and they weren't thrown to the floor when she and the professor battled."

Parma listened to Metit's translation, and sighed.

No answer would come from her lips, but her expression betrayed the knowledge that Bolan had figured out her deception.

"Does that mean you're going to untie me?" Holt asked.

"Don't push your luck," Bolan answered.

Metit asked Parma a question, and Parma sneered as she responded. Metit took a step backward, then started to raise her Glock. Bolan snatched the pistol from her hands.

"She said that I should never have returned if I'd wanted to live," Metit translated. "They were going to ask who you were, then kill me. They were going to torture me."

Bolan looked at Parma, then to Holt. "Was that true?"

"You're asking me?" Holt asked.

"You supposedly work at the university. If you don't know the language—"

"That's exactly what she said," Holt cut him off.

"We don't shoot unarmed and bound prisoners," Bolan told Metit. "The only reason we don't have campus security up here is because we didn't open fire. And if we had to mix it up with campus security, we might have hurt people we're supposed to be helping."

Metit frowned, her lower lip quivering.

"You'll get your chance to fight, if you stick with me. But you have to have the right mind-set to stay with this operation," Bolan told her.

Metit took a deep breath. "All right."

Bolan stuck the Glock into his pocket, finger straight on the trigger guard to keep material from snagging the trigger safety. "You'll get this back when I can train you on it."

"American military," Holt spoke up.

Bolan looked at her.

"All the rules of engagement and concern for noncombatants. If you were a conventional intelligence operative, you wouldn't care who you had to blow through," Holt explained. "So you have to be former military, and American, from your accent. You hold yourself to a high standard, and you're going to do the same for your allies."

Bolan returned his attention to Metit. "You all right?"

"Still a little nervous," she replied. "What about Parma?"

"We'll leave the guns for the authorities to find. The law is very hard when it comes to illegal firearms," Bolan told her. "I have photos, and we can check who they are while they're incarcerated."

"And what about me?" Holt asked.

"That's what I was asking myself," Bolan answered. He looked at his PDA. It had vibrated in his hand, indicating an incoming message. He ignored it. The message would be stored on his device, even though a few moments of conversation had given him all he needed to know.

"That should be your people with my identification and credentials," Holt said. She sounded nervous.

"I don't need it," Bolan said. He looked at the screen anyway. "Your plastic surgery is fantastic. My people don't have a clue who you are."

"That depends on how good your people are," Holt returned.

"They're good, but not that good. It's been a while since Afghanistan." Bolan looked up at the woman, and squinted. "I thought I'd seen the last of you."

"Eartha, now," she answered. She blinked, those fierce green eyes staring out through a new face. "I was afraid you'd recognize me. Still sharp as ever…"

"Cooper," Bolan replied. "Parma was that good of a fighter?"

"I took a knock to a soft spot on my head," Holt replied.

"Who is this woman?" Metit asked.

"An old colleague. She's with the Israeli Mossad," Bolan returned.

"I don't see you rushing to take off this cable tie," Holt noted.

"Observant as ever, Eartha," Bolan returned.

"Come on, Cooper, I'm still on your side, despite the new face," Holt returned.

"Are you going to explain what's going on?" Metit asked.

"She could have made her identification a lot easier by admitting who she was," Bolan answered. "Why keep things quiet, Eartha?"

Holt made a face, hearing the emphasis on the hollowness of her new cover name. She wriggled, wishing that she could get out of the cable tie.

"We were never supposed to meet again," Holt replied. "After the second time we worked together, I'd offended my bosses deeply."

"By working with Hamas operatives who were out seeking true justice for their people," Bolan countered.

Holt nodded. "They gave me a new face and a new cover, and told me that I had to stay low profile. No more direct action."

"What are you doing here at the university?"

"I convinced my bosses that there were elements of terrorist groups who were increasing their spending power by using stolen artifacts," Holt replied. "Hence they set me up as a British archaeologist."

Bolan frowned. "You're working alone. On something you shouldn't."

Holt sighed. "This thing is more of a family issue."

"The conspiracy we're dealing with?" Bolan asked.

Holt looked at Bolan. "What do you know so far?"

"They have access to good weaponry, state-of-the-art vehicles and they're interested in shutting down every lead that could bring us to their attention," Bolan said.

"They're called the Spear of Destiny," Holt said. "And they've been around a long time."

"How long?" Bolan asked.

"As far back as World War II," Holt explained. "My grandfather was in the SS, and he worked in Egypt interfacing between the Axis powers and the Wafdists."

Metit groaned. "Anti-British imperialism. They nearly handed our nation over to the Nazis."

"The things that my grandfather saw haunted him deeply, so much that he converted to Judaism and eventually joined the Stern Gang," Holt replied.

"What things?" Bolan asked.

Holt sighed. "There was a Wafdist splinter group called the Spear of Destiny. They had provided SS scientists with a steady supply of ricin that could be weaponized according to ancient chemical means lost over the millennia."

"We're looking at an organization close to five thousand years old?" Bolan asked.

Holt shrugged. "It depends. It simply could have been revived with the recent return of interest in ancient-Egyptian history that came in the late 1800s."

"I can buy that," Bolan said. "I've had my share of encounters with resurrected cults like the Thuggee and the Assassins. The Spear of Destiny is an interesting name from a Nazi point of view. It's no secret that Hitler claimed to possess what some called the true Spear of Destiny, the weapon that pierced the side of Christ as he was crucified. Allegedly, any man who possessed it would be invincible in battle."

"Which sounds like the beginning of World War II," Metit mentioned. "Rommel's forces pushed almost to the Nile. The Nazis were kicked out of North Africa, but by then, Egypt was a mess politically, with rioting and civil strife all the way through 1945."

"The troubles continued to 1948, with the final expulsion of 'imperial' rule in the wake of Egypt's first war against Israel," Holt added. "And in that battle, the Arab nations made good use of former Nazi intelligence and military officers to guide their battle against Israel."

"An influence that faded over the years from public sight and knowledge," Bolan concluded. "But I'm looking at this Spear of Destiny group and seeing too many bad things. Ancient, weaponized poisons, a cult that has resurged in power, if not public acknowledgment, and these two."

Bolan nodded at their prisoners. Parma glared at the Executioner, hatred in her eyes.

"You will learn nothing from us," she whispered. "Especially you, slave."

Holt sneered at Parma, and Bolan stepped between the women. Even with both of them tied up, there was a possibility that they would go after each other with a vengeance.

"I will tell the law of what you have done here," Parma said. "And my master will ensure that no charges will stick to me."

"Redjedef wouldn't be so merciful to someone who had betrayed his secrecy," Holt spoke up. "He might not let you into his tomb to be his pole polisher in the afterlife."

Bolan saw the Egyptian woman blanch in shock, then dissolve into snarling fury at the implication that she was nothing more than a sexual servant for him. "Blaspheme not against the Eternal Pharaoh!"

Bolan looked out of the corner of his eye at Holt, who smirked. Bolan winked to Holt.

"Redjedef, that sounds like a familiar name. Is it a different spelling of Djedefre?" Bolan asked.

Parma bit her upper lip. "I'll say nothing more!"

"Too late," Metit answered. "Yes, Redjedef is another name for Djedefre, son of Khofu."

"Your grandfather again?" Bolan asked.

Holt nodded. "I've looked for references to him in the Mossad's data banks, but there's been nothing at all. The only tentative links were between the ancient poisons that the Spear of Destiny provided to the SS, and the fact that they came from ancient tombs hidden around the country."

"I've been updating my information on Egyptian-based terrorist and criminal operations, and the Spear of Destiny don't register on those fronts," Bolan said.

"You don't have to look that up on your little PDA?" Holt asked.

"No," Bolan answered with a chill in his voice. "Whoever Redjedef and the Spear are, they've kept themselves well hidden."

"So what this murdering bitch said is true," Metit said, looking down at Parma, fury smoldering in her dark eyes.

"Go ahead, take your gun back," Parma said. "I willingly die for my pharaoh."

Metit sneered. "Then why make you happy, bitch?"

The young archaeological student turned and walked back toward Professor Qam's office in a huff.

Bolan smiled, then produced a pair of pocket pliers. With a snip of the wire cutters, Holt's hands were free once again.

"Heck of a girl you've got there," Holt mentioned.

Bolan nodded. "She'll do."

CHAPTER TEN

Khaldun stepped onto the campus, frowning at the police activity around the archaeological offices. He flashed his badge and was allowed through to the crime scene where two Egyptian nationals were being held for firearms-law violations. He found the two.

Ubu Ratik sat in a chair, a paramedic wrapping his head with gauze, and from the glassiness of Ratik's eyes, he was suffering a major concussion. Parma Mutfi glowered as she was checked over by another paramedic.

"Let me talk to the woman," Khaldun said.

The paramedic looked up from the bruised and battered Egyptian woman, then nodded, assenting to the authority of Khaldun's badge.

He took Mutfi by the shoulder and walked her to a quiet spot in front of the ambulance, away from prying ears.

"What happened?" Khaldun asked.

"One of the students, Rashida Metit, returned from the archaeological dig," Mutfi answered. "She looked a little jumpy, and not in the best of health."

"So why does Ratik look like he ran face-first into a freight train?" Khaldun asked.

"Because, for all intents and purposes, he did," Mutfi replied. "There was a man with the student, over six feet tall, his skin baked from the sun, his hair black as night, with cold blue eyes. He moved with speed, an efficiency of motion that thwarted Ratik's every attack."

Parma Mutfi sighed. "He was a magnificent example of humanity."

"He beat you up?" Khaldun asked.

"He kicked me in the ribs and in the shoulder, but only to contain me. I had been lunging for a weapon at the time," Mutfi admitted. "He used only enough force to stop me, not kill me. He was uncertain who was on his side and who was not."

"But you said he was with the student, correct?" Khaldun asked.

Mutfi grimaced. "The conflict that drew his attention to us was with a professor from the university. Eartha Holt."

Khaldun's brow wrinkled. "A teacher left most of these bruises?"

Mutfi nodded. "From the conversation I heard, she admitted that she was actually an operative for the Mossad."

"Mossad?" Khaldun asked, his voice showing more alarm than he'd originally intended.

Mutfi looked nervously at him. "If it is any consolation, she is not looking into our group at their behest. She had confirmed that the enemy do not know the names Redjedef and the Spear of Destiny. She is only aware of us through personal history."

"She… Did you speak?" Khaldun asked, gripping the woman by the chin. Her dark brown eyes widened with horror at the force of his grasp.

"No… She already knew," Mutfi answered. "I remained silent. Her grandfather was with the SS. He had dealings with the Eternal Pharaoh years ago, during our struggle for independence from Britain!"

Khaldun released Mutfi and stepped back. "The SS… The Eternal Pharaoh had dealings with the Nazis in Germany?"

"According to what the Holt woman said," Mutfi replied. "I also have a name for the American who manhandled Ratik so thoroughly."

Khaldun was reeling from the implications of what the Spear's eyes on campus had said. Only the mention of a possible name brought him out of his daze. "What is that name?"

"Matt Cooper," Mutfi replied. "Though, it may just be a cover identity."

"Obviously," Khaldun returned. He got out his cell phone and fired off a trio of text messages. The first was to colleagues hundreds of miles away in Syria, containing the two names, Eartha Holt and Matt Cooper. He repeated the same message to friends in Cairo. The third text message had Cooper's and Holt's names as well as a quick sentence. SS from WW2 remembers you. We are known.

That last message went to a blind text drop that would be relayed to Redjedef, the Eternal Pharaoh himself. Once he'd finished texting, he shakily put his phone away.

"You are certain you said nothing?" Khaldun asked.

"I reacted to the mention of our master's name. Holt was wholly certain of what was going on, and may actually have been aware of a blackout to the dig in Sinai," Mutfi replied.

"No surprise there," Khaldun answered. "A simple phone call from Holt to Qam would have raised a flag when no one answered."

"I didn't say a word," Mutfi repeated.

Khaldun rested his hand on her shoulder and smiled. "I know. There is no way that we could have foreseen an old acquaintance of our Eternal Pharaoh showing up on the radar. Redjedef is immortal, and no man walks through the halls of history without touching thousands of lives. Those echoes are impossible to plan for."

Mutfi nodded, relief seizing her. "Thank you, Spear of the Pharaoh."

"I'll arrange for you to get out of further questioning," Khaldun said. He took her by the wrist and turned the corner. There, he was encountered by a military officer who was small, wiry and seemingly cut from tanned leather.

"Are you the officer in charge?" Khaldun asked.

"Colonel Atef Gahiji," the officer answered. "We received a phone tip that there may have been a terrorist incident on campus."

Khaldun nodded. "There was, but it appears that this woman and her companion were the victims of an attack."

"Really?" Gahiji asked. He didn't press the question, and looked at the young woman. "She took quite a beating. Makes me wonder why she wasn't shot with one of the firearms left behind."

"Because I told them what they wanted to hear," Mutfi whispered softly.

"What did they want to hear?" Gahiji asked.

"That's classified," Khaldun cut him off.

"Classified?" Gahiji repeated. "In case you hadn't noticed, my credentials mean I outrank you. And cases of terrorism—"

"I'm working on my own investigation, which has higher levels of support than yours does," Khaldun said. "Or don't you believe that the potential for depriving the Brotherhood of the ability to make money on the black market is a viable solution?"

Gahiji took a deep breath, clearly perturbed by the implications. "And this woman, who remained silent until you came, she is one of your operatives?"

Khaldun nodded.

"And your man without the identification?" Gahiji asked.

"His badge and ID were stolen by the terrorists," Khaldun replied.

"But not his gun," Gahiji noted.

"They are too well supplied to need that, but they couldn't pass up the opportunity for legitimate-looking credentials," Khaldun replied.

"Perfect," Gahiji replied with a sigh. "Your man will have to go to the hospital. He received a severe concussion, and he does need to be stitched up."

"Take good care of him," Khaldun said.

"Are you certain that your operation won't need assistance from us?" Gahiji asked.

"Positive," Khaldun replied. "Come on, Parma."

Khaldun left the scene, knowing that the counterterrorism officer was plagued with questions, but given the nature of Khaldun's credentials, and who he claimed to be working for, Gahiji would never dare to speak his mind about his doubts. Khaldun had a powerful master, and Redjedef had followers in high places.

Indeed, Redjedef had been instrumental in separating Gahiji from his beloved Unit 777 in the wake of an incident that had almost brought Egypt and Israel to full-blown war. Redjedef had made an effort to strengthen his controls over the Egyptian government, and with the assistance of a renegade general who hated the Jewish state, the Eternal Pharaoh had created a crisis. The government sought a purge of anyone who had connections to General Nahd Idel, releasing them from service. The Spear of Destiny had picked up almost all of those who had agreed with the old warrior, putting them to work at building a new organization.

Idel's death and the failure of his attempt to reignite the fires of war between Egypt and Israel had given Redjedef the ability to restructure government agencies. That was how Khaldun had the power to pull a suspect away from a crime scene, as well as assemble a crew of commandos that would be the envy of the world's armies had they been known. The Eternal Pharaoh had spent the months since Idel's downfall assembling the beginnings of a bold new government that would bring Egypt forward as a major superpower.

All it would take was the prize wrested from the grasp of a group of archaeologists. Redjedef was moving the world to the brink of a new age, one where the Hebrews, who had once been the slaves of god kings, were stripped of their control of a piece of land that rightfully belonged to Egypt. The Arabs who had sought to usurp the true leadership of the Middle East would be next, falling before weapons that they had no chance

of protecting themselves against. Tel Aviv and Riyadh
would be turned into barren wastelands, destroyed ruins
voided of life by one of the most potent poisons in the
world.

Khaldun ordered Parma Mutfi into the shotgun seat
of his car, then slipped behind the wheel.

The concept of Redjedef's predecessor having been
an ally to the Nazis had thrown him off balance, making
him worried, but then he realized that at the time, the
Nazis had been the enemies of Britain. Britain, in the
beginning of the twentieth century, was nothing but
a leech on the Egyptian people, stealing their history
and the fruits of their labor. To side with the Germans,
who as the losers had lost any right to their character-
ization, was only logical. Since the Nazis had been the
enemies of the Jews, and had offered their services to
the Arab world to remove Israel as an imposition on the
region's purity, it was logical that they had been unfairly
demonized.

And even if the Nazis had been as wicked and cruel
as history said, history had also whitewashed the actions
of England and its imperial expansion and control over
the state of Egypt. One sided with whoever was the
strongest enemy of your enemy. And at the time, there
was no greater enemy than the Axis. Even today, the
Eternal Pharaoh had thousands of minions in the form
of the Muslim Brotherhood, terrorists who worshipped a
false god named Allah, and not the true gods, the sire of
the almighty Pharaoh Khofu, his eternal son, Djedefre,
and all who followed that pure, sun-kissed blood. The
Brotherhood were psychopaths, and thus fully malleable,

easily steered toward actions at the Eternal Pharaoh's bidding.

He drove away, knowing that the Spear of Destiny's greatest minds and computer experts were hard at work, giving him the ammunition he needed to engage in battle with the stranger who had dared to battle Redjedef's will.

That's when Khaldun's cell phone rang, and the Spear of Destiny leader received a nugget of information that had him grinning from ear to ear.

ORIF MASOZI SNEERED as he tried to get in touch with his head of security, Kamau. The Shabaab bandit leader wondered what the big man was up to, having disappeared over the space of the past couple of days. Masozi sighed as he leaned back in the white metal-mesh chair, colorful cushions conforming to his body as his long fingers stroked the sides of a sweating glass of ice water.

There was one other person he could get into contact with, and that was a man named Khaldun, a powerful Egyptian who had been instrumental in setting up the diamond mine on the other side of the continent, and who had also introduced Masozi to Mubarak. He dialed and caught the man on the second ring of his phone.

"Who is this?" Khaldun asked. Masozi recognized the voice from earlier conversations, but the man seemed distracted. From the background sound over the phone, it appeared that Khaldun was driving.

"I'm on a disposable phone. It's Orif," Masozi said. He didn't have to provide a last name, nor did he want to, not over an open phone line. Whatever had to be said would be relayed obliquely, with a minimum of conversation.

"Nice to hear from you," Khaldun replied. "What do you need?"

"Right now, I'm in town," Masozi explained. He didn't have to give the hotel, just that he was sharing the same zip code as Khaldun. "I was looking for an advance party that I'd sent up to look for something."

"Look for what?" Khaldun asked.

"Well, we had a little problem with Ibrahim. He brought something extra to our transaction," Masozi said.

There was a grumble as Khaldun remembered Mubarak's given name. "Extra?"

"A couple of extras," Masozi replied. "He had something he shouldn't have had possession of, and he brought a few party crashers."

Masozi waited to hear what Khaldun had to say about the "party crashers." It had been a few days, so Masozi had had time to think about who sent those killers after Mubarak. Masozi wasn't a world-class detective, but he did know that Khaldun had a lot of firepower and manpower at his command, and he wouldn't have liked Mubarak trying to make extra cash on his time. Mubarak had been the front man for Khaldun, the intermediary who allowed the Shabaab access to something more than leftovers from the cold war era weapons sent to destabilize African democracies. If Khaldun was behind the hit on Mubarak, Masozi would have to keep that in mind. After all, he was here for guns, revenge and a cache of chemical weaponry that could hold armies at bay. If it were Khaldun that Masozi had to battle, then there was a good possibility that the Shabaab was out of its depth.

"We'll have to talk about this in person," Khaldun replied.

"Has Isoba contacted you?" Masozi asked.

Khaldun grunted, trying to keep from betraying Kamau's last name. "No. He's in town, too?"

"I sent him on ahead to look for the guys who finished off Ibrahim. He and this guy, Matt Cooper, went up early while I made my own travel arrangements," Masozi said. There was no way to hide the white stranger's name, and he knew that he was dicing with the alleged electronic ears of the American intelligence community by saying someone's full name over the phone.

"Did I hear you right?" Khaldun asked.

Masozi snorted. "You want me to repeat his name and get all manner of trouble mixed into our business?"

"And you say that Isoba's with him?" Khaldun asked.

"Yeah," Masozi answered. "Why?"

"I think you might want to rethink your hiring practices, Orif," Khaldun replied. "The guy you mentioned just stuck his nose in the middle of my business here."

"Here where?" Masozi asked.

Khaldun paused for a moment. "I had some people at one of the universities keeping an eye on things."

"Really?" Masozi asked. He wasn't familiar with all the colleges in Alexandria, but he was aware that at least a few of them had archaeological departments. A little research would tell Masozi where, but that wasn't relevant. What was important was that the first thing that popped into Masozi's mind was an archaeological dig, just as Mubarak had mentioned. "Was it because you sent Ibrahim a message?"

"No," Khaldun answered. Either the Egyptian was a good actor, or he honestly had no clue that the American, likely a spy, was accompanied by a towering mass of muscle like Kamau. "I'm going to have my people keep an eye out for Isoba."

"And if you find him?" Masozi asked.

"Bad luck for him," Khaldun answered. "Because if he's working with the white guy, then he's kicked over a nest of hornets. You just have to determine if he's that close a friend, or if he's been fooling you for a while."

Masozi frowned. He'd either just ruined himself, or Kamau had been hiding something over the past year. Had the Shabaab strongman made a mistake in trusting Kamau?

"Thanks. I'll try to get in touch with him and see if he's alive and kicking," Masozi replied.

"You haven't gotten through?" Khaldun asked.

"No."

"Then he might not be working with my pain in the ass," Khaldun surmised. "He could be dead and in a ditch. All I know is that the guy who's given me trouble has been alone, or with a young woman."

"Let me know if you find anything out about the guy I mentioned," Masozi said. He was anxious to ditch the phone, but until he received a callback from Khaldun, all he could do to ensure his privacy was to end the call.

It wasn't a good day, Masozi thought. He tried Kamau one more time, not knowing whether he wanted the Somali giant to answer or not.

KAMAU CHECKED his phone, and while he didn't recognize the cell-phone numbers, he saw that a familiar code accompanied each call. It had been the three-digit string attached to each of the calls sent by Masozi when they were trying to get in touch over a new phone, usually a disposable, or a landline connection in a new area.

The fact that Masozi was calling meant that he had arrived in Alexandria, and most likely had brought at least a dozen gunmen, if not more, to join him on the search for the source of the ricin. Kamau sighed just as he saw Bolan pull into the garage off to the side of their safe house. He knew that he would have to get in touch with Masozi sooner or later, but something told him that communicating with the Shabaab boss would be the wrong thing to do.

Bolan entered with Metit and a new woman, a brunette with fierce green eyes.

"Something wrong?" Bolan asked.

"Masozi's rung my phone three times. And some instinct is telling me that answering him would be a bad move," Kamau replied.

"You're sure it's Masozi?" Bolan asked. "He didn't waste time getting here."

"How'd your trip go?" Kamau asked.

Bolan pointed to the new woman. "Meet Eartha Holt. She's a friend of the family, so to speak. And she's got some interesting information regarding the owners of that tomb Metit's people uncovered."

"Really? That seems to be a big help," he replied, looking Holt over. She appeared to be uncomfortable at the new scrutiny paid to her, and he stopped evaluating her. Instead, he provided a friendly smile to Metit, who returned it.

She was a brave young woman, still managing a grin after all she'd been through. He tried to push thoughts of a relationship with the Egyptian woman out of his mind, but there was nothing he could do in that regard. Metit was beautiful, smart and around his age. Kamau sighed, and sought another round of conversation to distract him from the student. "I'm thinking, Masozi's in town, he might want to talk to Mubarak's supervisor."

"Khaldun is the only name you have for that man?" Bolan asked.

Kamau nodded. "It was in the information I'd sent back to Ethiopia, but their files aren't that extensive. Have your people sent you anything about him?"

"So far, we're looking at dead ends everywhere," Bolan answered.

Kamau's phone rang again. Both Bolan and he looked at the screen.

"What's that code at the end of the number?" Bolan asked.

"It's a code we give to each other when we're talking through unfamiliar lines," Kamau said. "It's something that Masozi picked up from American drug dealers. This way we can hit each other up with disposable phones, reducing the chances we could be traced by them."

"Smart," Bolan said. "You don't think you should talk to him?"

"No," Kamau said, his voice deep and somber. "Mubarak worked for Khaldun, and Masozi will have been in contact with him."

Bolan nodded. "And if Mubarak had gone off the

reservation under Khaldun, it might have been Khaldun who had sent the commandos after him down in Kismayo. Since the voices and faces I heard were Arabic, it's likely we encountered Egyptians."

Metit looked at the phone. "So are you going to answer it?"

Bolan picked up the phone. "Quiet."

He turned on the phone, and he heard Masozi on the other end. "Isoba, pick up. I'm worried about you, brother."

"Sorry, Kamau can't make it to the phone right now," Bolan said, his voice full of menace.

"What did you do with him?" Masozi asked.

"I let him off in the middle of the desert yesterday," Bolan replied. "He was asking too many questions, and I don't like running around with an albatross around my neck."

"Bastard," Masozi snarled. "So you just got back from the desert?"

"I've been in town for a while," Bolan answered. "In fact, I got to see the sights."

"Like at the university," Masozi said.

Kamau, listening on the other side of the phone, grimaced. Bolan's face remained impassive, however. The soldier released a chuckle. "You have a pretty good grasp of what's going on."

"Yeah," Masozi answered. He sounded disappointed.

"Listen, I'm getting closer to—" Bolan began.

"Fuck you, Cooper," Masozi replied. "Our partnership is over."

The phone clicked off.

"That got under his skin," Kamau answered. "What now?"

"Masozi's pissed off," Bolan said. "And as long as I have this cell phone, he'll be able to track me down."

"We're still playing the bait game?" Metit asked.

Holt rolled her eyes. "Again with painting the target on your back?"

"It's the best way to get the enemy close enough to me so that I can find out what they're doing," Bolan answered. "Besides, we're well positioned here."

Holt sighed. "Got some weapons I can use? My university gig was strictly a no-direct-action job. Observe and report only."

"I can arrange something on the fly," Bolan said. "An old friend got it for me."

Metit took a deep breath. Instinctively, Kamau wrapped an arm around her shoulders.

"Since I have Holt," Bolan began. "You and Kamau can—"

Metit shook her head, cutting him off with an angry stare. "I'm staying."

"I'm in this, too," Kamau answered. "If Masozi knew you were on campus, then they'll be expecting you and two women. He still thinks I'm in the middle of the Sinai."

Bolan nodded. "It's going to get ugly. Let's get you down to the cellar where you can practice."

Metit raised an eyebrow.

"Trust me, I've been training people to shoot for a long time," Bolan told her. "And you're going to have to know what to do fast."

CHAPTER ELEVEN

Khaldun sat in his car, smoking a cigarette. He'd arranged for a meeting with Masozi as soon as the Somali militia leader called back with news that Matt Cooper had abandoned Kamau to his death in the arid wastes of the Sinai Desert, miles from nowhere. The Shabaab chieftain was flanked by two burly Africans who wore loose jackets that obviously concealed considerable firepower.

"Have a seat in the car," Khaldun told Masozi.

Masozi nodded and slipped into the passenger seat. Khaldun was glad he'd dropped off Mutfi. She had been relegated to his information coordinator, essentially a glorified secretary. There, she'd continue to interface between Redjedef and Khaldun as he worked the angles of the Eternal Pharaoh's bid for power and sought out the threat that had loomed on the horizon in the form of Matt Cooper.

Masozi pulled out a cigarette and lit it. "So, who the hell is Matt Cooper?"

"We can't find anything on him. I'd say he's off the books, a military contractor," Khaldun replied.

Masozi frowned. "Explains his expertise with weapons, his marksmanship. He didn't miss, even under fire himself."

"You're certain that he said he left Kamau to die in the desert?" Khaldun asked.

"He was in the Sinai, and he took Kamau's phone and drove off, presumably with the girl, or he was on his way to rescue her," Masozi replied.

Khaldun thought about it. "You said you also had something."

"One of the things you sold us was a cell-phone cloner," Masozi answered.

Khaldun nodded. "And one of the things it can do is locate another cell phone by GPS coordinates."

"When Cooper phoned me, he didn't destroy or ditch the phone," Masozi replied. "Its chip is still active."

Khaldun narrowed his eyes as he looked at the coordinates and a street map of Alexandria that Masozi had procured. "This is the warehouse district."

Masozi nodded. "The bastard's either completely clueless, or he's using Kamau's cell as bait."

"A guy like Cooper? He's setting up an ambush for us," Khaldun said. "That's what I would do."

"Me, too," Masozi replied. "Trouble is, how much are we going to run into when we pay him a visit?"

Khaldun looked at the map. He knew the area. Just to make certain, he pulled his notebook computer to his lap from its spot on the backseat. With a few clicks, he had an aerial view of the address, at least as current as it had been when a popular search engine's satellite photos had been most recently taken. "Looks like there are a lot of fields of fire open to make any assault force pay for every step they take."

Masozi nodded. "We've had setups like that in Kismayo. They're as close to impregnable fortresses as you can get. Mine was like that, and except for the guys who killed Mubarak, and of course Cooper, we were untouchable."

"You think that Cooper was working with the squad that went after Mubarak?" Khaldun asked. He wanted to continue to keep the Somali from equating his operation with the one that had struck him with such vicious force only a few days earlier.

Masozi shook his head. "No. They fired on him as well as on my people. I'd just gotten caught in a three way."

"Cooper snuck in, and then this commando squad, and you called your place impregnable?" Khaldun asked.

"He entered alone, most likely. And we were distracted by the meeting with Mubarak and his people," Masozi said. "You try maintaining a secure perimeter when someone's driven a transport truck full of rocket launchers onto your premises."

Khaldun sighed. "I wish we had that kind of distraction for Cooper."

Masozi looked at the photographic aerial view. "What kind of manpower can you get on short notice?"

"What quality?" Khaldun asked.

"Ideally, I'd like an excellent knockout team, and we can throw rabble as our main diversion."

Khaldun smiled. "I can scrounge up a lot of rabble."

"Good," Masozi answered. "The more, the merrier. They don't even need guns. In fact, it'd be better if they weren't armed."

"You think he'll open fire on the crowd?" Khaldun asked.

"Who knows? If he does open fire on the rabble you bring to this party, then he's busy wasting ammunition and attention while some stone-cold killers sneak up behind him. Either way, it's a win-win situation."

Khaldun grinned. "Cunning."

"He called down the lightning when he tried to screw me," Masozi answered. "I'll see him dead."

Khaldun nodded. "Let me make those phone calls. You want in on the kill?"

"I've got a small squad," Masozi admitted. "I'm not going to have anyone to spare when it comes to dealing with Cooper and whoever he has on his side. We'll hang back and see what works."

"Why save anything for a second round?" Khaldun asked. "This isn't some action movie where we build up bigger and bigger fights until the hero has exhausted our resources, while he gets the chance to rest between battles."

"You've got a point there," Masozi answered. "But my boys, while hanging back, could provide some proper cover for the good troops we send in. Let's face it, the Shabaab gunners aren't brilliant assault troops, but we can hammer the hell out of defensive positions like Cooper's warehouse."

Khaldun nodded. "Snipers?"

"With RPGs."

Khaldun frowned. "Rocket-propelled grenades are going to draw a lot of attention."

"You're worried about that? When we're going to throw a knockout punch at Cooper?" Masozi asked.

"Besides, this part of the city isn't going to draw attention, at least rapid response by law enforcement. A few explosions and gunfire can wait until morning."

Khaldun nodded. "Point taken. I remember a while back, nearly eighty members of the Brotherhood were wiped out in this city. There were explosions and automatic weapons then, and the police stayed out of it. It was an abandoned hotel complex, and no one was in the neighborhood who didn't belong. The cops stayed away and picked up the corpses the next morning."

"There've been a few such incidents in this city," Masozi replied. "Think this is the same one who shit on your parade?"

Khaldun thought of it, and similarities to other wipe-outs that had hindered the Spear of Destiny's operations over the past few years. The biggest blowout happened to have been a massive one in the Sinai desert, where Unit 777 forces had launched an all-out assault. Khaldun, thanks to his rank in the Egyptian intelligence community, had heard details that the crack counterterrorism troops had been present only in a support mode. The real work had been done by two people.

A man and a woman. Europeans.

Like Matt Cooper and Professor Holt, Khaldun thought.

"You look as if you had just seen a ghost," Masozi said.

"I'll get some RPGs for your teams," Khaldun said. "My people will be prepared for the fireworks."

Masozi swallowed. "You're scared."

Khaldun nodded. "You reminded me of a debacle I

hoped never to repeat. We have to strike hard and strike fast."

Masozi left the car, rejoining his men. No one wanted to speak anymore. It was time to act, before they lost the nerve.

IT WAS CLOSE to evening, and Bolan was satisfied with the progress that Rashida Metit had made with the Beretta 92 she had been given. Her fingers had been long enough to comfortably hold the pistol, and the superior crispness of the Beretta's single-action trigger made it easier for her to remain on target than the mushiness of the Glock 19's design. Added to the fact that the big eight-and-a-half-inch-long Beretta soaked up recoil like crazy, carried fifteen shots and was as smooth as glass was that Metit had taken to the new gun much better. It wouldn't fit in a small purse the way the Glock had, but she wasn't going to need concealed carry, not if Bolan was correct about how he'd baited Masozi.

After burning through three hundred rounds of 9 mm ammunition in the basement, their hearing protected by earplugs, Metit was able to empty fifteen shots into a three-by-five-inch card without missing. Bolan loaded six magazines for the student, and she carried five of them in pouches on her belt. Bolan loaded a round into the chamber and filled the magazine well.

"Ninety-one shots," Bolan told her, thumbing on the safety. She took the weapon, flicked off the safety and holstered the pistol in a thigh sheath. "I hope you don't have to use any of them."

"What's going to happen?" she whispered.

"The way I set up this safe house, there are only a

few good strategies to get in here. Kamau and I have set up trip wires and alarms to alert us in the event of a stealth approach, and we've given the enemy a good corridor to come at us."

"You have?" Metit asked. "Because this place looks like a fortress."

"I've been at this for years, and I've been on the receiving and giving ends of ambushes," Bolan said. "It's an art of subtlety and misdirection. I've set up the perception that they'll have an easier time taking the route I've chosen."

"What if they try another method?" Metit asked.

Bolan pointed to his rifle. "I have a grenade launcher on my rifle that has loads for vehicles if they try to come in with some improvised tank."

Metit swallowed. "Tank."

"That's a marginal possibility," Bolan assured her. "A more likely approach would be a mob."

"A riot," Metit surmised. "No wonder you gave me nearly one hundred rounds for this pistol."

"A hundred rounds isn't going to handle an angry throng," Bolan replied. "Even if I were to allow you to fire into the crowd."

Metit frowned. "I would think that if Masozi and his friend throw a few hundred people at us, the disparity of force would be enough to warrant killing them."

Bolan was surprised at her assessment. "You're right. A mob can overwhelm an armed force and trample them into pudding. But if we get into that kind of fight, we'll be blindsided, and we don't have the necessary fire-power to put down such an assault without making the local military and police aware that there's a full-scale war going on."

"So how would we deal with a mob?" Metit asked.

"Ideally, I'd love to have tear gas and nonlethal rounds, but I don't carry that kind of firepower. We were lucky to score regular ammunition and 40 mm shells for our rifle launchers," Bolan replied. "Kamau and Holt have pooled gasoline and flammable material at choke points in the alleys. We can ignite the piles…"

"And the mob is halted by the fire," Metit answered.

"It's not a perfect scenario. There's a chance that innocent people swept up in the crowd could end up burned, but it's the maximum amount of force that I'm comfortable with when it comes to noncombatants," Bolan told her.

Metit smirked.

"What?" Bolan asked.

"You care enough to be concerned about people who, by all rights, would have no problem kicking you in the head until your skull was crushed," Metit replied.

"My fight isn't with disenfranchised civilians," Bolan said. "It's with the scum who manipulate them for their own twisted ends. The bastards who pull the strings and profit from the blood they shed are the same ones who cause the conditions that breed poor and violence-prone people in the first place."

"So when I get my shot at the bad guys…" Metit said.

"It'll be a pure, clean shoot, because I've made sure of it," Bolan concluded for her. "Come on, let's head topside. You're as good as you'll ever be on the limited ammunition we had to train with."

"Am I good?" Metit asked.

Bolan nodded. "Good enough to live to fight another day."

"Then that's pretty good," Metit agreed. She looked at a door on one side of the basement. It was an improvised one, made of plywood, and she could see chunks of brick missing around the wooden panel put up. "Is that our escape route?"

"Yes," Bolan said. "On my signal, cut down that corridor. I'll be the last through the hole, to close the door behind us."

"Close the door," Metit repeated. "Something loud?"

"Very," Bolan confirmed.

Metit grinned. "Good. It's been a while since something went boom."

Heading up the steps, they ran into Eartha Holt at the top.

"Something up?" Bolan asked.

"Kamau spotted a crowd forming," Holt replied.

Bolan checked his watch, just to make certain of the timing. "There's no way Masozi could have set this up. He must have gotten in touch with whoever was in charge of Mubarak."

Holt nodded. "They definitely are locals. Not a black African among them."

Bolan slid past her and went to join Kamau in his roost. While they had been at the campus, Kamau busied himself. Bolan had to hand it to the big Ethiopian. He'd designed a blind that hid his bulk, and had room for a large man like Bolan, as well. The blind also blended in with the vent structures on the roof, making it a good, covert observation post, complete with a pathway that obscured the travels of people to and from the blind. On all fours, the warrior scurried to join Kamau, who handed him a pair of binoculars.

"It's a mix of ages down there, but it's generally fifteen to thirty, as far as I can tell," Kamau informed him.

A quick scan with the glasses confirmed Kamau's estimation. "Good eyes."

"You can thank Leupold, too," Kamau said, tapping the binoculars.

Bolan grinned. "They're going to come after us under the cover of a mob."

"The petrol and lighter fluid left behind by your friends came in handy in that case. They're even staging right where you thought they would," Kamau added.

Bolan turned in the blind and scanned in the opposite direction. "No sign of the real attackers, but they won't show up until they have the cover of darkness."

"You certain that we shouldn't leave me up here to give them a welcome?" Kamau asked.

Bolan shook his head. "No. I've set things up to make dead certain I can handle it all myself."

"So we do all the grunt work, and you get to have all the fun." Kamau sighed.

Bolan raised an eyebrow. "This isn't going to be enjoyable. Besides, I've got plans for you."

"Protecting Metit, right?" Kamau said. He seemed dejected, as if he'd had his invitation to a party revoked. Bolan could sympathize with him, which is why he'd brought a phone up with him to the blind. Kamau took a deep breath and shoved his disappointment aside. "What about Holt?"

Bolan frowned. "She can handle herself. There's a reason why the Israelis send her places by herself."

"She's not going to love that you've given away her allegiance," Kamau said.

Bolan shrugged. "Holt isn't necessarily a patriot. Especially not with the stuff she's been through, and the roads she's been forced to walk down alone. She had to clean up one particularly nasty mess for her bosses, something that would have made things tough."

"Really?" Kamau asked. "And how could Israel's opinion slip further than it has?"

Bolan nodded. "You would be surprised."

"If you were of a mind to go into details," Kamau concluded.

"Exactly," Bolan said.

"So is she hanging with you, or is she coming with us?" Kamau asked.

"Knowing her, she'll be sticking with me," Bolan answered.

"How deep is your history?" Kamau pressed.

"Friends only," Bolan replied.

Kamau knew he wasn't going to get anything else out of the big American. "They won't start making their moves for another hour or so. They're still streaming in."

Bolan looked at Kamau. "I've got one more thing for you to do. This should throw Masozi a curveball."

Kamau raised an eyebrow. "What?"

Bolan handed the big man the cell phone and a small folded piece of paper. "That's just an outline I wrote while Metit was familiarizing herself with the Beretta."

Kamau looked over the paper. A big grin split his face. "You are an evil man, Cooper," and began dialing.

KHALDUN AND MASOZI knew better than to be within a mile of the raid on the warehouse. Depending on the reputation of the lone warrior and his capacity for mass destruction, they were best served far away from proximity to the battle. Rather than leave things to chance, however, the pair had created an improvised command center in Masozi's hotel room. There they had a communications scanner, as well as a cell phone hooked to the GPS signal tracker, ensuring that they were certain of Bolan's location.

That's when another phone warbled. Masozi reached into his pocket and pulled it out. Then his face blanked, as he looked at the readout on the screen.

"What is it?" Khaldun asked.

"Kamau's code," Masozi answered.

Khaldun plucked the phone from Masozi's grasp. "It's the same phone as we're tracing to. Maybe Cooper got the code from Kamau?"

"I doubt it," Masozi replied. "It was Kamau who made up these codes in order to keep us secure from electronic surveillance. He added whole new layers of safety and privacy to our pirating operation."

Khaldun looked at the phone as it went to voice mail. "I don't believe this shit. It has to be Cooper trying to mess with us."

"For what reason?" Masozi asked.

Khaldun shot the Shabaab militia leader a harsh

glare. "I don't know. He sees a few hundred rioters assembling a few blocks away and maybe he wants to get us off of our game."

"Message is saved to the voice mail," Masozi answered, pointing to the screen. "At least hear what this alleged ploy is supposed to be."

Khaldun handed off the phone as if it were a dead rat. "Talk on the other side of the room. I don't want to wear your brains if it's some form of trick."

"This Cooper is a sorcerer," Masozi replied. Still, he walked toward the bathroom to take the voice-mail message, not wanting to risk passing too near a window in case Cooper had taken up a position as sniper on a roof near to the hotel.

He punched in the code and listened to Kamau's brief message.

"Orif, it's Isoba. Pick up. Cooper said you'd called while I was out getting supplies," Kamau's voice said on the other end. "I dropped my phone in our SUV, and that's how Cooper found it."

Masozi strode angrily toward Khaldun and put the cell on speaker, replaying the message.

Khaldun's face twisted in puzzlement. "What is that?"

"I don't know. You're supposed to be the big bad professional when it comes to this," Masozi answered. "But with an answer like that, it's apparent you don't have a clue."

"Answer the phone the next time it rings," Khaldun replied. "I'm going to tell our people to hold off on making their move."

"Sure," Masozi answered.

Get FREE BOOKS and a FREE GIFT when you play the...

LAS VEGAS GAME

Just scratch off the gold box with a coin. Then check below to see the gifts you get!

YES! I have scratched off the gold box. Please send me my **2 FREE BOOKS** and **gift for which I qualify**. I understand that I am under no obligation to purchase any books as explained on the back of this card.

366 ADL E373   **166 ADL E373**

FIRST NAME

LAST NAME

ADDRESS

APT.#

CITY

STATE/PROV.

ZIP/POSTAL CODE

7	7	7	Worth TWO FREE BOOKS plus a BONUS Mystery Gift!
🍒	🍒	🍒	Worth TWO FREE BOOKS!
🔔	🔔	☘	TRY AGAIN!

Offer limited to one per household and not valid to current subscribers of Gold Eagle® books. All orders subject to approval. Please allow 4 to 6 weeks for delivery.

◀ DETACH AND MAIL CARD TODAY!

® and TM are trademarks owned and used by the trademark owner and/or its licensee.

The Reader Service — Here's how it works:

Accepting your 2 free books and free gift (gift valued at approximately $5.00) places you under no obligation to buy anything. You may keep the books and gift and return the shipping statement marked "cancel." If you do not cancel, about a month later we'll send you 6 additional books and bill you just $31.94* — that's a savings of 24% off the cover price of all 6 books! And there's no extra charge for shipping! You may cancel at any time, but if you choose to continue, every other month we'll send you 6 more books, which you may either purchase at the discount price or return to us and cancel your subscription.

*Terms and prices subject to change without notice. Price does not include applicable taxes. Sales tax applicable in N.Y. Canadian residents will be charged applicable provincial taxes and GST. Offer not valid in Quebec. Credit or debit balances in a customer's account(s) may be offset by any other outstanding balance owed by or to the customer. Offer available while quantities last.

If offer card is missing write to: The Reader Service, P.O. Box 1867, Buffalo NY 14240-1867

BUSINESS REPLY MAIL

FIRST-CLASS MAIL   PERMIT NO. 717   BUFFALO, NY

POSTAGE WILL BE PAID BY ADDRESSEE

THE READER SERVICE
PO BOX 1867
BUFFALO NY 14240-9952

NO POSTAGE
NECESSARY
IF MAILED
IN THE
UNITED STATES

The cell rang again, and Masozi answered before the first moments of its chime ended. "Isoba?"

"Shit, boss, I was worried about you," Kamau said over the airwaves. "You sound tense."

"Of course I sound tense!" Masozi answered. "What the hell did you think I'd sound like when I had the conversation I did."

"What conversation?" Kamau asked.

"The one where he said he left you out in the Sinai Desert to die of exposure and starvation," Masozi answered.

Kamau laughed. "Cooper said that? It's real funny. I've been keeping busy all this time. Hell, I was going to tell you about the cuties we picked up in Sinai, where Mubarak said his boys were."

"Cuties? As in multiple women?" Masozi asked. Khaldun listened intently to the conversation over the speakerphone. His message to his field commander had been brief, allowing him to pay attention to what was going on.

Kamau chuckled in response to Masozi's question. "Yeah. We drove into this archaeological camp yesterday. Not a sign of Mubarak's gang, or any 'vast stores of ricin' like he told us he had."

"But he said… And he was at the university," Masozi said, confused. Khaldun frowned as Kamau's version of events didn't jibe with what he'd personally experienced, nor what Parma Mutfi had told him. Khaldun made a motion to cut the call off, but Masozi wasn't having any of it.

"Yeah. We took them by the university offices earlier today. I waited in the car while they went in to check on their fellow professor's notes," Kamau said. "We picked up a professor and her teacher's assistant. Her name is Holt, and the assistant is a girl named Metit."

Masozi looked at Khaldun, suspicion wrinkling his forehead. Khaldun kept making the motion to hang up. "Where are you at right now?"

"We set up a warehouse," Kamau said. "I even have the address here."

He rattled it off, and Masozi felt a tremor go through his body.

"Put Cooper on," Masozi ordered angrily.

"Sure," Kamau replied. "Are we still cool, Orif?"

"You and I are Shabaab brothers. We will die for each other."

Khaldun covered his eyes with one hand, squeezing his brows together.

"Orif?" Bolan's voice spoke up on the phone.

"What the fuck was that noise you spouted earlier?" Masozi asked.

"I don't know. You hung up so fast—" Bolan began.

"Cooper!" Khaldun spoke up. His patience had worn threadbare at this point, and at the sound of his alleged enemy's voice, he finally lost his control.

Masozi sneered at his "partner." "Shut up, Khaldun!"

"Whoa! Whoa!" Bolan added. "What's with all these proper names over an unsecured phone?"

"Why did you tell me you dumped Kamau in the desert?" Masozi asked.

"I think your headscarf's wrapped a little too tight,"

Bolan answered. "I was joking, and all of a sudden, you fly off the handle and slam down the phone."

"Then why didn't you call me back?" Masozi asked.

Bolan sighed. "Because I didn't have your new number. And even if I did, you wouldn't answer me because I don't have those top-secret digits Kamau gave me."

"You miserable liar!" Khaldun bellowed. "You killed five of my men at the dig!"

"Unless you're talking about scorpions that got too close to my boots... Who the hell is this guy, Orif? You called him...Khaldun?" Bolan asked.

"You had men at the dig site?" Masozi inquired. "Is that the shit storm that came down on your operation?"

"Who is this guy?" Bolan continued to ask.

Khaldun threw up his hands in frustration, pacing back toward the bathroom.

"They're saying they saw nothing there," Masozi shouted after him.

"Sorry, Cooper."

"Who's Khaldun?"

"He's the guy who was supposed to be in charge of Ibrahim," Masozi said, returning to his phone discipline of not using family names. Given names would be harder to trace, but unfortunately, no such identifier was in Masozi's vocabulary for Khaldun. "I've been buying product through the man for years from Khaldun."

"Why are you listening to this liar?" Khaldun asked.

"Next thing you know, he'll be accusing me of

fighting off a half-dozen helicopter gunships as well as executing his men," Bolan chided.

"There were four," Khaldun growled. "Not a half… Masozi…"

"Listen, just because we don't have a given name to call you by doesn't mean you can drop my name on an unsecured conversation!" Masozi answered.

"You guys want to come out to the warehouse?" Bolan invited. "We'll try to work out something better than what Mu—Ibrahim tried to arrange. And we still have a bunch of mystery men on our asses."

"Cooper!" they heard Kamau over the phone. "Cooper, it looks like there's a mob down the street. The natives are getting restless."

"What?" Bolan asked. "Orif, did you hear anything about this?"

"I'm going to try to straighten this thing out," Masozi answered. "Just sit tight."

"Will do," Bolan said.

Masozi hung up, then switched the phone to text messaging.

"What are you doing?" Khaldun asked.

Masozi glared up from the cell phone.

CHAPTER TWELVE

Khaldun watched as Masozi's thumbs ran over the keyboard of his cellular phone, contacting the leaders of the mob with a change of plans.

"I asked you a question," Khaldun said. As far as Masozi knew, the Egyptian was no more a friend than the American who dropped way too many questions in the Somali's lap.

"I'm going to have my men meet up with Cooper and Kamau," Masozi answered. "It's a last-minute change of plans."

Khaldun groaned.

"Did you have people at that camp Kamau talked about?" Masozi asked.

"We did. I hired Mubarak as someone to keep people away from something we'd stashed in that area," Khaldun replied.

"Castor beans?" Masozi asked.

"What could we do with ricin?" Khaldun asked. "They've been trying for over a hundred years, since World War I in fact, to make a weaponized form of ricin. The only ones who ever got close to it were the Soviets, and even then, it is only useful for assassinations. That's where we kept our stash of weapons."

"So what's this big helicopter battle Cooper talked about?" Masozi asked. "And the five men you bitched about? Were you the one who sent those bastards to raid my people in Kismayo?"

"No," Khaldun lied. He was tense and thrown off his game. "Why are you sending your men in there?"

"To see what the hell is going on," Masozi answered. "I'm also texting Kamau now to let him know some of his buddies are dropping by the warehouse. If something unusual is up in there, they'll get a message to us."

Khaldun took a deep breath. "It's a trap. You've been lied to."

"If that's the case, then my team will know about it," Masozi replied. "You can't get these kinds of impressions through a phone conversation. What you can do, though, is send your men in on my group's heels. This can be the perfect distraction, like what Cooper used to get into my compound."

"And the mob?" Khaldun asked.

"Keep them in reserve. You can throw them at Cooper anytime you want," Masozi said. "While your commandos and my team slip out the back, they can choke the area in case the police do show up. As a bonus, we won't make as much noise without a rocket-grenade bombardment, and you get to save ammunition."

Khaldun nodded. "That actually sounds good."

"Of course," Masozi said. "My Shabaab have been some of the most successful pirates off the Horn. You don't get to that position without having a few plans."

Khaldun nodded, but he fumed. Cooper was up to something, and right now, he'd pulled off a major deception, nearly shattering Khaldun's own secrecy. If it hadn't been for the fact that Masozi only knew him by a generic title, unrelated to his true identity, long buried, he would have been worried about the betrayal of his name. It was only by dint of acting that he showed concern over their using it.

Cooper had a plan, and it had gummed up the wheels of Khaldun's plot to eliminate a threat to the Eternal Pharaoh's plan of conquest.

WITH ONE PHONE conversation, Bolan had achieved a few leaps in figuring out what was going on. He had gotten a few shreds of information regarding the leader of the opposing group from the Sinai dig site. The leader was a man named Khaldun, a name that Bolan had sent through to Stony Man Farm for referencing. He had also delayed things. From his spot in the roof blind, he saw that the throng of would-be rioters were no longer focused and on edge. Someone had told them that there was going to be a delay in their plan. The longer the crowd remained bored and unfocused, the less likely they were to run desperately into the walls of flame he'd set up to stop them from assaulting his warehouse.

Kamau had also informed him that Masozi was sending in his militiamen in order to evaluate what progress the pair had made. Bolan smiled.

That had to have put Khaldun off his game, but it also made certain that the mystery commandos would sneak into position to observe the meeting between "Cooper," Kamau and the Shabaab. Since they were originally supposed to arrive under the cover of a riot, the altered plan would also throw off the infiltrators. Remembering his time in the military, any last-minute changes to strategy usually cost a strike team precious moments in reaction time. Against the commandos Khaldun regularly employed, those precious moments wouldn't be much, but they'd be enough for the Executioner to gain the upper hand, or at least avoid being blindsided by a sheet of automatic fire.

Bolan had attached a wireless headset to his ear, enabling hands-free conversation through the PDA. Aaron Kurtzman had been burning up the Internet, trolling for information, trying to confirm slivers of data that had been provided by Masozi, Kamau and Holt over the past day. As the PDA had powerful encryption software installed, there was no worry on Bolan's part that the conversation he was having would be intercepted by the enemy.

"So far, we've got nothing in any Egyptian counterterrorism database relating to a Khaldun," Kurtzman said. "Though we did receive a quick e-mail message from Colonel Gahiji, through the usual dump address you'd given him."

"What's that?" Bolan asked.

"An intelligence official named Faslif showed up at the campus and vouched for Parma and the big man you knocked out," Kurtzman replied. "Right now, we're trying to figure out who he could be."

"Judging by the conversation I just had with Masozi and Khaldun, it sounds like Khaldun was the same guy," Bolan said.

"Hell of a risk you're taking," Kurtzman noted.

Bolan chuckled. "I've used myself as bait so often, I think I'm turning into a night crawler."

"Sooner or later, a fish is going to swallow you, Striker," Kurtzman warned.

Bolan shrugged. "If that happens, I won't worry.

I learned how to get out of a fish's belly years ago. Any news on how the ancient Egyptians might have weaponized ricin in a manner that could be utilized today?"

"We've been burning up the search engines and our data files in that regard," Kurtzman replied. "One thing we found was that tombs had walls that were coated in an unknown poison, usually accompanied by the phrase 'Let death with her swift wings strike down any who disturbs this place.'"

"Which sounds similar to the voodoo zombie powder concoctions utilized to turn *houngans'* enemies into their slaves," Bolan said. "They'd put the powder on windowsills or where the man would be walking barefoot, and through skin contact with the concentrated poison, they'd end up comatose and paralyzed to the point where they looked as if they were dead. The only trouble with that defense was that the Egyptians hadn't expected four millennia to weaken the concentration of ricin toxin."

"Much of the looting of the Pyramids and other tombs occurred long before nineteenth- and twentieth-century explorers showed up, Striker," Kurtzman said. "A few sacrificial lambs crawled down the wrong hole and stirred things up enough for the rest of the looters to slip past, or at least put on sufficient protection."

"So how would that work in a modern environment?" Bolan asked.

"One problem is that ricin is a poor poison to contaminate water supplies. While it can kill with a dose the size of a grain of salt, it isn't water soluble, and thus can't disperse through that particular vector," Kurtzman said. "Also, since it's insoluble, it can't be mixed into a suspension and aerosolized."

"I'd heard that they have tried with artillery rockets and shells," Bolan said.

"Sure, you can get a localized cloud, but the kill radius wouldn't be much larger than the shrapnel zone of a standard artillery shell," Kurtzman answered. "There are more efficient poisons that can be made airborne and carried along the wind. Hell, you've even encountered a variant or two of certain diseases that have been turned into a respiratory vector as opposed to their traditional infection method."

Bolan sighed. "I remember that all too well."

Holt was at a table, finishing her adjustments to a rifle she'd field-stripped and reassembled. The woman wanted to be as certain of the action of her weapon as she could be. Thus, she had broken it down and looked at every part that could go wrong. Upon putting it back together, she adjusted the sights using a laser bore sight.

"Talking to your people?"

Bolan pointed to the wireless earphone. It was a black metal bar that had a hook contoured over his ear.

"Say hi to Eartha for me," Kurtzman said. "I'll sign off and keep digging through data."

"My computer guy says hello," Bolan relayed.

"Hi, Bear," Holt said, leaning in so her lips were next to the microphone on Bolan's earpiece. Bolan pulled away from the closeness of her lips to his cheek.

"I'm not going to bite you, Cooper," Holt told him.

"We'll talk about your intentions when we get to that," Bolan said. "How's everything?"

Holt ejected the cartridge-shaped laser emitter

from the breech of her rifle. "I can make do with this. Granted, it's only sighted in for twenty-five yards, but the way you operate, we're not looking at much more distance when trouble comes calling."

"So you're sticking with me," Bolan presumed.

Holt nodded, and began loading her magazines.

Bolan handed her a headset. "We'll all stay in the loop."

Holt put it on. "I wasn't sure you still cared."

"I was sure you were dead, or crippled."

"That's what the bosses wanted it to look like," Holt answered.

Bolan waited for her to put on the earpiece. "Sometimes, it just pays to tell management to go to hell. It's better to ask forgiveness than beg permission."

Holt smiled at him. "Then do you forgive me for not letting you know I was all right?"

Bolan nodded. "Do I get forgiveness for not looking after you?"

"It wasn't your fault I got hit in the head. And it wasn't your fault that you had to move out to another mission immediately," Holt replied. She reached out, her small hand touching his. "Listen, if you're worried about this being some form of personal vendetta…"

Bolan gave her fingers a squeeze. "I know all about personal vendettas. I also can see that you've got it under control."

"This has been in my family for decades," Holt continued. "My grandfather handed it down to my father. My father gave it to me. And my grandfather was there when my dad died, reinforcing the fact that I had to keep an eye on this particular corner of the world."

"Except for a trip to Afghanistan," Bolan replied.

Holt remained silent.

"There was something related there, too?" Bolan asked.

"Redjedef may have been looking through some of the old Soviet facilities," Holt answered. "When World War II ended, quite a few Nazi files and weapon designs fell into Soviet hands. And the Soviets were testing chemical and biological weapons in Afghanistan like crazy. Because I had been in the area following up a lead, I caught the Dagger cleanup."

"Had they developed something with the ricin?" Bolan asked.

Holt frowned. "There wasn't anything that was in computer records, but a lot of the scientists preferred old pen-and-notebook work anyway. There are still spots in Afghanistan that haven't been searched since the Soviets retreated."

"Redjedef wouldn't have sided with the KGB anyway, would he?" Bolan asked.

Holt narrowed her eyes. "Redjedef's predecessor sponsored dozens of SS operatives and put them to work for Arab governments who didn't like having Jews in their midst. The KGB was the same cake, baked in a different oven."

"I thought as much," Bolan said. "Of course, this Redjedef probably inherited his role and title from others."

"I shudder to think that there's someone 4500 years old running around," Holt replied. "But everything seems to point to the Eternal Pharaoh being a symbolic title, and his group, the Spear of Destiny, is aware of this. But since he's from a holy bloodline, he's considered a living god, like the old pharaohs were."

"Knowing what the problem is and being able to corner it are two different things," Bolan said. "What is he going to do with all of that ricin?"

"You're certain it's ricin?" Holt countered.

Bolan nodded. "I know what castor beans look like. Part of my weapon-of-mass-destruction training."

"And only ricin?" Holt asked.

"I saw that they'd taken five vases. I'd assumed that since they resembled the cask that Mubarak had brought to Somalia, they had the same contents. What were you thinking?" Bolan asked.

"Some form of natural resin, perhaps," Holt said. "I heard you talking about fluid suspension on your headset. What if, instead of an aerosol, they utilized a frangible material that, upon sufficient impact, turned to dust instead of mist?"

"Which could create areas that seem free of poison gas, but would behave in the same way that *houngan* zombie powder can be distributed in trap form," Bolan concluded.

"Redjedef had already tried it with modern nerve gas," Holt added. "But when we took down Idel, we had enough good people on our side to stop the release of it. Maybe Redjedef felt that using twentieth-century technology wasn't the way to set himself upon his throne."

"We'll figure that out when we get more information," Bolan said. He looked over Holt's rifle. She'd put a suppressor onto it, and she had finished loading her magazines while they'd talked. "Everything looks fine. Head up to the catwalk. And be alert."

Holt picked up a pair of night-vision goggles and tucked them atop her forehead. "You don't have to tell me, Matt."

She made an effort to stand on tiptoe, in an effort to plant a kiss on his cheek, and Bolan bent to meet her halfway. The brief moment of affection helped him to feel better. The taste of her mouth would be intoxicating if he weren't expecting the arrival of armed pirates in his safe house

Holt climbed the ladder up into the shadows of the warehouse ceiling.

KAMAU WAS WAITING when he saw some familiar faces at the dock entrance. There were six of them, but Masozi wasn't among them. If the Shabaab boss were going to be present, he'd be coming much later. All of the men were armed, but they'd obviously left their rifles behind at the staging area for their attack. Still, they each had a handgun, a machete, or both. When Kamau remembered what the young men did with their machetes, his thoughts turned dark and grim. If he had to open fire on these men, even if he had lived and laughed among them, he wouldn't lose a night of sleep because of it. The Shabaab militiamen were bullies, rapists and murderers.

"Isoba, what's up, brother?" Tejinn, a reedy Somali nearly as tall as Kamau, greeted him. "The boss man says you find yourself a woman."

Kamau pushed out a barking laugh, not feeling it as he did. "You're going to have to get your own. I'm not going to make Orif take his turn after you dirty bastards."

Tejinn sighed. "You wound me, Isoba."

Not yet I'm not, Kamau thought grimly.

"What about the white bitch? Or is she off-limits, too?" another of the Shabaab asked.

Bolan stepped into the open. "If you want to go through me, you're welcome to try."

The other men looked at the Executioner as he arrived. Clad in a black, athletic shirt that clung to his long, lean muscles like a second skin, sleeves down to just the top of his forearms, he looked as if he were carved out of night itself. The threatening steel of Bolan's voice had elicited a few bug-eyed gulps as a response.

"We'll find something else tonight," Tejinn spoke up, slapping the loudmouth who had raised the ire of the towering American.

Bolan narrowed his eyes. "You do that."

Tejinn glanced to Kamau and grimaced.

"Oh, you've got a shiny," Tejinn spoke up, pointing to the wireless headset tucked over Kamau's ear.

"Americans bring the best toys to work," Kamau replied. "He has a crate ready, for about as many as Masozi would bring."

"We get some?" Tejinn asked.

Bolan nodded. "Sure. Come on in and we'll set you up."

"'Course, you better shut off your phones, even the walkie-talkie function," Kamau said. "The feedback will be a bitch if you try them on without calibrating everything."

Tejinn nodded. "Sure."

He looked doubtful as he reached down to the cell phone he wore on his belt, but with a swipe of his thumb, he killed the signal. They'd be in the warehouse, and as far as Khaldun's people knew, there were only two to four people inside. Tejinn and his men outnumbered them, and they were stone-cold killers. There were two women inside. Tejinn knew that there wasn't a woman in the world who could fight a true warrior of the Shabaab.

As Tejinn walked through the door, he released a surprised gurgle, then was jerked out of view. The two behind him rushed forward to see what had happened.

As SOON AS the "leader" of the Somali fighting men was in the doorway, Bolan whirled and speared his hand across Tejinn's throat. His rigid fingers flexed Tejinn's windpipe, making him gag and lose his breath, nerves misfiring as the violent impact stunned him. Bolan grabbed a handful of shirt and hauled the skinny Shabaab fighter around, bashing his face into a brick wall.

Two more figures, startled by the sudden disappearance of their comrade, rushed into the doorway. Bolan didn't waste time with the battered and dazed Tejinn. He shifted his attention to them, and before they could register his presence, he clawed at both of them. His right hand wrapped around the throat of one of the Somali gunmen, strangling back a cry of dismay. Bolan's left hand came down like a lion's paw, his hard fingernails tearing the other's forehead and ripping at his eyelids.

The blinded Somali staggered past Bolan, screaming and clutching at his face, leaving the Executioner to attend to business with the other militiaman. With a savage twist, the warrior yanked his opponent into the warehouse with him, and rammed the gunman into the back of his blinded compatriot. Skulls clunked against each other, and the two staggered off balance. Bolan released the man he was choking, leaned back and speared his heel into the Shabaab raider's sternum. Bones cracked and he folded over, collapsing atop his blinded friend.

A fourth Somali appeared in the door, his hand wrestling to unsnag the front sight of his pistol from his waistband. Bolan turned to him and drove the sole of his foot into the gunner's pistol and hand. Finger bones crunched against metal, and a dull roar informed the warrior that his opponent could not have had his trigger finger in register. The muzzle-blast, driven into the loins of the Somali, was mostly soundless and contained.

The Executioner knew that even if the man had shot his femoral artery, there were still a few moments of fight in the Shabaab gunner. Bolan sank his fingers into the muscles on either side of the wounded shooter's neck and yanked down hard, bringing up his knee to meet the Somali's face. The crunch of his nose collapsing under incredible force was all the warrior needed to know. Splinters of bone had rocketed through the man's brain, killing him instantly. His suffering ended, the groin-shot militiaman tumbled lifelessly to the ground.

Bolan turned to see the man whose face he'd gouged had smeared the blood from his eyes. The Somali's lips were peeled back in rage, and he had yanked the handle of his machete, a foot and a half of bare, dull metal glimmering in the shadows. Bolan kicked the blade man in the knee hard enough to bend the joint backward, the simple strike keeping the rest of his body out of range of the militiaman's swordlike chopper. With the leg lost from beneath him, the knife man toppled crazily against the wall, throwing both hands up to catch himself.

Bolan didn't bother scooping up the fallen machete. It would make too much of a mess anyway. He took a step closer to the Shabaab gunner with the scratched-up face, and elbowed him in the ear. Between the wall and the force of his elbow strike, he shattered the neck of the hapless Somali militiaman. Whatever sins he'd committed escaped in a wail of dying regret. Bolan didn't want to think about what judgment the man would receive, but considering the horrors of the Somalian civil war, he'd be in the darkest corner of hell.

Tejinn slapped at the wall, trying to regain his feet, but Bolan kneed him between the shoulder blades, flattening him to the floor. It was a delaying action so that he could check on Kamau. So far, no gunfire had erupted, but that could have meant that the remaining two Shabaab murderers had used knives on him.

Looking into the loading dock, Bolan saw Kamau twist the head of a Somali 180 degrees with the power of his thick forearms. The other Shabaab soldier lay on the ground, wheezing and clutching his chest. The Ethiopian turned and brought his foot down savagely on the fallen man's chest once more. Ribs crumpled under three hundred pounds of force.

"You injured?" Bolan asked.

Kamau shook his head. He bent and grabbed his last kill by the ankle and dragged him to the deepest part of the loading-dock ramp. He moved back to where he'd engaged the two enemies and looked around. Fortunately, the entrance was well shielded from prying eyes by an extended roof and door panels. Nothing could be seen from another rooftop. He gave Bolan an okay signal, and the Executioner turned back to Tejinn, who was on his hands and knees.

"Sorry about all this," Bolan said, sounding genuine. He grabbed Tejinn by the collar, and, twisting the fabric into a noose, hauled the Somali to his feet and led him into the warehouse. Outside, Kamau covered the corpses with a tarp, then closed the door behind him.

The safe house would look quiet and peaceful for at least a few more minutes. Bolan needed to secure a Shabaab prisoner for the time being.

More trouble was on the way, and Bolan didn't want to leave Eartha Holt alone with a team of stealthy commandos for longer than he had to.

The Executioner took up an Uzi submachine gun, its muzzle fitted with a suppressor, and handed Tejinn off to Kamau. "Take this guy down to Metit. I've got an appointment to keep."

"Good hunting," Kamau offered, dragging the militiaman by the scruff of his neck.

In a target-rich environment like the safe house, it would be too easy for the Executioner to reach his bag limit.

CHAPTER THIRTEEN

As Bolan climbed the ladder to the rafters, his silenced Uzi hanging from a strap around his neck, his wireless headset issued a beep. Khaldun's commandos were on their way, having crossed a laser trip wire that he'd set up.

Unlike in the movies, laser trip wires and electric eyes were entirely invisible. No amount of steam or smoke would make them show up in the visible spectrum, and as light-amplification goggles didn't operate in the infrared section of the spectrum, rather the ultraviolet opposite end, there were no means of detecting Bolan's early-warning system. The cheap electric eyes, well hidden by rooftop debris, had been simple to install.

From the sound, Bolan also knew exactly how much time he had before the enemy arrived. He keyed his headset.

"Hear that, Eartha?" Bolan asked.

"Counting down to impending gunfire, Matt," Holt replied. "Kamau and Metit okay?"

"In the basement," Bolan returned. "With an extra package."

"Shabaab militiamen aren't going to have a lot of information for us," Holt replied. Bolan was on the catwalk with her, and she had her eyes peeled on the likeliest entrances for Khaldun's team.

Bolan picked up the slack, extending the stock on his Uzi for maximum stability and control. With the weapon set up like that, and his sharp senses and innate understanding of the subgun, any opponent within its range was a doomed target.

A dull thud sounded on the ceiling and Bolan homed in on it. Holt's rifle was also aimed at that part of the roof.

"You've got a Shabaab gunner. Are you interested in anyone from Khaldun's group?" Holt asked over the headset.

"I've already gone over a set of fingerprints from another captured bit of flesh," Bolan replied. "These guys have been erased from the records."

"That sounds familiar," Holt said bitterly.

Bolan grumbled. "Focus on the job at hand. We didn't join this fight to whine about our legacies."

"I'll be satisfied with just living to old age," Holt whispered.

A low-pitched whine filled the air. If Bolan hadn't been up in the catwalks, he wouldn't have heard it on the warehouse floor, and even now, it was barely more than a dull hiss accompanied by the subtle ring of metal scraping metal. The carbide saw that carved through the aluminum roof of the warehouse had been treated not to spark, so the only way that Bolan could locate the direction of the team cutting through the ceiling was by sound.

Three sets of gloved hands slipped through and bent the thick sheet of metal back. It took all that strength to pry open the panel, and once that was done, a short rope descended through the hole. Bolan and Holt remained still, their weapons trained on the improvised hatch, when Bolan's observational skills kicked in.

"Eyes shut!" Bolan hissed over the headset.

He clamped his eyelids shut. The blinding flare of a dangling flash-bang grenade, producing an orange sheet of light, illuminated through his lids. Holt, on the other hand, had light-amplification goggles. A flash grenade tended to cause major damage when it came to looking at the eruption of the distraction device's fireball. Bolan had used that vulnerability against opponents who hid behind the lenses of those goggles on many occasions, turning watchful sentries into stumbling liabilities. The fighting woman on the other side of the catwalks could have been knocked out of the fight with little means of getting to the ground. "Holt?"

"I turned my head... One eye's seeing nothing but fireballs," Holt replied. "I can see with my left, but depth perception sucks big-time."

"Cover," Bolan whispered as he peered through the darkness, watching men rappelling onto the crosswalks above the warehouse floor. He slithered behind a sheet of metal in time to evade the harsh blue blaze of an under-the-barrel lamp, amped up to stunning luminescence. The Executioner knew that the enemy was not only in full paranoia mode, but was working its hardest to destroy the night-vision abilities of the defenders they sought.

The commandos had to have caught a glimpse of Bolan's diving form as suppressed gunfire sputtered downrange. Behind the metal panel, the soldier's hearing was knocked out by the clank of slugs on corrugated aluminum. He poked the Uzi around the corner and rattled off a couple of bursts, then withdrew behind his shield. The enemy was using conventional pistol-caliber weaponry, incapable of punching through the cover he'd taken. However, the constant rattle meant that an entire army could be flanking him, and he wouldn't hear them walking up on his blind side.

The Executioner decided to fight fire with fire. He pulled out his pocket flashlight and set it to its maximum strobe effect. The compact Surefire had the power to blind targets as well, despite being no longer than his fist was wide. Thumbing the switch, Bolan poked the light up and over the shield, releasing a pulsing flicker of blinding glare.

There were a couple of cursed grunts in Arabic, informing the warrior that the powerful little torch had disoriented some of his enemies. With a lunge, Bolan evacuated his compromised cover and charged to another section of railing that had been shorn up with two-by-fours. A single burst of slugs chased him, thunking against the wood, other weapons snarling with little direction, the rounds flying off target. Bolan knew that he had only one capable opponent who could see him. With another strobe blast, he hoped to feint that enemy. Peering around with the Surefire, he saw the gunman throw his arm up in an attempt to shield his vision.

Bolan triggered a burst of Parabellum rounds that ripped the gunman from navel to sternum. He let out a burbling cry as he flipped over the railing and tumbled to the ground, thirty feet below. If he hadn't died already from the eviscerating power of Bolan's machine pistol, the Egyptian had been finished off when his skull cracked open, vomiting brains on the concrete floor.

"To your right," Holt whispered.

Bolan turned just in time to catch two Spear of Destiny hardmen crossing a walkway parallel to his. The Executioner opened fire on them, snaking behind a light fixture that exploded with sparks from the enemy's weapons. The big metal collar of the fixture shuddered as subguns snarled out their payloads. Bolan held his fire, knowing that he'd be wasting his ammunition, but the Egyptians were working under the theory of suppressing fire. He took the opportunity to reload his weapon and scan for Holt. Her depth perception had been compromised, but she still was able to call out threats looming against Bolan. He was set to return the favor for her.

Holt's Uzi snarled in the distance, the thuds of suppressed bullets escaping her silencer allowing the warrior to triangulate her position. She might not have been operating with both eyes, but she still had managed to dump a load of lead into another of the Egyptian raiders. Bolan spotted another gunman attempting to circle around her, bringing him within the warrior's line of sight. A trip of his subgun's trigger caused the would-be murderer to jerk under the impacts of several 9 mm rounds.

"Thanks," Holt whispered. "My one eye is clearing up, and those goons are still on the other side of your light."

"Got a clear shot at them?" Bolan asked, sweeping the catwalks for more movement. He wasn't certain how many professionals Khaldun had decided to throw at the safe house, but it had to be more than five.

A clamor of voices sounded through the hole in the

roof, and Bolan realized that it had to have been the rioters. He slid his hand into the pocket where his detonator for the flammable barriers had been secreted. He thumbed the trigger, knowing he had to get those fires up and roaring quickly if he wanted to minimize the harm inflicted by the flames.

The detonation he'd been expecting was superseded by a much closer blast, a section of domed roof buckling as a thunderbolt struck it. The aluminum bulged, expanding like a balloon. Bolan had enough reaction time to throw himself flat as the bubble of metal burst open, ragged petals flaying widely as a concussion wave burped through the hole.

It was like a volcano had formed, upside down in the warehouse, but instead of flowing lava, a rain of shrapnel sparked and pinged on the concrete below.

"That wasn't me," Bolan said, as he scrambled to his knees.

The Uzi had been jarred from his hands, so he swept up the Smith & Wesson .45. The RPG rocket that had struck the roof had just torn the light fixture that separated him from the Egyptian gunman from its moorings. It had happened so suddenly, and on the heels of the crash of a 77 mm explosive warhead, that the two commandos were caught by surprise as the Executioner fired his pistol at them. The 230-grain hardball rounds didn't have the same punch as his preferred .44 Magnum Desert Eagle, but they were still renowned man-stoppers. The .45 slugs tore through flesh and bone without hesitation, Bolan's four shots taking down his two opponents. One of them tumbled to the ground, but the other dangled, folded over the railing. Bolan pulled

the partially spent magazine from the pistol and pocketed it before ripping a new one and slamming it home.
Seven rounds of .45 Auto might have been plenty for
some situations, but the Executioner wanted all eleven
shots on hand. He slid the Smith & Wesson back into
its hip leather and retrieved the Uzi on its sling.

"Holt?" Bolan called.

"I'm just a little rattled," she replied. "It looks like
we're alone up here. I took out another shadow after their
friends turned this warehouse into a convertible."

Bolan looked at the ruptured ceiling. "More like a
moon roof."

Holt sighed. "If you have time to joke, you have time
to shoot."

"Get down to the floor," Bolan replied. "These guys
called in an artillery strike to take us out. Once the RPG
gunners don't hear from their friends, any restraint's
going out the window."

As if to punctuate Bolan's point, another blast hammered the curved roof. He grabbed the side rails of the
ladder and slid down its length. Out of the corner of his
eye, he saw Holt taking the same rapid descent. The
two hit the concrete, flexing their knees to absorb the
impact as a third and fourth detonation shook the top
of the warehouse.

"We weren't expecting that kind of firepower, were
we?" Holt asked as the two met up near the basement
entrance.

"I'd be lying if I said I did," Bolan answered. "I
was sure they'd be a little more restrained in an urban
environment."

Holt shrugged. "Let's hope your flame barriers went off. Otherwise..."

A side door imploded, and angry yells filled the air. Bolan grimaced as he smelled singed hair and clothing.

"They went off, but Khaldun must have thought ahead," Bolan surmised.

Holt spun the suppressor off her Uzi and the Executioner followed suit. The kind of force that they were facing might be broken by the rattle of assault weapons, or at least slowed for a few seconds. The warehouse shook again and Bolan wrapped his arms around Holt's shoulders. Burning-hot bits of aluminum peppered his back, but the tough fabric of his skintight shirt kept his skin from being cooked and lacerated. A sharp splinter had sliced across the back of Bolan's hand, but it was a mere cosmetic scratch. He'd been lucky that the hand deflected the shard of aluminum from his skull.

Holt squirmed from under Bolan's shielding form and fired a long burst over the heads of the rioters who were feeling the heat from the shrapnel that used to be the roof. Gunfire and burning splinters of metal proved too much for half the mob at the door they'd kicked in, and they turned tail and ran. The others scrambled, looking for cover from the hot rain that threatened them.

"I hate warehouses," Holt groaned. "Every time I get near one, it's smoke, flames, bullets and bodies all over the place."

"Every time?" Bolan asked with some slight bemusement. He triggered a burst at some crates that were sheltering a portion of the irate mob, the rioters keeping their heads down.

Holt pursed her lips. "Come to think of it, any building I end up with you in develops that problem."

"Get down the stairs," Bolan ordered. "Joke time later."

Holt turned and descended the steps as the Executioner guarded the doorway. More RPG shells hammered the building, this time striking the walls of the warehouse. Dust and rebar crashed to the floor, stealing the will of more rioters. The rest squirmed, trying to navigate rows of crates while the world crashed down on their heads.

Bolan closed the basement door behind him and flipped down a steel bar to jam the door shut. The improvised bolt wouldn't last long, but with the building being shaken apart by the hammering of high explosives, there wouldn't be much need for it to hold out indefinitely. Besides, once he reached his bolt-hole, no one would be able to follow them.

As Khaldun's men unleashed mayhem on the warehouse, the Executioner and his allies would make their getaway.

TEJINN BLINKED, his whole body aching from the manhandling he'd received from Bolan. He knew that his wrists were bound behind his back, tight enough to keep him from moving, but loose enough to allow circulation to his fingers. Whoever had hog-tied him had done a damn good job of it.

Bolan stood in front of him, wringing out a rag, then continued cleaning his face.

"What are you doing?" Tejinn asked.

"Cleaning the cuts you received," Bolan answered. "I don't want them to get infected."

Tejinn looked around. Except for a lone lightbulb over the pair, the room had been darkened, blacked out. He'd only seen rooms like this in movies, but the oppressive claustrophobia of the scene was starting to weigh on him. "You're not going to torture me, are you?"

"I don't believe in torture," Bolan admitted truthfully. "You have to have a proper setup, lots of background information and corroborating evidence to verify that you're not just squealing to keep me from slamming a flatiron into your testicles."

"W-what about water boarding?" Tejinn asked.

Bolan grimaced. "I've had it done to me, and it's definitely a tongue loosener. But anything said while you're upside down and trying to breathe through a waterfall is gibberish."

"So, you're not going to water board me either?" Tejinn asked.

Bolan shook his head. "There. All clean."

"Where am I?" Tejinn asked.

"Still in Egypt," Bolan said.

Tejinn looked around. "So what is all this for?"

Bolan stood up and put the bloody rag into the bucket by his foot. "Well, I don't believe in torture for gaining information. But I do believe in an eye for an eye."

A curtain was pulled aside, and Tejinn saw two women, scarves wrapped around their heads and faces, enter. Angry eyes, one set dark and smoldering brown, the other fierce and brilliant green, glared at him as if he were a piece of meat. Tejinn could see the glimmer of sharp knives in their delicate hands.

"You told Kamau that you wanted a crack at raping this girl," Bolan said. "They told me that they want a crack at you."

Tejinn swallowed. "You've got to help me."

Bolan rubbed his chin for a moment. The furious women orbited the pair, their hard stares looking over the Somali prisoner. "No, I really don't have to. Nor do I want to."

"I can tell you anything that you want," Tejinn said.

"What can you say?" Bolan asked. "I want to know what the Egyptians are up to, but they wouldn't let you in on that. You're just someone from down the coast. In fact, the hard-line Arab Muslims you claim brotherhood with consider you nothing more than walking, talking cattle."

"Mmm. Meat," Rashida Metit whispered with menace.

"You think he's got anything worthwhile under those pants?" Holt asked.

Tejinn swallowed hard. "Listen, Kamau knows that I've got a lot of useful stuff in my head. He might have been chief of security, but I have rank, too. Sure, I don't know Khaldun or his people, but Masozi let a few things slip as we were setting up the raid on your warehouse."

"You don't have anything to bargain with, and you're a rapist," Bolan said. "Honestly, this is just going to be the equivalent of a night at the show for me."

"You miserable asshole!" Tejinn shouted. "There's a convoy heading out in the morning!"

Bolan paused. "A convoy." He made a point of rolling his eyes.

"Khaldun wanted Masozi and the rest of us to accompany him to somewhere in the desert," Tejinn said.

"Know where?" Bolan asked, dubious.

"Neither of them wanted to let too much out of the bag, in case one of us ended up…like this," Tejinn answered. "They kept us in the dark."

"Then my advice is to go toward the light as fast as you can," Bolan told the Shabaab terrorist. "Or the woman can have free rein."

"Listen, we can cut a deal," Tejinn pleaded. "I don't know where the convoy is going, but I know where it's staging from."

Bolan tilted his head. Holt glided the flat of her knife along Tejinn's shoulder. The Somali was sweating, his forehead shimmering in the glow of the lone lightbulb.

"Call these bitches off!" Tejinn shouted.

Bolan winced as Metit walked quickly toward him. He barred her progress with his arm. "You're calling women you wanted to rape, who have knives and the desire to see you carved up *bitches?* I thought you wanted to live."

Holt dug her fingernails into Tejinn's scalp and rested the cold edge of her blade on his cheek. "You can stop the little Arab girl, Cooper. But what are you going to do to me?"

"I don't know," Bolan answered. "What have you got for me, Tejinn?"

"Save me…"

"Give me something," Bolan growled.

Tejinn spoke. He told everything he knew about the garage where the convoy would be leaving from. As he did so, he realized that Holt had let go of his head, stepping back.

It was too late now. The die had been cast, and Tejinn gave up every shred of information that he could muster. No one had done more than leave a few fingernail scratches in his forehead, and Tejinn had broken down.

Tears flowed down his cheeks once he was out of words. He sucked in deep breaths, his shoulders heaving. Even when Holt cut the duct tape wrapped around his wrists, he remained in the chair, his eyes clenched shut.

Bolan leaned in close, whispering in his ear.

"You have a chance to turn your life around. You've seen the poison pumped through your ears has put you on the fast track to suffering and oblivion," Bolan said. "But there is a better path. I suggest you take it."

Tejinn looked up, eyes rimmed with tears. Bolan and the women left him to his thoughts.

CHAPTER FOURTEEN

Metit got into the car with Bolan and Holt. As soon as she sat down, Kamau pulled away from the curb.

"You still up to sticking with us?" Holt asked the young woman.

"I'm in this for as long as you all are," Metit answered.

"Good," Bolan said. "We'll head to our hotel and get some sleep. I need everyone rested if we're going to keep up with Khaldun and Masozi."

Metit sighed. "Sleep will be good."

It had been a long day, and she hadn't even seen an enemy up close, at least until Bolan's staged interrogation of Tejinn. She remembered the feel of the knife in her hand, and thought about her willingness to use it. She could also see the restrained fury in Holt's eyes as she caressed him with naked steel. The Somali militiaman had inspired a bottomless level of rage in both women.

It was a simple matter of Kamau mentioning that the man wanted to rape Metit, too. It had ignited a fury within her that frightened her on an elemental level. Metit rubbed her hand, trying to dispel the phantom memory of the knife handle. Sleep would distract her from the memories of the fury that had been awakened. She made a silent vow to herself to control her anger.

It frightened her more than the thought of death at the hands of Khaldun and the Shabaab.

The hotel would give her a chance to try to clear her head.

ORIF MASOZI and Khaldun looked at the smear of smoke on the skyline of Alexandria with the predawn glow of sunrise. Khaldun took a sip of coffee, cold and grown bitter from sitting too long.

"Do you think they could have gotten out of that?" Masozi asked.

"I had my men disable and block the vehicles of the archaeologists in the Sinai. And still he managed to get at least two SUVs working and out of the canyon," Khaldun said. "I had gunships scour the earth around the camp with heavy machine guns and missiles, and yet he was untouched by all of that firepower. This is no ordinary man we're up against."

Masozi lit another cigarette and took a deep drag on it. "You sent those people to my compound to assassinate Mubarak."

"Only to assassinate Mubarak, and to retrieve or destroy the castor beans he brought with him," Khaldun said. "But since you are my ally, my orders were to minimize the breakage."

Masozi frowned. "Cooper claimed he only shot at my people in self-defense. But he's the one who dropped the hammer on Mubarak."

"He killed that traitor?" Khaldun asked.

Masozi nodded. "And he gunned down my people, under my nose, and I let myself fall for his lies so badly, he tricked me twice. The first time to keep me from executing him for violating my compound, and just last night."

"Your friend Kamau isn't your friend," Khaldun added.

Masozi shook his head, waving smoke away from his face. "He's the one who helped to sell me that second lie. All these months, I treated that man like a brother, and he ends up killing six of his comrades."

"We're not sure if they were all dead," Khaldun said. "We never recovered Tejinn's body."

"Didn't you see what those rocket grenades did to the warehouse?" Masozi asked. "I'm surprised we found as many body parts as we did."

"I've learned, from Cooper, never to assume that anyone is dead if you haven't seen the corpse. Even worse, even if you did see the corpse," Khaldun said. "He stuffed two of Mubarak's men into an SUV, and their corpses and the vehicle became target practice for my helicopters. What we found gave us the impression that we'd killed someone."

"Don't get superstitious on me," Masozi replied. "This sorcery crap is going to get on my nerves. Cooper is a man. A skilled man, a clever liar and a ferocious fighter. But he's a man. And he can be killed by a bullet or a knife just as you or I can. Right now, he's outthought us. But even if he has Tejinn as a captive, there is nothing that I've told him that could compromise our next move."

"Nothing at all?" Khaldun asked.

Masozi sighed. "I'm not you. I don't lie to my allies every chance I get."

Khaldun's eyes narrowed in anger.

"Don't give me that," Masozi answered. "You spun so many lies that you tripped over them, and gave Cooper the perfect opportunity to kill dozens of our people. If you hadn't lied, maybe his body would be under the remains of that warehouse."

Khaldun winced at the reproach. "All right."

"We leave later for whatever trip you have planned. You don't have to go home, but no way am I letting you sleep in my hotel room," Masozi replied. "So go. I'm going to get some rest."

Khaldun nodded and got up. "Maybe after your nap, you'll be a little more polite and a lot less cranky."

"Unless Kamau brings me Cooper's severed head and the resurrected soldiers I lost, I doubt I'll be happier," Masozi answered. "But I will make an effort to be more polite."

"That's all I ask," Khaldun said.

Masozi was glad when he was finally alone in the room. He had arrangements to make before he could succumb to the luxury of sleep.

KHALDUN COLLAPSED behind the steering wheel of his car just as his cell phone warbled to life. He clapped his hand to his forehead, groaning in disdain at the shrilling little electronic device. He looked on the screen and saw that it was his master, the Eternal Pharaoh, wishing to speak with him. He opened the device and put it to his ear.

"Your servant awaits your command," Khaldun said, instantly regretting the dullness of his voice as he spoke.

"You have been through a trial this evening, my first

among immortals," Redjedef said to him. "That is the only reason I shall forgive your lax reception of my word."

"You're talking to me over a cell phone," Khaldun groaned. "How holy can this interaction be?"

There was a chuckle on the other end. "You have me at that point. Have you learned anything more of Cooper?"

"I've learned plenty," Khaldun replied. "I've learned that he can derail an assault on his premises and scurry away as a building's collapsing around him. I learned that he can light a fire that wasn't strong enough to cause more than a few burns, yet make it look bright and menacing enough to scare off half a riot."

"Your work shall be cut out for you in the coming hours," Redjedef told him. "Anything else?"

"It turns out that Masozi's chief of security has sided with Cooper against us," Khaldun added. "I don't know how he turned Kamau, but he did."

"He did not change the allegiance of the Ethiopian," Redjedef replied.

"Ethiopian?" Khaldun asked. "Since when can't an IOC splinter cell tell the difference between an Ethiopian and one of their countrymen?"

"Since Kamau is obviously an ethnic Somali who had taken residence in Ethiopia," Redjedef answered. "It has taken my people some digging, but they have discovered communications between—"

"You couldn't have told me this sooner?" Khaldun asked, with impatience sharpening his words.

Redjedef sighed. "No. I could not have. Some of us

have to hide our agendas. I spoke with you at my earliest opportunity."

Khaldun winced. "My apologies, my king."

"Accepted," the Eternal Pharaoh answered. "You've been under enormous stress, and I have only added to it."

"Only slightly," Khaldun replied. He frowned, thinking of what Masozi had told him about Tejinn and Kamau. The two men had apparently become fast friends, so the disappearance of the Somali seemed doubly suspicious. Khaldun doubted that Masozi had more than one mole in his militia, but the bonds of friendship allow one man to see the weaknesses of another.

"Khaldun, are you awake?" Redjedef inquired.

"Just thinking of something," Khaldun said. "That is what you have picked me for, sire. My mind is never still, always seeking that which may threaten your bidding."

Redjedef sighed. "You are returning to form. What thoughts troubled you?"

"Kamau might know how to break a prisoner that Cooper might have taken in the confusion at the warehouse," Khaldun answered. "Masozi tried to assure me that he didn't give his militiamen any information that could have been used against us, but his promises seemed hollow."

"Perceptive," the Eternal Pharaoh complimented. "What threat can this pose to your journey?"

Khaldun ran over the numbers in his head. "Cooper was prepared, but he only seemed to have a few people at his disposal. If he were to know the location of the convoy, it would be relatively useless in terms of an attack. All he could do would be follow and observe."

"I shall give you the means to check your shadow, in that instance," Redjedef promised. "I may not be Ra, but I too have eyes that peer down from heaven."

"Satellite observations," Khaldun translated. "Excellent, and thank you, Master. I worry that the cost of this operation may stress your resources."

"This is not a matter of cost. Indeed, the satellites are practically free."

Khaldun raised an eyebrow at the implications of that statement. He didn't wish to press the point, though. He had to prepare for his convoy. "Have you any news of Cooper for me, sire?"

"Just that he only wears the trappings of authority. He is not a servant of any leader, and answers only to himself," Redjedef replied. "Thus, he is an enemy who is more dangerous than we've ever encountered. This is a man with his own agenda and belief system, and it has carried him around the world."

"He has not fought a god," Khaldun countered.

Redjedef groaned softly. "Perhaps. Perhaps not. Just know that what you are fighting has established his existence as a myth, a legend, a nightmare."

"Has he a name?"

"None known to any who yet live. He is only a reputation," Redjedef explained. "But he is a professional, and he is very capable."

Khaldun managed a smile. "A professional, you can plan for. You know how they're going to react to a crisis."

The Eternal Pharaoh chuckled. "Your strength has

been restored, warrior. Prepare the Spear of Destiny for its ultimate thrust."

Khaldun bowed his head, even though he was aware that his master couldn't see it. Redjedef was correct; his spirit and strength had been renewed with a few wise words. And with that hope, his reverence for the mysterious and powerful son of kings and gods swelled. "As you bid."

Khaldun still possessed one of the best armies of professional soldiers and the best equipment that money could buy. One man was nothing compared to such power.

He turned off the cell phone, started the car and went to prepare for his pharaoh's victory.

KAMAU COULDN'T SLEEP, and he had figured why. He had been too hard on Metit, snapping angrily at her when all she was trying to do was give him a slender thread of hope and laughter in a sea of turgid blood and violence. He sat up in his bed and groped for his discarded T-shirt. Pulling it on, he stood up and listened for the sound of Bolan's breathing in the next bed.

"You're not disturbing me," the man said.

Kamau felt a shiver go up and down his spine. "Then why are you talking in your sleep?"

"I'm relaxed, but aware," Bolan replied. "You might want to put on some pants and shoes if you're going out to see Rashida."

Kamau smiled in the shadows of the darkened hotel room. "I'll be fine barefoot. The soles of my feet are like elephant hide."

"Fair enough," Bolan said. "Just don't make too much noise. Other people are more sensitive than me."

Kamau shrugged as he pulled on a pair of cargo shorts. The thought that someone else could be more sensitive than "Cooper" was something the big Ethiopian couldn't believe. The soldier who had dropped back into a catnap between the time Kamau bent over for his shorts and then stood up was alert to the finest nuances of behavior. In a matter of seconds, he had ascertained that Kamau wasn't a true member of the Shabaab.

Walking on the ratty carpet in the hallway, he looked up and down the corridor. The hotel had seen much better days, and none of them had been since the turn of the century. Still, its lower standards of maintenance extended to the relaxed attitudes of the desk staff. Kamau could smell alcohol and hashish smoke, most of it stale, some of it fresh. Few would expect two white people to be hanging out in such a hovel. Its lower class provided a shield of anonymity for the cadre.

Kamau felt a wet spot and he realized why Bolan had suggested shoes. He wasn't certain what the moisture was from— spilled drinks, or urine, or something worse. He kept walking, reminding himself of his boast of feet as tough as pachyderm armor. He reached Metit's door and bit his lower lip.

He wondered if he should knock when he heard the sound of breaking glass. "Rashida?"

There was whispered feminine cursing.

"Rashida, are you okay?" Kamau rasped through the door, trying not to wake the entire hotel.

"Hang on," came her muttered response. The door opened and Kamau saw that the young woman was cradling her hand below her breastbone. Her knuckles had been split, and blood dripped freely from several cuts.

"Watch out, I broke the mirror," Metit mumbled, letting Kamau into the room.

Kamau looked at the mirror on one wall, and saw the radiating cracks that came from a hard punch to the reflective surface. "Got tough feet. Are you all right?"

Metit shook her head. "No. I'm bleeding, and I tried to punch myself in the face."

Kamau sat her down, and then grabbed some towels from the bathroom. It took a few minutes to verify that there weren't any splinters stuck in her skin, and he tore a length of bath towel to wrap around her injured fingers. Still keeping some cloth underneath the bloody hand, he guided her to the sink to rinse off the cuts to prevent a chance of infection. For all the squalor of this hotel, at least it had clean pipes and water that looked potable.

He bandaged her fingers, and once he was done, she rested her head against his chest, taking a deep breath.

"I'm sorry," she said.

"I'm the one who came over to apologize," Kamau replied, stroking the thick, black silky locks that poured halfway down her back.

"It wasn't my place to badger you so," Metit told him. She looked up at him, and even though the whites of her eyes were red veined from a bout of tears that had only barely dried, the glimmering pools of darkness drew Kamau in. He cupped her chin.

"You were only trying to help," Kamau whispered. "I want to thank you."

Metit managed a crooked smile. "Kiss me, please."

Kamau did so, softly, feeling as if he was taking advantage at first. Metit was vulnerable, reeling from torments that he couldn't even begin to imagine. Only a day ago, she had been a prisoner, left for dead because she'd been knocked out during the commission of an unspeakable act against her. But she returned his kiss, arms snaking around his neck.

Kamau held her gently, guiding her back to her bed. She, like so many other women he had known, was tiny in comparison to him, but the strength she exhibited, cleaving to him as if he were an anchor in a stormy sea, told him that this was something she wanted.

Kamau gave in to the more primitive side of his affections for her. He'd never expected to be the lover of the pretty, young student, not in the wake of the violence that she'd suffered. But given the chance, remembering the words of gentle support she'd given him, he was pulled into her life.

The lust that underlay his affection was tamed by the knowledge of the pain she'd experienced. She had been pushed to an edge few people had ever experienced, she'd seen her own darkness, and she wanted to be reassured that there was good in the world.

Kamau and Metit lay together, baring their bodies and spirits to each other. With subdued passion and gentle caresses, they began a process of healing, the kind that only came from a lover's touch.

CHAPTER FIFTEEN

Colonel Gahiji waited in the hotel lobby, sipping lemon water and regretting his decision to stop smoking so many years ago. He was a healthier man for it, but cigarettes went a long way toward numbing nerves that built up during waits for covert meetings. He was early, by about an hour, and there was still at least forty minutes before "Matt Cooper" was due to show up. The early arrival was a necessity in order to make certain no one had staked him out. He was in counterterrorism, and thus, he was a known subject for surveillance and counterespionage. All manner of terrorist groups and the governments who sponsored them kept an eye on his movements.

Gahiji was certain that he hadn't been trailed, his seemingly paranoid countershadowing precautions having cleared his back trail, and any other avenue by which he would have been followed. His eyes were keenly peeled, and even then, he almost didn't notice the presence of the Executioner until he was ten feet away. His uncertainty at the first appearance of the soldier had tensed him up, but Bolan's reassuring hand rested on his shoulder. Gahiji looked up at the familiar, friendly features of a man who had done much for Egypt against the savages who would corrupt her leadership and usurp her justice.

"Matt, it is good to see you," the colonel said softly. A woman slipped into a seat across from him. At first he didn't know her face, but a pair of sharp, fiery green eyes provided all the identification that he required. "My emerald-eyed terror…"

Holt smiled and nodded in acknowledgment. "Professor Eartha Holt."

Gahiji took her hand and kissed the back of her fingers. Bolan sat beside them. "Atef…"

"Gahiji, now," the veteran military man replied. "Sorry for the change."

Bolan waved it off. "I know my friends, no matter what new names they take."

Holt smiled at that last statement, and Gahiji felt comfortable at last.

"After communicating with each other through phone calls and passed messages, it's good to finally talk face-to-face," Gahiji replied.

"I wish we had the time for pleasantries," Bolan admitted. "You've been looking up Khaldun?"

"I haven't had to, but I didn't want to risk it except in person," Gahiji said. "Khaldun is my replacement, and he worked his way up through the ranks as a shooter."

Bolan frowned. "A soldier on the same side."

"Far from it," Gahiji replied. "The man took two terror suspects and presented them as his operatives."

"Which suspects?" Holt asked.

"Parma and her big friend," Gahiji explained.

Bolan nodded. "You trust me that much?"

"You've prevented this country from entering a war which would have slain millions, at the risk of your own life," Gahiji said. "I trust you more than I trust Khaldun."

"Is that his real name?" Bolan asked.

"Are any of our names real, 'Cooper'?" Gahiji asked, looking between Holt and Bolan.

Bolan managed a smile. "I guess not."

Gahiji sighed. "His name is real enough for government work, just as yours is, Cooper. Same with you, Holt."

"No doubt," Holt answered. "He's good?"

"He's been good enough to have survived a round with me," Bolan admitted. "Two rounds, in one evening."

"The way you describe it, neither case was a direct confrontation," Holt noted.

"He was good enough and had the right caliber of men to keep me on the run and off balance," Bolan said. "You helped me set up a trap a few hours ago, and he made certain to stay on the other side of town."

"You're not showing your nerves, are you?" Gahiji asked. "You attacked a small army with only a few people. An army buried in a mountain."

"No, I'm not showing my nerves," Bolan said. "I'm being realistic, however, about my opposition, so I don't underestimate him. If I take anything for granted, I end up dead, and worse, Khaldun and whoever he works for wins. When they win, hundreds, maybe thousands, suffer or die, as well."

"Whoever he works for...I think is Redjedef," Holt spoke up.

Gahiji narrowed his eyes. "A first-dynasty pharaoh?"

"Someone who took his name, or more or less his title," Bolan said. "A lot of these self-described masterminds pick old names in order to grant themselves greater authority for the dimmer and more superstitious. They identify themselves with pharaohs, gods, ancient sorcerers, even prophets."

Gahiji and Holt nodded in unison. Some of the most terrifying insurgents in the world had been led down their paths of violence by imams who twisted the tenets of an entire religion. Both people, and Bolan himself, had engaged in bloody combat with the dupes of these false prophets. This new lead conspirator, Redjedef, was of the same cloth. Whether the man believed he was truly a reincarnated pharaoh or was using a convenient identity to hook his agenda on, dozens had already been murdered under his orders, maybe even more. There was no doubt, however, that the death toll would increase exponentially upon this madman's whim at the first sign of failure.

Suddenly Bolan's assessment of Khaldun's skills and threat level was driven home. The Executioner was serious about this mission, as he was with every operation he went on.

"I have a trusted observer watching the convoy setup," Gahiji spoke up. This wasn't a time for debate, it was time to get going on solving the crisis that Khaldun was trying to cover up. "There's a lot of busywork going on, preparations for a large move."

"As you said, busywork," Bolan replied.

"You're thinking this might be a trap?" Gahiji asked.

"It's the only thing I have right now," Bolan told him. "My own people are looking for something that would provide a good target to further anyone's agenda that could be disrupted by a release of biological toxins."

"Narrowing that down isn't going to be easy," Gahiji replied. "I've been scouring the news, but we're in a fairly packed time of year. You've got tourism, international negotiations, the continued mess of the Israeli occupied territories…"

Bolan's face drew into a grim countenance of dark contemplation. "How about the people left behind at the dig?"

"I haven't been able to recover anyone without attracting the attention of Khaldun's department," Gahiji replied. "I've only been able to place a single sentry on-site, just to keep the students and university faculty from being desecrated by vultures and other scavengers."

"If Khaldun's people show up in force, make certain…" Bolan trailed off.

Gahiji and Holt tilted their heads as Bolan's features blanked out. Except for the flash of his eyes as thoughts spiraled in his mind, he had gone motionless.

"Cooper?" the two people at the table asked him.

"Colonel, under no circumstance is your man to engage Khaldun's men if they show up," Bolan said. He quickly drew a sketch map on his napkin and handed it to Gahiji. "There should be a cave here that your man can retreat to. Tell him to leave no footprints to betray his presence."

"What's wrong?" Gahiji asked.

"It's only been two days since the students were murdered," Bolan told the Egyptian officer. "Khaldun's people have me looking here in Alexandria for trouble, while in the meantime, he has been cleaning up the site in the Sinai. This is why he downplayed my presence at the university and in dealing with his operatives."

Gahiji's forehead wrinkled at the thought. "He's going to make it public knowledge that there was a terrorist incident in the Sinai Desert, and that while there may have been terrorists killed, Egyptians lost sons and daughters to needless violence?"

Bolan's lips drew into an angry line. "Trained commandos with helicopters and most specifically 5.56 mm weaponry."

"As opposed to Egyptian or other Arab-region weapons in 7.62 mm COMBLOC or 5.45 mm for the more recent copies of those weapons," Gahiji concluded.

Holt took a deep breath. "Khaldun and his forces made the hit look like an Israeli strike team."

"Mossad counterterrorists making a strike on Egyptian soil would be more than enough to sway the military toward anger at Israel," Bolan said. "With innocent students caught in the cross fire, you've got an increased potential for the people to voice their outrage against them, too."

"Then the ricin was simply a distraction?" Gahiji speculated.

"No. I remember how this operation worked before. We've got Egyptian-based materials producing a virulent toxin," Bolan said. "It gets used on Israeli soil, and suddenly Tel Aviv has its own incentive to act against Cairo."

Holt grimaced. "That means I'm the only chance of telling the Mossad about a threat about to erupt in their backyard. But I'm currently on shit duty."

"So what about Khaldun's 'convoy'?" Gahiji asked.

"I'll take a look," Bolan offered. "But I need you to arrange some transportation for me."

Gahiji nodded. "Anything."

"Holt, Kamau and Metit need to get to the dig to support whoever you have up there," Bolan said.

"What about my bosses?" Holt asked.

Bolan caught her green eyes flashing with conflicting emotions. "I need a seasoned fighter at the dig. There's going to be something going on there, I can just feel it. Meanwhile, I'll have my own people go through back channels to keep the Mossad apprised of what's going on."

"You seem in a hurry," Gahiji replied.

"If this distraction is what I think it is, then I'm definitely on a short time line," the Executioner answered. "One more thing, you seemed extra distressed by the mention of Redjedef, something more than just the recognition of an old pharaoh."

"Back when we were sifting through the wreckage of General Idel's mountain stronghold—in the Sinai Desert—I picked up communications between Idel and the Syrians referring to an intervening agent, phonetically called Reg," Gahiji replied. "I thought it might have been an abbreviation of another name, though there were other hints that there was some kind of royalty involved, so I'd also assumed it perhaps indicated regent."

"Because you didn't think that the second pharaoh of Egypt would be chosen as a code name for someone working with the Syrians?" Bolan asked.

"Because we, like the Israelis, have enough shit

coming out of our ears concerning the twenty-first-century version of fanatics for a historical figure," Gahiji replied. "Accepting the addition of Egyptian fanatics following a millennia-old god king without a ton of evidence would strain credibility."

Holt looked to Gahiji.

"Could you help with the back-channel warnings to Tel Aviv?" Bolan asked. "And do what you can to stem the spread of information about the Sinai massacre, at least until we can pin it on the true perpetrators."

"We'll keep their fingerprints out of the news," Gahiji replied. "But can you bring down Khaldun and Redjedef?"

Bolan didn't answer for a moment. "I'll do everything I can."

The Executioner rose from the table. "Eartha, I'll meet you at the dig, if everything goes right."

BARBARA PRICE'S VOICE greeted Bolan as he slipped on his earphone, driving through Alexandria to where their prisoner had said Khaldun had set up a convoy.

"Striker, what's going on?" Price asked.

"We're working against a deadline," Bolan said. "And Khaldun has official backing."

"We've got that from our records," Price replied. "It took some digging. His real name is Menes Benipe."

"It wasn't something my old friend Gahiji could give me," Bolan replied. "Mainly because he's been kicked out of those circles after he was so successful in shutting down Redjedef's initial operation."

"You think his promotion was deliberate," Price stated.

Bolan looked at the case that sat in the leg well of his SUV's passenger seat. Gahiji had left him a few extra gifts in the loaned vehicle. While the wiry, leather-skinned old soldier may not have had command of Egypt's finest counterterrorism squad, he still had sufficient resources to assist the Executioner. "I know his promotion was deliberate. Khaldun and his unit were essentially pushed in to replace the commandos who had assisted me against the last round of war starters."

"You might have a point," Price responded. "We've been trying to track the paperwork on the change of service, but it's a muddled mess."

"A lot of envelopes under the table and favors in back rooms, likely," Bolan returned.

"So Redjedef profited from the reassignment of Gahiji."

"He had to do something in the wake of that defeat," Bolan returned. "It was unlikely that he could chase me, we never leave much behind to trace, thanks to the work of the cyberteam."

"Gahiji wouldn't have given you up, especially after all you'd done for his son," Price added.

"So Holt and I were shielded in that regard. Unit 777 got a major win against a renegade force, and we faded into the shadows," Bolan said.

"We've still worked with the Unit in the time since that mission," Price noted. "Have we compromised the Stony Man teams?"

"No. Gahiji was promoted out of the Unit, but the operatives are still trustworthy," Bolan said. "But you should have that kind of information from after-action reports by Calvin and Rafael and how they did with them."

"True," Price replied. "But you can never be too careful."

"The Unit was replaced by Khaldun's government intelligence operation, but they still work under military matters and they acquire their own intelligence, and have proved to be good allies for my work in Egypt," Bolan said, looking at Gahiji's gift package.

"We found out something about Mubarak," Price spoke up.

Bolan didn't wait for the news. "He's been tied to the Israelis as an asset."

"You knew we found information about him in the Mossad's records?" Price asked.

"Why else would Mubarak be in charge of an operation that would have drawn the attention of Israeli counterterrorism commandos?" Bolan asked. "Redjedef learned from his previous efforts with General Idel as his instigator. Now, he's been playing it so that there's sufficient evidence of interference from Israeli agents and Egyptian operatives. He appeared enough in rumors to draw the attention of Holt, who had told me she and her family had been keeping an eye on him."

"So it's a multigenerational conflict?" Price asked.

"That's the only way I can see it. The title of Eternal Pharaoh had been handed down from father to son, at least since World War II when that version incited violence to assist the Nazis in destabilizing Egypt," Bolan told her. "There have been other chesslike moves since the forties, but they've been countered, thankfully."

"How do we know that?" Price asked.

"Because we're still fighting the madman," Bolan said.

"All we have to do is keep the Egyptians and the Israelis from overreacting to whatever threat Redjedef unleashes, and we'll be fine," Price offered.

"That keeps the war from sprouting in the long run, but in the real world, we've got the problem of whoever the pharaoh and Khaldun want to target to begin this mess," Bolan countered. "Right now, I'm on my way into a trap, to see what I can spring loose."

"I don't suppose it would do any good to tell you to be careful, would it?" Price asked.

"I'm going in hot, fast and nasty," Bolan said. "I can't play around, not with a potential deadline counting down."

"What kind of deadline?" Price asked.

"The trouble will start the moment the news of the Sinai massacre is revealed," Bolan said. "Then something is going to happen to Israel to set them off."

"I'm already coordinating with the Mossad to keep them from going off half-cocked," Price explained.

"There's only so much an intelligence agency can do to salve the wounds inflicted by a full-blown attack," Bolan replied. "These people have launched all manner of deadly assaults, including the fully mechanized destruction of half a city by a tank force."

Bolan pulled to the curb and shut off his engine. It was nearing sunset, and he was within walking distance of Khaldun's convoy. He was far enough away right now that he wouldn't be noticed, but close enough to see the distant activity, meant to lure the Executioner into the jaws of a superior opponent.

"So what do you have in mind?" Price asked.

"I've got a few local resources on hand headed to the dig to keep an eye on it," Bolan said. "Khaldun is most likely going to want to be there, personally, directing the cameras to maximum effect."

"Because televised corpses will be so much more impressive," Price replied. "What's to say Khaldun hadn't already taken video immediately after the massacre?"

"Unlikely. The bodies wouldn't have had time to decompose enough," Bolan replied. "He wants this gory and lurid. That means carrion flies, discolored flesh and dried blood."

"Disgusting," Price growled.

Bolan made a grunt of agreement. He opened Gahiji's package and saw a pair of micro-Uzi machine pistols inside, with a leather, double-shoulder harness setup to carry them. There were six loaded 32-round magazines for each weapon, and with a quick check, he noted that the mini blasters themselves were loaded with short, concealable 20-round magazines and ready for action. The Executioner allowed himself a smile. "Thanks, Atef."

"Got something?" Price asked.

"Some extra gear," Bolan told her. "A care package of sorts."

"Good news, especially since we haven't been able to supply you," Price replied.

"I've been able to make do with local black-market purchases and gear acquired in the field. I started out operating hand to mouth, and spent a long time working without a net. You don't have to hold my hand at all times, Barb."

"Striker, we're only worried because you're an American in the middle of an international-crisis situation," Price told him. "They find a white corpse somewhere, you're it. They drag your burned carcass down the street as a propaganda banner..."

Bolan slipped into the double harness. Gahiji had also provided several loaded, 10-round magazines of .45ACP for Bolan's M&P 45. The Egyptian colonel may not have had access to a Desert Eagle, but he had managed to scrounge up the ammunition and accessories for the weapon. It couldn't have been easy, but once again, the soldier was in his veteran counterpart's debt.

"If they use me as a propaganda banner, there's going to be too much else going on for people to notice. If I die, I'll either be dead stopping it, or failed at my efforts. If I've stopped it, millions will be safe from war and a coup that puts a psychopath in charge of a nation. If I haven't, too many other people will be dead for my corpse to matter in the equation. But right now, I've got a trap to spring."

"Why not just avoid it?" Price asked. "Or let the police or army take care of it?"

"Because you have a bunch of nervous hired gunmen ready to shoot someone. If I don't show up, they might look for someone else. If the police or Egyptian army show up, they take bullets meant for me," Bolan explained.

"So you're volunteering to take the heat."

"I told you. I'm putting out a fire," Bolan said. "I

may get singed, but the arsonists will definitely be burned."

The warrior killed his link with Stony Man Farm, pulled out an AKM and went to work.

CHAPTER SIXTEEN

Orif Masozi was enraged. He had lost too many men to Cooper, and he personally wanted to be part of the team that would draw that man into a trap and spring it shut on him. It didn't take much mental math to have calculated that Cooper was the man who had pursued him across Africa, looking to shut down his diamond pipeline. That he was behind much of the destruction at his Kismayo headquarters was beyond a shadow of a doubt now.

Masozi had lost track of the number of his Shabaab warriors over the past week. Was he not a dedicated warrior of God? Didn't his efforts of liberating Somalia from the wicked and disease-ridden concepts of sexual equality and race mixing count to that God in granting him a modicum of success against one American man?

Cooper had to have been an American. No other white would possess the cowboy attitude to dare confront the Shabaab militia alone.

Perhaps there was something to Khaldun's ominous pronouncement of Cooper being far more than just a soldier, but Khaldun hadn't spoken to this man face-to-face or touched his hands. Despite the calluses on his fingers and palms, he was made of flesh and blood. Cooper was merely a man, and men died every day.

Here, in a construction site that had shut down due to the world economic crisis, Masozi vowed to feel Cooper's blood soak his fingers. Looking at the unfinished attempt at creating a modern structure, the Shabaab commander knew that the United States had brought about this kind of desolation, creating an economic structure that shattered once accountability had been demanded. How many children had starved while the men who were supposed to work here were forced into other jobs, or worse, unemployment, because of the squandering of money in the decadent U.S.? Cooper had attacked Masozi and his diamonds because he wanted the glimmering gems for his nation in an effort to revitalize their economy. That had to be the case, another instance of white men stealing from Africa, caring not for who suffered or starved in their wake. Cooper was the face of that greed.

The American, however, wasn't the focus of Masozi's greatest fury. That was reserved for the traitorous Kamau. Khaldun had finally dug up information about the man. Kamau was an ethnic Somali, but an Ethiopian citizen. Worse, instead of following the true prophet, Kamau was a Christian.

Masozi trembled, trying to restrain his urge to smash something. The man that Masozi had elevated to the rank of brother, the chief defender of the Shabaab's security, worshipped a Jew who didn't even keep the faith of the Jews. That disgusted Masozi far more than the knowledge that Kamau was a spy for a government that had turned its back on the true Muslim revolution throughout Africa.

Khaldun said that his organization, the Spear of

Destiny, had been devoted to restoring Egypt to what it rightfully should be. That was the only reason that Masozi was still in Alexandria. The Shabaab was working toward making Somalia a perfect Islamic republic, just as the Taliban had been in Afghanistan. This wasn't a war for territory, this was a battle for the souls of people who didn't know the grace and mercy of God.

Masozi could never see that such "mercy" was a joke. He couldn't put together the contradiction that he and his "soldiers" committed rape and murder on whim, destroying anything that showed the slightest hesitation of turning to Islam. Masozi couldn't admit to himself that it wasn't God that he worshipped, it was the reckless abandon that holy war gave him. No restraint would stop and no regret would hinder Masozi as he continued enslaving West Africans to dig precious stones out of the ground with bloody fingers. No logic would crack through his worldview of forcing women to be nothing more than sexual playthings that were genitally mutilated and deprived of education and dignity. No ounce of compassion would creep through to see the sailors that his pirates murdered were hardworking men who left behind families to grieve and suffer without their fathers' or brothers' paychecks.

Holy war had given Masozi a clean slate on his soul, and blinders against the inconvenient facts that his "crusade" was nothing more than the accumulation of wealth and the commission of violence to feed his bloodlust. He let the words of a prophet give him his license to do whatever he pleased. That was why his "God" would not grant him victory, but he'd never see that. All he would see would be an angel of wrath, clad in black, dispensing cleansing flame from the muzzles of his weapons.

Masozi sat and fumed. Cooper and Kamau would be on their way, and even if they expected a trap, Khaldun had bolstered his remaining militiamen with additional forces from the Muslim Brotherhood, as well as extra weapons and booby traps, which would even the odds.

"Even the odds," Masozi grumbled. "Dozens of us here, and we have to even the odds against two men?"

He reached for his glass of lemon water, but a powerful hand clamped down over his wrist. Another callused paw smothered his mouth, pushing his head back until he could see up into a pair of cold, blue eyes. Masozi struggled, trying to break free, but the Executioner had too much leverage on him.

"Not two men, Masozi. One," Bolan told him in a harsh whisper. "It doesn't take more than one man to destroy a nest of parasites."

Masozi tried to open his mouth enough to bite at Bolan's hand, but the force of his palm kept the Somali warlord's lips and jaw shut tightly. Before he allowed himself to surrender to panic, Masozi kicked the table in front of him, the jug of water that would provide his refills crashing on the concrete floor.

Bolan looked up, and smiled. "Thank you, Orif."

Masozi's eyes widened.

"This way, they're all shooting inward, not outward where innocents may be hurt," Bolan whispered.

No! Masozi thought. No one could be that good of a planner. This was just a single man, mortal and vulnerable to the dangers of the world! But even as the thought entered his head, something primal at the base of his soul had shifted uneasily. He had looked into the eyes of a true warrior and seen a spark and fire that he hadn't believed possible in a human.

The Islamic militia, far from its home in Somalia, had been found lacking in mercy and justice. The force of nature that gripped him so firmly, immobilizing him completely, had levied a death sentence, one that Masozi wouldn't face immediately. A hard punch to his temple ended his musings as he slipped into unconsciousness.

MACK BOLAN LET the unconscious form of the Somali warlord collapse to the floor. Masozi would be dealt with later. He scooped his rifle from where it hung on its sling and leveled it at the door to Masozi's trailer. The Shabaab were veterans of the civil wars of Somalia, but that didn't confer any expertise. They had set up a perimeter of booby traps and trip wires in order to catch Bolan in case he had tried to slip in through some unconventional pathway.

If the Somalis had more experience with the security systems, or had arranged booby-trap ambushes for enemy forces more sophisticated than Third World soldiers, they might have slowed the Executioner's path through their "fortifications." Instead, Bolan had slipped through the enemy's back door, gathering a bagful of "party favors" he'd culled from their jury-rigged grenades and trip mines. Bolan had been through areas of the world where true masters of sabotage had turned forests into death traps, and skilled madmen had turned parked automobiles or small stuffed animals into weapons of destruction capable of killing veteran soldiers. That skill, coupled with the knowledge that he had been

led into a trap, had given Bolan the forewarning to find
and disarm the Shabaab's mechanisms.

"Masozi? Is everything okay in there?" a voice bellowed on the other side of the trailer door.

Bolan remained quiet, his finger resting a half inch
from the trigger of his assault rifle. Masozi lay, drool-
ing, still breathing, on the carpet. The Executioner could
hear the rustle of a pistol being wrested from its leather
holster, the clack of rifle bolts on the other side of the
door.

Bolan's finger came down on the trigger, and he got
off three short bursts on full-auto. The thin sheet-metal
paneling of the door was no impediment to the storm
of 7.62 mm rifle rounds. He instantly took notice of the
grunts of two men as they took the slugs to their chests,
knocked to the ground dead or wounded. A slash of
autofire tore through the trailer immediately.

After a quick glance to see that Masozi was still
alive, Bolan rose and leaped to the hatch in the roof
that had been his original entrance to the trailer. With
another kick and the shrug of powerful arm muscles, the
Executioner slithered onto the roof as another salvo of
rifle fire stabbed into the trailer. Bolan reached for his
bag of collected weapons and plucked a standard hand
grenade. He tugged out its pin and flipped the bomb
over the edge of the roof.

Darkness had fallen, and it was now Bolan's time.
In the shadows of the construction yard, he was just
another blur of black in the night, hardly worth noticing
when there was the eruption of Kalashnikovs all over
the place. Men were running to the aid of their compa-

triot, alerted to trouble by the sight of two of their own cut down.

"Be careful! Masozi's still in there!" one of the militiamen sounded just before the fuse on the borrowed grenade burned through completely.

That caution was thrown out the window as a shock wave edged in serrated, razor-sharp metal swept through the half-dozen men who had responded to the action at their warlord's trailer. Bodies, sliced to ribbons by high-velocity shrapnel and crushed by the intense pressure of several ounces of military-grade explosives, were knocked about like tenpins in the path of a bowling ball.

Cries of dismay suddenly erupted throughout the camp as everyone turned toward the column of smoke that rose from the grenade's blast center. Something had just struck in their midst, and suddenly, their well-orchestrated ambush had to turn itself around, facing into the construction site, not outward.

Bolan knew that he didn't have a lot of time to deal with the bloodthirsty gunmen who were present. The Egyptian police and military were going to respond quickly to the sound of gunfire and explosions, even in that part of the city. He felt around in his satchel and withdrew a squat, tuna-can-shaped PMN-1 antipersonnel mine. The soldier plucked out the ring pin on its stab detonator, then sized up a machine-gun nest on the far side of the compound. With a smart flick of his wrist, he sailed the mine through the air.

The flat, circular bomb had the potential for varying its explosion delay thanks to the tension on a steel wire that cut through a lead strip within its mechanism. Bolan had loosened it slightly to give it a more grenadelike fuse, and the PMN landed just short of the machine-gun nest of Egyptian Brotherhood terrorists as they struggled to turn their PKM heavy automatic weapon. On the second bounce, 240 grams of TNT were triggered as the lead wire finally snapped inside. The resultant explosion decapitated one of the gunmen, shearing his neck flush to his shoulders. The other gunman howled in agony as his right arm disappeared under the shock wave.

Bolan hated to allow an opponent to suffer so, but he had too many other threats to deal with before he could administer mercy to the gravely wounded terrorist. A Shabaab gunman shouted and pointed at the Executioner as he perched atop the trailer. Bolan silenced the alert militiaman with a quick blast of autofire to the upper chest. The muzzle-flash of his rifle betrayed his position, however. The Executioner snatched up his satchel and hurled it toward the center of the camp before he leaped off the roof of Masozi's temporary headquarters, jumping away from where the bag had flown.

The ripple of Kalashnikov fire filled the air, bullets striking sheet metal and punching readily through the roof of Masozi's trailer, seeking Bolan's flesh. Providence had been on the side of the Shabaab and their Brotherhood allies, as no one had taken a shot at the sack of grenades and mines hurling through the air. Bolan landed safely on a dirt mound, knees flexing to absorb his impact, momentum sending him into a somersault that put him over the peak of the mound and behind a concealing berm.

The Executioner let his AKM hang on its sling and drew his Beretta 92. The pistol was fitted with a suppressor, thus leaving him less exposed when he fired it from concealment. The bright flare of the muzzle-flash was buried in washers and expansion chambers through the length of the can, letting him snipe with impunity. He lined up the Beretta on the head of one man and triggered the pistol. A full-metal-jacket round had sufficient mass and density to shatter the militia soldier's right eye socket and stab into the tender, spongy brain beneath. The "silencer" had stolen too much velocity from the bullet to allow it to exit the doomed killer's skull, so the slug rebounded, whipping gray matter into a foamy froth that jetted past the punctured and deflated eyeball.

A second Shabaab warrior turned at the sight of his friend, yelling in surprise at the gusher of gore that erupted from his face. Bolan fired a second round from his Beretta, this bullet taking the Somali through his open mouth. The round-nosed slug course corrected off his upper-left molars, ricocheting into the thick column of stacked bones that joined his head to his torso. The sudden wrench of one vertebra ground the two discs of bone against each other, scissoring his spinal cord and rendering him a paralyzed mass of flesh. The Somali collapsed atop his dead friend, and began the slow process of bleeding down his windpipe. Bolan spared him the slow demise with a third shot that dimmed his lights forever.

Two enemies down, and the riflemen weren't paying attention to what was going on, rushing to surround Masozi's trailer. Their shouted communication to one another and the rattle of reloading had completely muffled the carnage that had exploded in their midst.

Two Somalis and a pair of their Egyptian counterparts swung around the back of the trailer, and Bolan greeted them with two quick shots from his Beretta. One Somali was cored through the heart, the full-metal-jacket 9 mm round slicing through the tough muscle of the organ, rupturing two ventricles and inducing high-pressure exsanguination from the entrance and exit wounds. An Egyptian was silenced forever as Bolan's second 9 mm round struck the bridge of his nose and turned the knot of bone there into a volley of splinters that accompanied the copper-jacket projectile in destroying his brain.

The other two gunmen halted in their tracks as the men in front of them stopped violently. That pause of surprise was enough for the Executioner to line up his two next shots, another pair to the face that took the fundamentalist gunmen down swiftly.

"Come on out, Cooper! And we'll be merciful to you!" a voice shouted off to Bolan's left.

The Executioner had seen the Shabaab's idea of "mercy." He'd sooner be beaten like a mule. Instead of responding with a bullet, Bolan kept to the shadows, sneaking up behind the spokesman.

"We know you're in there!" the Somali militiaman shouted.

The only living soul inside the trailer was Masozi, and even that was contingent on the hope that none of their rifles had swept along floor level. Bolan wondered how good their fire discipline was, especially in regards to keeping their warlord alive. He returned the Beretta to its holster and folded the stock on his AKM, cinching its sling so that he could fire the weapon one-handed. He had a target in mind, and Bolan wanted to have a shield to reach his best angle of fire. He reloaded as quietly and calmly as he could, his hands sure and steady.

The Somali hissed something in his native language. Bolan couldn't make out the words, but he got the meaning. "Have you idiots finished readying your weapons?"

Bolan snaked his forearm around the Somali's throat and yanked back hard, cutting off any attempt to cry for help. The militiaman was about a hundred and sixty pounds, and too skinny to make a truly effective human shield, but for now, it was all he had to work with. With quick, sure-footed strides, Bolan angled himself so that he was in sight of the satchel of mines and grenades. He extended the AKM, using the tension of the sling against his shoulder to stabilize his aim.

"Cooper…" the militiaman rasped. "Cooper's here…"

It was too soft, too late. Bolan triggered a short burst that struck the satchel of high explosives, and the night split asunder, bright light and high pressure pouring out of the erupting bag. Bolan twisted and slammed into the ground, keeping the Shabaab gunman relatively safe.

Screams filled the air from shrapnel injuries, while groans from shock-wave injuries formed a dull background to the cries of pain. Bolan checked on his prisoner, who aside from looking stunned and caught in a headlock, was fine.

"I want you to tell your men something for me," Bolan growled.

"The hell with you, Cooper," the Somali replied.

Bolan turned the AKM's muzzle under his chin, its hot barrel burning his skin.

"Wait! Wait!"

"Tell them that God hasn't abandoned them. He was never with them. That's why so many of them have died at my hand. If they wish to live, they must reexamine their spirits, and seek a more righteous path," Bolan told him.

The Shabaab man looked at Bolan in surprise as he was released. "You would blaspheme?"

"Look around," Bolan told him.

The militiaman turned, and his shoulders sagged at the sight of carnage having ripped through thirty trained and prepared men, fighters who had pledged victory against Cooper in their holy war. He took a deep breath, then did as he was told.

The survivors, those who could still walk, left the construction site as quickly as their injuries could allow them. There were a few wounded remaining, but with the most recent eruption of explosives, the authorities would be on hand, and they would receive first-responder emergency medical care. Bolan's former prisoner looked, sunken-eyed, at the Executioner.

"Go home," Bolan said. "If we meet in battle again, there will be no mercy."

The Shabaab fighter threw down his weapons and walked away.

Now it was time to check on Masozi.

ORIF MASOZI GRUNTED to consciousness as he flopped into the trunk of the automobile that Bolan had salvaged from the convoy. His eyes blinked, blurs sharpening to crystal focus almost instantly, recognizing the warrior who had haunted him across an entire continent.

He sputtered and reached up, but Bolan slapped his hand away.

"What are you doing with me?" he murmured, his mouth cottony and dry.

"Taking you for a ride," Bolan told him. "We're going to see Khaldun."

Masozi tried to generate some spit to moisten his dry, numb tongue. Only with a little dampness did he manage to release the next few words. "What do you think you can do with me at your side?"

"At my side?" Bolan asked, then snorted in derision. "I'm just making certain that if I die, you die. He lights up my car, you're going to be perforated, and perhaps even roasted."

"Why not just shoot me?" Masozi asked.

"Because I'm not Shabaab. I lack the soul rot to murder a helpless prisoner."

"Bastard," Masozi growled. "I am a warrior."

"Is that why you're loaded like luggage into a trunk and your fellow Somali militiamen are either dead or running for their lives?" Bolan asked.

Masozi reached up again, but Bolan grabbed his wrist in an iron grip. The soldier's other hand speared down, his thumb crossing the Somali's windpipe. Pressure began to build at an exponential rate inside Masozi's head.

"Don't act indignant," Bolan told him through clenched teeth. "You're a coward, a predator and some-one who revels in bloodshed as your addiction of choice. You murder, rob and terrorize. I am your judgment, finally come due."

"Khaldun…" Masozi croaked as Bolan lightened the

tension on his throat. "Khaldun told me nothing that would be useful to you."

"What about his phone?" Bolan asked. "I'm sure you looked at his number."

Masozi coughed. "I know it."

He rattled off the number. Bolan's grasp on him eased off, and Masozi drew his hand away from the Executioner, massaging his throat. A gun flopped heavily onto his chest.

"What's this?" Masozi asked.

"I'm not rotten enough to execute an unarmed man. But I'll be damned if I allow you to walk around. Consider this your chance," Bolan told him.

Masozi turned over the handgun in his grasp, cautious to keep his grip from encompassing the handle, so that it looked as if he was ready to fire.

"No safeties, a round in the chamber. All you have to do is pull the trigger. Now, get out of the trunk and fill your hand," Bolan told him.

Masozi stayed in the trunk, but turned the big Smith & Wesson .45 so that he could put a bullet under Bolan's chin. The Executioner slapped the handgun aside with the back of his fist, and speared his hand back down to Masozi's throat.

"I offered you a chance to fight honorably," Bolan growled as his fingers dug into the flesh around the Somali's windpipe. "You chose a different path."

Masozi felt his mouth fill with blood as he struggled to point the pistol at Bolan's head. A powerful hand clenched around his forearm, the death grip on his throat excruciating. Masozi pulled the trigger, and the Executioner winced as the booming roar of the .45 auto rattled his left eardrum. He missed, and the muzzle-blast's deafening sound and pressure hadn't done anything to the American.

Masozi's chest gyrated, trying to suck in breath. He felt the skin on his neck tear, hot fluid splashing down over his shoulders. More sticky, coppery blood poured over his lips. He tried to spit, but no air issued through his mouth or nose. His larynx crunched and crumbled under the Executioner's killing grip.

The world blurred out, and he felt the grip of the pistol pivot in his fingers, their strength gone.

Bolan withdrew his stranglehold, and Masozi tried to speak. It was no go for the Somali. His windpipe had been irreparably crushed and mangled. No final words, no dying curse would haunt his killer.

Bolan retrieved his Smith & Wesson, then slammed the lid on what would be the warlord's coffin.

The Shabaab leader would find out if his life truly was holy and just.

The Executioner had other fish to catch.

CHAPTER SEVENTEEN

Bolan checked his pupils in the mirror of the car that served as Masozi's casket. The .45's muzzle-blast, so close to his ear, hadn't caused a concussion, and a scan of the shell of his ear showed that no blood leaked from a burst eardrum. He had a ringing going on, but that was a natural reaction to the increased noise and pressure at such close range. He felt lucky that it hadn't been his usual Desert Eagle in the Somali warlord's hand. Otherwise he truly would have had a punctured eardrum. As it was, Bolan took a couple of aspirin, which would deal with minor aches and deal with swelling from his assorted bruises and lacerations incurred in the past few minutes.

He'd been in battle in the desert, in Kismayo, and across Alexandria. Now, he had to make certain that Khaldun and the rest of the Spear of Destiny would be stopped cold before the madman could make public the massacre allegedly committed by a squad of Israeli assassins.

Using his combat PDA, Bolan punched in the digits that Masozi had given him before the struggle that resulted in the Somali's execution. He transmitted the number to Stony Man Farm in an effort to locate Khaldun and perhaps get a record of the telephone calls that had been made from the Egyptian's phone in order to track down Redjedef, the Eternal Pharaoh. It all seemed a mess, because as long as the Executioner had been looking for clues about this man, even the Mossad and Egyptian intelligence agencies had come up short on the mystery man who was nothing more than a ghost as he manipulated the government, even employing generals to kick off his schemes.

The soldier paused before leaving the construction site, then got Stony Man Farm on his speed dial.

"What do you need, Striker?" Price answered.

"I need to pick Gary's and David's brains," Bolan said, referring to Gary Manning and David McCarter of Phoenix Force. His options for information had grown thin, and there were two people on the planet who could possibly come up with something. The Canadian and British members of the Stony Man operations team had high levels of intelligence and a great deal of experience in dealing with the kind of people he was involved with.

"What could either of them have that would be any use to this case?" Price asked.

"They have more experience with Nazis than anyone else," Bolan answered. "Gary with his time helping out the GSG-9 in Germany, and David because he's a World War II historian. Are they in the field?"

"No, they're at the Farm," Price said. "I'll have to wrangle them up."

"I'll be on the road in any case," Bolan told her. "But we're losing precious minutes."

"We'll take care of this," Price told him. "Anything in particular you're interested in?"

"Eartha Holt came into this situation because her

grandfather was aware of a secret cabal that was willing to work with the Nazis," Bolan explained. "Move forward a couple decades, and West German terrorist groups got very cozy with groups like Black September, providing manpower to back each other up, training and funds to help out on joint operations."

"The Palestinian Liberation Organization disbanded Black September in 1973," Price countered.

"Officially," Bolan said. "But Hamas, Fatah and Abu Nidal popped up much later."

"Either way, the Palestinian terrorist groups are allied with Communist organizations, not fascists," Price interjected.

Bolan scanned the street. Something was wrong. "But Arab states neighboring Israel picked up a lot of former SS officers in the late forties in an effort to do something about the so-called Jewish problem. Those original officers are too old to be a menace today."

"But some have revisited the sins of their fathers?" Price asked.

Bolan spotted a car with two men sitting inside. His instincts focused on it. The vehicle was dirty, but it showed none of the signs of distress, such as dents or rust, like other cars and trucks parked along the street.

"Got to cut this short. My dance card's not empty yet."

He ended the call and pocketed the PDA, jogging across the street in long, loping strides. His right hand rested on the grip of his reloaded Smith & Wesson .45. The vehicle looked far too new for the neighborhood, so he concluded it had to have been a government sedan, dusted just enough to blend in with the dirty urban environment.

The two occupants of the vehicle hadn't moved an inch when they had seen the Executioner, laden with weaponry, leaving the scene of a violent altercation where automatic weapons and explosions had abounded. That was another clue for the warrior that something wasn't right about the two men in the car. Though their faces were shaded, keeping them from being identified, he knew that they weren't ordinary citizens of Alexandria out on an evening jaunt. Bolan finally reached his SUV and knew that the moment he started it, he'd have them on his tail.

Khaldun had been able to have one of his men, an agent who Gahiji had identified as Ratik, operate plainclothes within the city since he was with Egyptian intelligence, rather than uniformed military. These two were likely the same kind of men, plainclothes operators who had military backgrounds, but had proved to be ruthless and thuggish enough to operate under Khaldun's type of operation.

Bolan slipped behind the wheel, and looked through his mirror. The shadows knew that he was aware of them. The question was how to deal with the operatives. They may have been simple men who were under orders, unaware of what they were involved with. Bolan doubted that, though. There had been an earthshaking battle that had gone on. If they were honest federal agents, they would have called in the police. As it was, Bolan didn't even hear sirens in the distance. He had been expecting the arrival of the proper authorities, especially to help the wounded left behind at the construction site.

There were two ways to take them on. One was to lead them on a chase, then run them off the road. The other was the one Bolan had chosen. He fired up the engine on the SUV, then threw the gearshift into Reverse. He revved the engine for a few seconds, building up the RPMs in the engine as he held down the brake. Bolan gave the steering wheel a slight twist, then released the pressure on the brake.

The SUV rocketed backward, sailing toward the enemy vehicle as it sat parked. In the rearview mirror, Bolan could see one man waving his arms in panic as the other struggled to start up. It was only a brief glimpse, however. The two men had been jolted into sudden activity by Bolan's unexpected tactic. The rear bumper of the big four-wheel-drive vehicle connected with the sedan's grille with crushing force. The driver and his partner were wildly jarred, even as Bolan bounced against the restraining web straps of his seat belt. Had the pair picked a more appropriate vehicle for the environment, they wouldn't have been noticed. Even worse now, the unsettled men were battered by the rapid expansion of air bags from the steering column and dash panel. The superinflated bags were known for battering and bruising drivers and passengers in accidents, but the stunning force was less harmful than the smashing impact of chests against steering wheels or skulls against dashboard panels. As it was, Bolan's two opponents had been stunned and dazed by the very systems meant to save their lives in a catastrophic collision.

Bolan popped his seat belt and scrambled out of the driver's seat. He didn't have long before either of the two agents recovered their senses. A protracted race would have simply taken too long and risked too many bystanders' lives. Accelerating into their grille had been his best, quickest choice. The Executioner was working against a deadline, and he had no wiggle room.

Tearing open the driver's door, he encountered a token amount of resistance from the stunned driver. Bolan snapped a hard cross to his jaw, jolting the man into unconsciousness. Left insensate, he no longer struggled against the warrior's manhandling, and was dumped limply into the road. The other man, not quite as engulfed by his already deflating air bag, scrambled to reach into the backseat for the handgun that had flipped there.

Bolan lunged into the car in an effort to keep the man from arming himself. A foot rose to meet the soldier as he dived toward the second agent. He twisted in an effort to avoid most of the impact. The big American succeeded as the man's heel bounced off Bolan's shoulder. It was a jarring blow, but no bones were broken. The kick had slowed Khaldun's agent, and gave Bolan the opportunity to grab a handful of belt and shirt and yank the man out of the backseat. A wild elbow scythed out of nowhere and glanced off Bolan's cheek, snapping his head around. The panicked flail had done more damage than a skillfully placed, measured martial-arts blow, as the warrior hadn't anticipated it and adjusted for it as he had with the kick. It was only a stunning strike, but it bought Bolan's opponent the time he needed to launch himself halfway into the backseat, fingertips clawing for the Glock 17 deposited on the cushions.

Bolan fired off a short-range punch that struck the Egyptian just over his hip. The stroke folded the man in pain, his hand drawing away from the pistol he sought. Bolan didn't want to turn the agent into a corpse, even if he was as crooked as Khaldun. He snagged the Egyptian's belt again and hauled back, pulling the man halfway out of the car before the stunned agent recovered enough of his senses to release a kick into Bolan's stomach. Still smarting from the blow that had crashed into his cheek, the Executioner didn't have enough time to harden his abdominal muscles in response to the kick and he felt the breath knocked from his lungs.

The Egyptian gave up on the weapon he'd lost in the backseat, and he reached out, both hands with fingers hooked like claws coming down on either side of Bolan's head. The Executioner moved with the force of the agent's pull, taking a page from David McCarter's war book. He speared the dome of his forehead into a spot between his opponent's eyes. The impact hurt Bolan, a sharp sting as skin was mashed between two rolls of bone, but the dome of his skull was hard and curved, preventing the impact from stunning him. Meanwhile, the agent's central nervous system received a rocking shock from the hammer blow that struck him. The hooked fingers released from Bolan's scalp, fingernails scraping skin and blood in their passage from their broken death grip.

Bolan followed up with a punch that struck the man just under his sternal notch, an impact that forced the wind out of his lungs. The Egyptian, gasping for breath, was on the receiving end of the very breathlessness that he'd wanted to inflict on the Executioner. Bolan's expertly launched strike left the agent gasping for air, but unable to inhale due to the shock inflicted on his stomach muscles. The shock wouldn't be permanent, and as soon as he collapsed into unconsciousness, his musculature would relax and allow for normal breathing again.

Bolan took the man by the collar of his shirt and dragged again, dumping him atop the driver, who was beginning to recover from his beating. The weight of a limp form pinned the first Egyptian to the ground, despite his thrashing.

Bolan saw the man try to snake his hand under his jacket, but he plucked at the man's wrist, twisting it into the open. The soldier drew his Beretta and pressed it to a spot just behind the agent's jaw. The hammer clicked ominously, seizing the Egyptian's attention completely. "Behave yourself."

The man looked up at the Executioner, understanding his intent, if not the words, behind them.

"Did Khaldun send you?" he growled.

The Egyptian sputtered. "We were to arrest you if you came out of the construction site."

"Khaldun gave the order," Bolan asserted.

The agent nodded.

"Why haven't you called for backup after this?" Bolan asked. "There's dead and wounded in that construction site."

"Because you are our priority," the Egyptian offered. "Are you going to kill me. too?"

Bolan lowered the hammer on his Beretta before he holstered it. "Count yourself lucky that you're a lawman. I won't kill you, but in the future, make certain you know the character of the man who orders you to ignore a battle in the middle of a city."

"Where are you going?" the Egyptian asked.

Bolan looked down at him. "To get the man who sent dozens of terrorists to their death tonight."

"Khaldun?" the driver inquired. "He said he was on his way to the Sinai tonight. With a team."

Bolan pushed the man's unconscious partner off him. He helped the driver to his feet. "Let me guess, he received a tip about a situation at an archaeological dig?"

"We hadn't been told anything specific," the driver said. "But he told the department to be on full alert, to let you do your thing, and then we'd arrest you."

Bolan grimaced. "Give me your identification."

The Egyptian complied. He took out his PDA and got on the line with the colonel. "Gahiji, let me know if one of your people is straight or bent."

"Go right ahead," Gahiji answered. He listened to the rattled-off identification. "Yes. The kid's okay to leave on scene. He have a partner with him?"

"Yeah. He took a bit of a hammering, but I left him with all his bones and organs intact," Bolan replied. "But we'll need an ambulance on hand."

"I'll do what I can," Gahiji replied. "Still looking for that helicopter ride?"

"I'm working toward it," Bolan said. "What about your man in the field with my partners?"

"No signs of trouble yet," Gahiji answered.

Bolan grumbled. "Khaldun's on his way. I just have to check on something first."

"Don't take too long," Gahiji replied. "If Khaldun's heading for the dig site…"

"I'm not sure that's what he's after. Khaldun and

Redjedef are two slippery snakes who've avoided both
of our attention for years," Bolan warned. "There might
be something else out there in the peninsula."

"Worse than a ricin superweapon?" the Egyptian
colonel asked.

"Who knows, Colonel," Bolan answered. He killed
the phone link.

HAGAN ABELARD KNEW his father, Dierk, and his grandfather, Erich, would be proud of him. It had taken the
Abelard family the better part of a century to accom-
plish their goals of vengeance, taking over the ancient
cult of the Eternal Pharaoh during World War II.

Though the original Wafdist crusaders against foreign
rule would have gnashed their teeth and rolled over in
their graves at the thought that Colonel Erich Abelard, a
German national, had usurped the control of the Spear
of Destiny, the current Redjedef, Hagan Abelard, didn't
have to worry. The grave was a few hundred yards away
from the plateau, buried in the sands, and long forgotten,
a tangle of desiccated, mummified limbs that would
never rise again. The SS colonel E. Abelard and several of his men remained in Egypt, at first under orders
to seek out ancient artifacts and weapons, such as the
castor-bean base for deadly ricin or mythic accessories as the wands and staves of the pharaohs' sorcerers.
Hagan's grandfather saw the omen, the writing on the
wall, when the Allies began their assault on Normandy
Beach while the Soviet Union pushed back against the
forces that had permeated her borders.

The Reich was doomed as two unstoppable armies
surged against the Wehrmacht. Too far, too fast had been

the ruin of the Nazi regime's plans. Abelard summoned his family from Germany, utilizing the SS's protocols of setting up contingency seeds around the world to maintain continuity of government. A good deal of their compatriots had set up in places across South America, while others landed safely in corners of the Arab world, living as expatriates, or hiding out in Europe still. The Israelis had tried to hunt them down, but after the blatant failure of pure brute force, the survivors had learned.

The Abelard family, and their allies, had taken their time, disappearing beneath Egyptian culture. It helped that there had been a niche already carved out by the Wafdist splinter cell known as the Spear of Destiny. The cult had been started in the late 1800s, organized around the concept that modern religions, such as Islam, had failed the Egyptian people in making them bit players in someone else's empire. Back when Egypt worshipped the true gods, the descendants of the original Pharaoh Khofu, the nation owned an empire that stretched across the lower coast of the Mediterranean. The power and skill that the followers of those god kings possessed enabled them to bring literacy to the world with the first-ever written language, papyrus and architectural brilliance that transcended everything else on the planet. The Pyramids were one such example, but the magnificent temples and sprawling cities created by those first genius peoples put previous clay- and wood-based civilizations to shame. It was Egypt that had first forged bronze, tamed horses and touched the sky with their towering edifices.

Hagan Abelard knew that most of these beliefs of the Spear of Destiny were ethnocentric propaganda, no better than the lies spewed by the Nazi Party that pushed them to prominence in Germany. However, the fanaticism inspired by those lies had created an offshoot of the Wafdist extremists that were cunning enough to maintain their secret society. When Erich Abelard usurped the title of Eternal Pharaoh, a century of weight had accompanied it. The original cultists had funded themselves with treasures stripped from tombs, struggling to throw off the British who had come down upon them, turning them into just another colony to strip. The Wafdists hadn't created the same level of noise and conflict as cults such as the Thuggee, but they'd done their best.

Erich Abelard, however, knew how to do it better. He had created connections throughout the government, and set it up so that his son and his grandson and great-grandson could continue the legacy of power long into the future. Hagan Abelard wanted more, something that his father had instilled in him. Dierk Abelard had been the one who developed the ties to Syria that allowed them to refine the technology to disperse the ancient poisons.

Abelard smiled as he looked at the hermetically sealed tube containers of weaponized ricin ready to load into the Soviet-era missile launchers. It was an irony that the first traitors to the Third Reich had been so instrumental in the development of the tools that would bring them to ultimate ascendancy years after their own empire crumbled under the weight of their own failed economic system.

Though Abelard and the other SS descendants no longer considered themselves Nazis, the richness of their old enemies contributing to the Spear of Destiny's ultimate victory was hard to ignore.

Khaldun was on the cell phone. Abelard's own unit had to put up a filter in order to nullify the racket of the helicopter on Khaldun's end of things. With the money that the Spear of Destiny had made, selling surplus Egyptian weapons to warring African factions to replace their aging AKs and keep them in RPG shells, Abelard could afford such high-tech luxuries.

"Beloved Redjedef, eternal son of the most high Khofu, Matthew Cooper has taken action against our trap," the Tip of the Spear of Destiny said.

"And he yet lives, as I predicted," Abelard responded.

Khaldun sighed. "Blessed be unto your limitless knowledge and foresight."

Abelard rubbed his chin. Indeed, he and his family had been preparing, plotting, coordinating for a long time. It had taken a few decades to bring the Muslim Brotherhood to enough prominence as a renegade terrorist organization in order to help the followers of the Eternal Pharaoh to discredit all of Islam, while keeping enough tension against Israel and, by extension, her allies in Europe and the United States to add to the distrust of Judaism and Christianity. While Abelard wasn't remiss in taking the credit for his and his father's and grandfather's planning and foresight in assembling a coup to put them in power over one of the most powerful nations in the Middle East, he couldn't overcome the knowledge that he was behind the curve in dealing with Matthew Cooper.

By all accounts, he resembled the man who had

single-handedly derailed his previous attempt at a coup over Egypt. That too had the fingers of his Syrian allies in the pie. By trading the country three tanks, Abelard had been given enough nerve gas in order to make Israel crumble, but not before releasing a spasm of nuclear missiles that would have weakened Egypt enough for Abelard and Idel to take the country over completely.

"Sir?" Khaldun asked.

"I am thinking. Thinking dark thoughts, my friend," Abelard replied.

"Is everything going according to plan?" Khaldun asked.

"Except for Cooper. He is too much of a wild card. Too capable an opponent," Abelard explained.

"Redjedef, first son of the first pharaoh, we have come too far. Already, I am en route to expose the murders of innocent students," Khaldun replied. "And even if we are stopped, you have the missiles, and the capability to rain damnation down upon your enemies."

Abelard nodded, then realized that his minion couldn't see the silent, reluctant affirmation. "Yes, my warrior. May you speed on swift wings to your destiny."

"Blessed be thy eternal reign," Khaldun replied.

CHAPTER EIGHTEEN

The EAF H-60 Black Hawk screamed over the desert as fast as the pilot, a big brawny man named Nakti, could push it. Mack Bolan rode shotgun with him, eyeing the instruments.

"These birds are supposed to have a never-exceed speed of 355 kph," Bolan noted.

"You dare?" the pilot asked. Nakti looked toward the Executioner, a moment of grim and serious reproach on his face. It dissolved instantly into a smile. "Just kidding. We're holding steady at 340 kph. The engines are eating up fuel like crazy, but it's nowhere I haven't been before."

Bolan nodded. He did the calculations in his head, and got roughly 200 mph out of the equation. He wanted to get to the site of the Sinai dig as fast as possible. Khaldun was already in the wind, which meant there wasn't going to be much time to spare. Luckily, Gahiji had arranged for the Black Hawk to take Bolan anywhere he needed to go on a moment's notice. The Executioner was aware that the drop tanks were filled to the brim, giving the helicopter an increased range.

The H-60 was a different model than the UH-60 helicopter utilized by the U.S. armed forces, having less sophisticated military electronics in order to keep proprietary technology out of enemy hands. Similar to the surplus M-1 Abrams tanks that had been given to the Egyptians, the H-60 was merely second-rate gear, which the Egyptian air force had supplemented with its own purchases. Bolan figured that his pilot, Jack Grimaldi, would be able to tell at a glance which was third-party gear and what the U.S. military had shorted the Egyptians. Right now, the only thing that mattered was that the horsepower of the sleek, flat airship made it one of the fastest things in the air so that Bolan could catch up with Khaldun.

"Anything on the radar?" Bolan asked.

Nakti shook his head. "Not yet, but that doesn't mean anything. They could be flying nap of the earth, which is what I really should be doing."

Bolan watched a craggy peak whip past. He estimated the distance from the outcropping to be less than six feet from the cockpit. "Any lower, and we'd be much shorter at the end of the trip."

"Which is why I'm not flying low profile," Nakti replied. "But just to be safe, we're coming in on a J course to the Sinai dig."

Bolan frowned, then adjusted his helmet so that he could bring a pair of binoculars to his eyes. "How soon until we go dark?"

"I'll give it about five minutes," Nakti returned. "Why?"

"Then I can use the night-vision option on these binoculars to scan the terrain," Bolan said.

"For what?" Nakti asked.

"There was an ancient temple and military outpost that had been discovered there," Bolan explained. "Khaldun's men detonated an entrance to the place, but how many underground facilities have only one entrance and exit?"

"The closest thing is a pharaoh's tomb, but even those have all manner of air vents and pockets built in," Nakti replied. "If it's a usable facility…"

"That's what I want to look for. He dumped a mess on the top of that mountain, and even tried to close off one approach. But I believe there's more down below," Bolan said.

Nakti took a deep breath. "He'd be aware of the distaste we'd have for revisiting a site of such violence. We'd also focus our attention on the actual crime scene."

"While tunnels below would keep everything out of sight and out of mind," Bolan concluded.

"There's times when I'm surprised that the whole country doesn't collapse under its own weight. We've got so many underground tunnels just in the Valley of the Kings that even when they were burying their leaders, they had to make ornate twists and turns to avoid other spiraling tombs," Nakti said.

Bolan nodded. "Sophisticated subterranean construction methods. It's no wonder Redjedef was able to convince his followers that, under the pharaohs, the Egyptians were the mightiest empire in the world."

"Or at least the most technologically advanced," Nakti replied. "But religion doesn't mean a thing in terms of advancement. In many cases, it hinders progress."

"Not religion," Bolan countered. "Simply men trying to retain control instead of trying to adapt. Faith doesn't need proof, so it doesn't need to disprove science."

Nakti smiled again. "We're on the way to something where we'll be shot to ribbons, and I'm in the middle of a philosophical discussion that I don't feel the need to get wound up over."

Bolan returned the grin. "I'll keep you from getting blown to pieces, and I respect the belief and faith of all men who do not engage in violently forcing it upon others."

"That's impressive," Nakti returned.

Bolan saw another ridge loom, then disappear under the Black Hawk's cockpit. "Not as impressive as your flying."

The Executioner's PDA vibrated, and he pulled out the unit. "Striker here. Speak to me."

"Hey, Striker," McCarter's voice cut over the air. "Gary and I have done a little more digging and phoning around. I even bugged Katz's daughter to see if she had any information relating to Nazis, or gleaned anything from alternate files the old man kept in Israel. Since Katz never warmed to computers enough to trust putting data into them, we had to go through cardboard boxes by eyeball."

"What popped up?" Bolan asked.

"Well, some of the information we captured from an ODESSA operation in France had mention of brethren in Egypt," McCarter said. "That's why the Nazi bastards were able to recruit disgruntled immigrants into their cause."

"Rabble-rousing has always been a Nazi strong point," Bolan agreed. "And let me guess, there were more than a couple members of ODESSA's puppet team that were Syrian."

"French citizens, but of Syrian birth. We didn't have enough to pin anything on Damascus at the time, especially when ODESSA had an entire armed camp operating in the French countryside. Luckily, the records on those two men *are* in a computer somewhere."

"Sleeper agents," Bolan surmised.

McCarter chuckled. "Right the first time, Striker. They were doing a solid for their pals in ODESSA. In exchange, whatever they had in Egypt was doing business with Syrian intelligence."

Bolan's lips drew into a grim line at this news. "That was quite a while ago, David."

"This brings us to the next thing we discovered, going through information archives. The Nuremberg Trials were made difficult because the SS did its best to destroy records of their activities, but they didn't destroy enough evidence before the Soviets and the Allies kicked down their doors," McCarter said. "And they didn't believe that the information they had on the SS team that went to Egypt to foment dissent against British 'occupation' would have been used against them."

"That's where you picked up word on the Spear of Destiny," Bolan said.

"Local splinter group of the Wafdists who broke off because they didn't want to associate with Muslims," McCarter explained. "They didn't like Islam, but they worked closely with the Nazis."

"That's because much of the SS didn't like the new gods either. They preferred their deities dark, ancient and powerful," Bolan said. "Allah is too positive a figure to the Spear of Destiny."

"You don't have to tell me that twice," McCarter answered. "Though, outside your dance with the Order of

Thule, we haven't seen that crop up in the neo-Nazis we've fought."

"That's because evil like that tends to seep into the background," Bolan said. "Who were the agents sent to Egypt?"

"Colonel Erich Abelard," McCarter returned. "He and twenty other men slipped into Egypt. They worked on a deal involving castor beans—which you can extract ricin from—in exchange for support in overthrowing the British colonial government in Cairo."

"Any word on where Abelard went?" Bolan asked.

McCarter took a deep breath. "There are no records of him after World War II. No existing records. Something tells me that when the Nazis were scrambling to the four corners of the globe, they helped Abelard disappear forever into Egypt."

"We couldn't be lucky enough to assume that the Wafdists did away with them?" Bolan asked.

"If we were, you wouldn't be scotching another of their plans for world domination, would you?" McCarter asked.

Bolan managed a smile from the Briton's response. "So Barb's got enough to tie this to the previous crisis?"

"Yes. We also made use of the digital-camera footage you took to help Gahiji keep things under control," McCarter said. "Right now, Egyptian news is ready to broadcast an edited tape presented by Gahiji."

Bolan's mood was improved. "How about footage of Khaldun?"

"He's not there yet, Striker," McCarter replied. "But Kamau has those cameras you told him to bring."

"Good," Bolan said. "I'm not going to let Redjedef come out with anything useful. Striker out."

Nakti looked over at Bolan. "What are you going to do with two cameras that can't be done otherwise?"

"The cameras are remote-operated wide-pan digital models with a powerful transmitter that we can edit into the video that Gahiji will present," Bolan said.

"I thought you said a tape was already made," Nakti countered.

"It's a digital file, designed for quick-and-easy editing, specifically with breaks for the footage I hope to get," Bolan explained.

Nakti frowned. "Won't Khaldun just see the cameras? And how will your footage be usable?"

Bolan shook his head. "Disguised as rocks and they have night-vision capabilities."

Nakti nodded with comprehension. "That's how you're handling Khaldun?"

"That's how I'm defanging efforts to stir up national hatred toward Israel," Bolan answered. "I didn't haul a case of guns onto this bird to say hello."

"What about me?" Nakti asked.

"You'll have to sit on the sidelines. This bird isn't hooked up with weapons for a fight," Bolan told him. "We'll need you to take us home, especially if we have wounded."

"Or prisoners," Nakti added.

Bolan shook his head slowly. "This is the endgame. No prisoners."

The pilot swallowed. He continued the countdown to lights out, hoping he hadn't been seen as he raced to the Sinai massacre site.

KAMAU PUT HIS HAND over one ear as if it would help him to hear Bolan better.

"Isoba, we're en route. How are things holding out there?" Bolan asked.

"We're doing fine here. Cameras are in place, and Rashida has taken Eartha on a scouting mission down one of the cliffs," Kamau answered.

"You're alone, or is Gahiji's man still there?" Bolan asked.

Kamau sighed. "I sent him back on the chopper. I would have sent Rashida, too."

"I understand. He didn't get along well with you?" Bolan asked.

"How'd you guess that?" Kamau inquired.

Bolan sighed. "He was either uncomfortable working with a woman, or a black man, or both, if he was willing to leave his post and leave control of it to you."

"It was the women," Kamau answered. "Specifically Eartha."

The Ethiopian giant heard his ally chuckle over the radio. "She can be a little off-putting."

"How did things go in Alexandria?" Kamau asked.

"The trap was sprung, no significant casualties for our side," Bolan said. "You can report to your superiors that Masozi's sect of Shabaab raiders is done for good."

"How'd he die?" Kamau asked.

"I offered him a fair chance to live. Instead, he's folded into the trunk of a car, rotting," Bolan told him. "Are you all right?"

Kamau took a deep breath. The years he'd put into his undercover role had been put to an end. It was as if a weight had been lifted from his broad shoulders. He was free from the nightmare of pretending to be a friend and brother to genocidal militiamen and ruthless pirates. Kamau felt a little dizzy for a moment, off balance from the news. "I'll be fine."

"Good," Bolan answered. There was a brief pause. "Rashida is leading Eartha?"

"Yeah," Kamau replied. "She's been looking over the map, and was doing measurements of the altitude and its relief. Something to keep her mind focused, and she's come to the conclusion that the opening on the plateau was merely a vent dressed up by Khaldun to look like an important find."

"We've figured that out already," Bolan said.

"Yes, but you're not an Egyptologist," Kamau countered. "Metit knows where to look."

"Point made," Bolan replied. "Just be careful there."

"I hear rotor blades," Kamau said.

"That's not us," the Executioner replied.

"Sounds like the party will start without you," Kamau answered. "If I don't see you again, it's been an honor."

"Isoba…"

Kamau turned off the radio. He scooped up his choice of weapon, an RPK light machine gun, with a 70-round drum. He'd have a while to act, waiting for Khaldun to get his men into position for the sake of his footage exposing the dead bodies. If the murderous Spear of Destiny commander was going to take video of the corpses, then Kamau was glad that the cameras supplied to him by Cooper were equipped with not only night-vision capabilities, but computerized filters and parallel lenses that allowed the camouflaged units to take images in both black of night and through the glare of spotlights.

He keyed his com link to the others. "You two under cover?"

"Nah, I just figured we'd continue playing mountain goat and get swept by machine-gun fire," Holt answered sarcastically. "Where's Matt?"

"He's on his way, but he'll be late for the party up top," Kamau answered.

"That's all right," Metit whispered. "We've found another entrance to that hidden temple."

"Great news," Kamau said.

"No. Terrible news," Metit said. "There's something very big and ugly at the entrance."

"What's she looking at, Eartha?" Kamau asked.

Holt's response was reluctant and preceded by a groan. "A Soviet SCD missile."

Kamau struggled to control the tremor that shot through his body. "A Scud. Out in plain view?"

"No. It's inside, and we can only see a sliver," Holt replied. "I was going to risk getting a better view, but you and Khaldun's helicopters cut us off."

Reminded of their presence, Kamau scanned the sky with his night-vision goggles. His throat tightened. Six helicopters were in formation, all of them loaded with gunmen, from the looks of the figures hanging their legs out the side doors of the ships. "Khaldun brought the whole crew."

"How many men?" Holt asked.

Kamau didn't want to think about it. "How many can six Black Hawks bring?"

"Shit!" Holt exclaimed. "Stay low, Isoba."

"No," Kamau answered. "Matt's risked far too much, and I haven't done a thing."

"This isn't a game. In fact, get back on the horn to him. He needs to know what he's getting into," Holt ordered.

"How is that going to help?" Kamau asked.

"I've seen this man at work. He can adapt on the fly to any bad situation. Tell him exactly what he'll be facing, and he'll be on top of it in no time," Holt explained. "Do it now."

Kamau went back to the field set and keyed it to life.

"Matt?" Kamau asked over the radio.

"Still here, Isoba. How bad does it look?" Bolan inquired.

"Six transport craft, filled to the point where they're dangling their legs out the side," Kamau said. "Eartha said you'd know how to handle this."

"I'll need you where you settled in to give me cover fire the other day," Bolan answered. "Has Metit found anything yet?"

"A Scud sitting in the side of a mountain," Kamau told him.

"Good. We won't need to aerially scout the mountainside. Set your watch for four minutes and thirty seconds, then when you're both in position and the timer runs down, you open fire," Bolan said. "Set on my mark. Mark."

"Watch set," Kamau replied. "I'll attract a lot of attention with this RPK."

"You won't have it for long," Bolan replied. "Get into position."

The Ethiopian giant was on his way, sending a prayer that his allies escape this nightmare intact.

METIT LOOKED BACK to Holt, big brown eyes wide with horror at the thought that she might rush to Kamau's side, but also dreading leaving her lover alone on top of the mountain with Cooper minutes away.

"Don't worry, girl," Holt told her. "That man has a plan, and few of his plans ever involve the sacrifice of an ally. The only time I ever got hurt working with him was when it was my fault."

"So what are we doing?" Metit asked.

"We'll be his eyes," Holt explained. "Because that man is going to need to know what he's dropping into."

Metit nodded. "All right."

Holt prepared a video camera with a flexible periscope lens. "I'm going to have to use this to transmit real-time digital information."

"Let me be the camerawoman," Metit said.

"Why?" Holt said.

"First, you're a better shooter than I ever will be. Second, I am a trained videographer, recording information for later analysis for archaeologists not at the scene," Metit replied.

Holt didn't have to think about it long. Metit had a good point. She handed over the camera, then checked her M-16. While the AK-47 and its ammunition was obviously going to be in good supply, Holt was more familiar with this rifle, and had a 40 mm grenade launcher attached under its barrel. The Egyptian military Misr rifles and their AK-47 originals didn't have such attachments. Being outnumbered, Holt knew that there would be need for a big punch. She wore a shoulder bag that was stuffed with 40 mm grenades.

As much as she talked up Cooper to Metit, Holt was under no illusion that the man possessed mystical powers enabling him to carry the day. But what he lacked in magic, the man made up for with a level of skill and determination that could push him through any opposition. Holt still had faith in the lone warrior.

"All right, kiddo, let's go," Holt spoke up.

Together, the two women moved closer to the Spear of Destiny's cavern.

KHALDUN HOPPED OUT the door of his helicopter, Misr in hand, scanning the dig site. As soon as they'd flooded the place with light, he knew something was terribly wrong. Still, he'd committed to his task and stepped out onto the plateau. His commandos swarmed around him, looking at the corpses of dead terrorists, their hands wrapped around the grips of the wrong rifles.

"They were supposed to have had AKs," one of his lieutenants said.

Khaldun bent and picked up an M-16 with its markings in Arabic. A sneer curled his upper lip as he looked around the camp. "So now the hostage wounds match the rifles these scumbags utilized."

The lieutenant ran his hand across his forehead, looking down at the corpse that Khaldun had disarmed. "So with this substitution, we can't definitively put the blame on the Israelis?"

Khaldun threw the weapon to the ground. "That's a worn-out M-16, as well. It could be traced back to a stolen shipment, making it seem as if this was something that I could blow out of proportion."

"What are we going to do?" a cameraman who Khaldun had brought along said.

"Take as much video as you can, but don't let the weapons into the picture if you can," Khaldun ordered. "We've got to salvage this as much as possible."

"Where to start?" the cameraman asked.

Khaldun pointed at a tent. "There're five women in there. Young women make for more heart-wrenching images."

The cameraman, escorted by two of Khaldun's riflemen, went to their task. Dread twisted in Khaldun's gut, telling him that he'd been set up. "I want you to scour the area. This stinks to high heaven, and I don't want it to turn into a trap. Keep to your partners. No separation, and you cover each other! This has turned to shit somehow."

The commandos of the Spear of Destiny went about their task with professionalism. Khaldun wondered if he should have tapped more conventional forces, especially since the fleet of helicopters he'd brought gave him the potential to haul seventy soldiers, fully equipped. He had only half that.

Khaldun tried to dismiss his doubts, realizing that ten of these men had pushed Cooper to his limits, forcing him into retreat against a superior force. That didn't make things any more palatable. There had been twenty

Shabaab and another fifteen Muslim Brotherhood men at the "rally point" he'd set out as bait for Cooper.

They'd been taken down in, what his men had immediately reported, less than half a minute, first gunshot to last ground-shaking detonation.

"They were terrorists, not trained soldiers," he told himself.

"Sir?" one of his men asked.

"What's wrong?" Khaldun countered.

"The bodies of the hostages are gone."

Khaldun's eyes widened, his jaw trembling. It felt as if someone had plunged a knife into his chest. "Gather up! We're leaving now!"

A light machine gun opened up from one side of the camp, two of Khaldun's commandos writhing under the deadly hammering of a dozen rounds that sliced through their body armor. The muzzle-flash and the loud chatter was enough to anchor the attention of Khaldun and the thirty-three other Spear of Destiny gunners.

"Kill that fucker!" Khaldun bellowed.

Something thumped behind the leader of the small army, a sound that was audible over the racket of five idling Black Hawks. He turned to see what was going on when an explosion ripped through the side of one of the H-60 aircraft.

A smoke trail rose into the sky, but nothing was visible against the night sky at the other end of the curl of vapor.

That didn't mean anything. Any good helicopter with its running lights off could maneuver after someone fired off an RPG from it.

"We've got enemy aircraft!" Khaldun warned. "Take—"

Khaldun tried to finish his shout, but an explosion forty feet away from him ripped the words from his lips. Chaos ruled the site of the Sinai massacre.

Chaos, and the Executioner.

CHAPTER NINETEEN

Bolan's first round from the Carl Gustav M-86 recoilless rifle was planted in the center of the H-60 Black Hawk, reducing the aircraft to a blossom of flaming splinters that rocketed into the nearby craft. Nakti had the recoilless rifle—actually a rocket launcher with a reusable, rifled tube—on board at Bolan's previous suggestion. Kamau had left the big cannon behind because he preferred the extra mobility of his light machine gun. Multishot grenade launchers would have been among Bolan's favored gear, but the Egyptian military didn't issue any version of the Milkor ML-6. Luckily, they did issue the big, reliable rocket launcher, and Gahiji had arranged for one to be on board Nakti's Black Hawk.

Its back blast wasn't going to cause damage in the interior of the bird, and with its range of up to 700 meters, it would give Bolan exactly the kind of firepower necessary to even the odds against the Spear of Destiny forces. The first 84 mm high-powered shell had destroyed one of Khaldun's helicopters, the wreckage turned to shrapnel damaging the other birds. The 3.5-kilogram shell had enough explosive content to make things rough for the grounded fleet. He could see one of the rotors had spiraled into the cockpit of another of the choppers, the flaming blade leaving shattered, caved-in glass and mangled bodies in its wake. One idling pilot had managed to get his bird off the ground.

At that moment, the commandos on the ground were betraying their positions as they opened up on Kamau's muzzle-flash. Their influx of autofire paused as soon as one of their choppers disappeared in a ball of fire. It didn't matter, as Bolan had already targeted a group of renegade soldiers in the camp. He swiftly stuffed another HE shell into the breech of his recoilless rifle, then sighted on the spot where a clot of muzzle-flashes had erupted.

Bolan wanted to cause the most damage among the enemy as well as negate the possibility of the murdered hostages being used for Khaldun's propaganda, so he had a team that had come with his allies to load the friendly dead on board their transports. The bodies of the Egyptian archaeological team had been loaded onto the helicopter that Kamau, Holt and Metit had been aboard. The only things left over were the corpses of Mubarak's terrorist cohorts and the replaced rifles in their dead hands. No innocent bodies would be mutilated or damaged any further before a reunion with their families. Those relatives would have familial closure. The terrorists' families wouldn't.

Though he would have liked to have taken a shot at Khaldun himself, the Executioner knew that he needed to sow the most confusion. The largest group of riflemen were his primary target, and without precious remains to damage, the whole camp was a death trap for the men of the Spear of Destiny, a free-fire zone that Kamau and Bolan could harvest with scything blasts of full-auto fire.

Getting the second round into the breech was easy, as the Carl Gustav was a familiar ally. Bolan pulled the trigger where he'd seen a concentration of muzzle-flashes, then released his shell. The warhead stuffed with Octol explosives, a mix of HMX and TNT, struck with sufficient force to create a fifty-foot blast wave, a circle of smoke that expanded swiftly, violently knocking men off their feet as if they were tenpins.

Nakti maneuvered the Black Hawk with precision, pulling it away from line of sight, utilizing the column of smoke from the M-86's shell as concealment. There would be no doubt that there was an enemy aircraft overhead, but the shock wave put out by the high-explosive, dual-purpose shell left the survivors with ringing ears and overwhelmed senses. Bolan took a moment to stow the deadly pipe.

He'd pushed his luck with the weapon and Nakti's life as far as he wanted to.

"Godspeed, Cooper!" Nakti shouted.

"Thanks," Bolan returned. He reached out to the rope dangling from its winch boom, then kicked out the coils piled in the entrance, gravity straightening the long, strong cord. His hands, wrapped in leather and Nomex gloves, allowed the nylon rope to slip through, his two-hundred-plus pounds of weight and dozens of pounds of gear dragging him down its length. The gloves he wore were made of high-quality leather with the palms made of layers of Kevlar and Nomex. He wouldn't be able to have the tactile feedback he usually needed, but for the quick trip down the line, the fast-rope gloves would keep his flesh from being flayed. As he closed with the ground, he clamped the cord between his boots to add extra friction to slow his descent.

It had been only a sixty-foot drop, but it would have shattered his legs and even his spine had he not had the rope. That brief moment of time that he descended had made him hard to see, let alone hit with a rifle. It also minimized the time that Nakti and his helicopter was exposed to ground fire. With a hop, Bolan dropped the last five feet and came down in a crouch.

A gunman stumbled toward him as the rope slurped up, retracted by the winch. The Executioner hadn't had time to get his rifle into position where he'd cinched it for the fast-rope descent. Lucky for him that his opponent was staggered from the 84 mm warhead's detonation. The Spear of Destiny gunner poked his M-16 toward the warrior, but quick hands grabbed the Egyptian's weapon and wrenched it from his grasp. The fiberglass buttstock cracked against the man's jaw as Bolan whirled the weapon, shattering molars. Further stunned, the Egyptian began to backpedal, but the Executioner wasn't a man to leave an enemy to suffer needlessly. One hand grabbed the rifleman's load-bearing vest, while with his other, Bolan raised his Beretta, plunged the barrel under his enemy's chin and fired a 9 mm round.

Bolan reholstered the Beretta, then tore off his fast-rope gloves in order to get a better feel for things he gripped. His aim had been slightly off, otherwise the impact of the fiberglass stock would have been place for an instantaneous kill via a broken neck. As the gloves fell to the ground, his hand reached back, took the grip of his M-16/M-203 rifle/grenade launcher combination and swung it into action.

"Get him!" a familiar voice croaked. "It's Cooper!"

Bolan was tempted to turn to focus on his main enemy from the past few days, but he needed to keep his eyes peeled for oncoming threats. The familiar and reassuring chatter of Kamau's light machine gun split the night, bowling over two more Egyptian commandos, their bodies sprawling from the vicious impact of the heavy rounds. Secure that he had one part of his perimeter covered, Bolan turned and focused on three more men running through a cloud of dust. Three quick taps of the rifle's trigger drilled several 5.56 mm rounds into the men, the short bursts spread wide, causing internal injuries where they speared through body armor and splintered bone. Lung tissue and aorta walls were sliced apart by 79-grain rounds that cut through muscle and skeleton like power drills through soft cheese.

"Eleven o'clock!" Kamau's voice came over his hands-free headset. The warrior lunged into a somersault, diving below the murderous line of autofire that sought to rip him asunder. Bolan's finger was so quick on the trigger that he tapped out a single round that focused on a spot that was five inches above the gunner's muzzle-flash. The 5.56 mm bullet sent a body to the ground in a sickening thud, its head destroyed by a rifle bullet at close range.

As the Executioner had decapitated that threat, the snarl of Kamau's weapon signaled the reason why another four Egyptian riflemen were doing a jerky version of a jig. Their bodies hammered by dozens of slugs, the Spear of Destiny commandos collapsed as their torsos were shredded by the heavier 7.62 mm rounds from the RPK. Bolan calculated that he and Kamau had accounted for around twenty of the enemy force, and it had appeared that Khaldun had brought at least twice that. There was also the problem that a little over a mile away, there was an entrance into the side of the plateau that provided access to Redjedef's personal force.

Rifles chattered off to one side, and Bolan turned to see three of the Spear of Destiny gunners firing their weapons into the sky. A quick glance showed sparks of bullet strikes on an aircraft. Since Nakti had orders to get out of the area, and he'd seen one of the surviving Black Hawks take flight, he knew that this was a Khaldun helicopter. Bolan shouldered his M-16/M-203 combo, targeted the H-60 chopper and pulled the trigger on the grenade launcher. The M-433 dual-purpose round that flew from the fat tube beneath his rifle's barrel was designed not to only engage enemy personnel on the ground, but also to engage lightly armored enemy vehicles. It would take a skilled marksman with a grenade launcher to hit an aircraft, but the Executioner was one such sharpshooter. The 40 mm packet was a combination of a shaped charge with a wire mesh for fragmentation purposes. The shrapnel potential was handy as the shaped charge unleashed an explosive jet of force through the belly of the Black Hawk. Fragmented wire vomited through the hole torn by the shaped charge, and rebounded off the aircraft's roof. The Egyptian crewmen in the cockpit had their lives ended instantly as super-hot knives of metal lashed through their necks, shoulders and backs.

"Oh, shit!" Kamau's voice cut over the radio, and Bolan diverted his attention to see that the stricken aircraft nosed down in his ally's general direction. Flames spewing out shattered windows and doors, the H-60 groaned as it connected with the earth.

"Isoba!" Bolan called out.

"...fine!" Kamau croaked, obviously having caught a lungful of hot air or smoke, or both.

"Get to new cover, I'll handle the rest of this!" Bolan told him over the radio.

There was a moment of pause on the other end of the line. The big Ethiopian didn't want to leave the Executioner alone on the battlefield.

"New cover, not total retreat. Once you're clear, continue support fire!" Bolan added.

"Sir!" Kamau returned.

Bolan had a few moments while the pouring smoke and blazing flame of the shattered helicopter distracted the enemy soldiers. He didn't know exactly how many he and Kamau had taken out, but he conservatively estimated that there were about twenty left, providing he'd taken out two from the clot of commandos he'd hit with the M-86. Two of his opponents were backlit by the fire of a burning piece of wreckage.

The Executioner shouldered his assault rifle and took both men with head shots, one catching a pair of 5.56 mm skull-splitters, the other taking only one hit. He didn't want to waste ammunition, but he had the M-16 on full-auto, and at 800 rounds per minute, there was going to be a little waste. Either way, two more were down, and Bolan took a moment to feed a fresh magazine into the rifle even as he took concealment behind a tent.

A couple of weapons burped in the darkness, bullets ripping through the canvas. Bolan knew that the fabric wouldn't give him much in way of protection, but as long as they couldn't see him, they couldn't put their rounds on target. Bolan ejected his empty shell casing from the grenade launcher, then fed in a new 40 mm canister. This was a blunt can of buckshot, a little shorter than his other grenades, making it easier for him to distinguish it by touch. With the breech shut on the launcher, he now had an enormous shotgun under his rifle's barrel.

The Executioner threw himself prone and far enough away so that he could see the riflemen who had dumped bullets through the tent. The pair saw his movement, but one man was completely dry in terms of ammo. The other tried to sweep Bolan, but he came up empty in midaim. The two Egyptians were professionals, both transitioning to their handguns as their rifles dropped on their slings, and Bolan was impressed by the speed of their draw, but as soon as their hands touched the handles of their pistols, he triggered the M-203. A low, throaty roar split the air, and hundreds of pellets of buckshot swarmed at the men, a wave of body-shredding metal that tore and mangled the Spear of Destiny commandos. Their bodies tumbled backward, the life drilled from them by the payload of the launcher.

The unfortunate part of the grenade launcher's effectiveness was that it drew a lot of attention from the surviving gunners. Bullets whipped through the air over his head, the ground erupting as high-velocity projectiles tore into sand and rock. Luckily, Bolan had a low rise of stone to his right, blocking that vector of autofire. The gunmen to his left had only a sound, as the grenade launcher possessed no muzzle-flash, so they simply directed their fire in a general direction. Sooner or later, a lucky bullet was going to connect with Bolan.

The Executioner aimed his M-16 at two men to his left whose muzzle-flashes were the roundest, looking from his position. That pair of men had their weapons nearly locked onto him, hence the relatively circular streaks of superhot gases escaping from their barrels. On full-auto, but keeping his bursts short, the soldier unleashed two miniwaves of withering fire, the first 3-round salvo stitching through the upper chest of one gunman. The second man caught the second storm of bullets, only two, in the middle of his face. Bolan returned his sights to the first man, just in case the Egyptian commando was wearing an armored vest.

He didn't have much time for an evaluation as three more of the Spear of Destiny gunners adjusted their aim, forcing Bolan to move. The instant he'd evacuated his old position, it was hammered with a shredding rain of high-velocity M-16 bullets, dozens of rounds moving at 3000 feet per second. Bolan was literally milliseconds from having his body pulped by the high-velocity slugs.

On the move, the Executioner fired from the hip. He struck down one Egyptian gunman, whipping a line of five bullets into his abdomen. The 79-grain boattail hollowpoint rounds reacted violently with fluid mass. They had sufficient weight to punch through what bones were struck, but the sudden introduction of hydrostatic force to their hollow tips deformed the 5.56 mm bullets, rupturing their copper jackets and turning them into power drills through human flesh. The rifleman that

Bolan had struck folded over in agony, his stomach and right lung transformed into frothy puddles of disrupted organ tissue and blood.

The death of their compatriot pushed the other two gunmen to take cover, buying the Executioner a few more moments to achieve a tenable position on this chaotic battlefield. Unfortunately, having risen to his feet, he was now exposed to the riflemen on his right. He expected the chatter of automatic fire to precede his fall, but a deeper, throatier rumble split the air, raking toward the gunmen trying to track Bolan.

Kamau had returned to action, letting his RPK light machine gun silence the enemy before they could harm his new friend. Bolan heard him over the hands-free radio headset. "Sorry I let you take so much heat for so long."

"No need to apologize," Bolan replied, skidding behind a jutting boulder that sparked and threw off splinters of stone as Spear of Destiny shooters tried to refocus on their enemy. The big rock was a comforting weight against Bolan's back as he reloaded the grenade launcher.

"I think there are seven or eight left with some fight in them," Kamau counted.

"Unless some are holding their fire," Bolan answered. "We've made a big cut into their numbers, but they might want to underplay the force they have left."

"Fucking sorcerer!" a voice bellowed in frustration and rage. Bolan's battle-honed reflexes kicked him out of the path of a swath of lead from a small group of men who had flanked him.

The Executioner tracked his M-16 and took off the

top of one man's head. The dome of his skull shattered like a glass bowl under a sledgehammer, brains erupting in a mushy mess. There had been three of them, but the two survivors hadn't broken their charge. One man fired a huge pistol, while the other kept at it with his own M-16, rounds chasing Bolan as he ran serpentine toward a crack in the ground. Kamau's RPK hammered out its brutal death song, taking out the rifleman with a concentrated swarm of 30-caliber slugs. Bolan skidded behind cover as the pistol-packing gunman, and the rest of his surviving team, turned their attention toward the Ethiopian.

Fortunately for Kamau, he'd found a knot of stones that was sufficient to deflect any small-arms fire while he was able to poke the muzzle of his light machine gun over the top and fire off bursts toward the remaining enemy shooters. From behind the safety of his stony emplacement, Kamau chuckled over the radio. "It's like a tennis match or something."

"Hang on to their attention for a moment more," Bolan replied. He rose from his cover and saw that three of the remaining Spear of Destiny fighters had bunched up to take advantage of the cover provided by supply crates. They were only thirty yards away, but Bolan decided to risk his HEDP grenade from the M-203. The 40 mm shell spiraled out of the barrel, and the Executioner dropped prone as the high-explosive charge connected with the trio of gunmen. Several ounces of efficient mixed plastique and TNT detonated, a mesh cone of copper meant for cutting through light armor transforming into a fan spray of shrapnel that lacerated and mutilated what hadn't been broken by the powerful pressure wave put out by the grenade. Limbs flew everywhere, bodies transformed into mangled mockeries of what they used to be.

Kamau rolled out to take advantage of the thunderous distraction of the grenade blast, cutting down another of the Egyptian renegades, a line of full-auto slugs sending the gunner to await his pharaoh in the afterlife.

One man broke from the battle scene, the pistol-packing loner who had tried to flank the Executioner. Unfortunately, there was no way that Bolan could pursue him with three riflemen continuing to struggle for their lives. Unlucky for the Spear of Destiny conspirators, they were in a cross fire between Kamau and Bolan. At right angles to each other, the two men had nearly unlimited fields of fire with no danger of hitting each other. When the last of Khaldun's handpicked soldiers fell under the coordinated attacks of the two warriors, Bolan was able to return his attention to the fleeing man.

Bolan's PDA vibrated in his pocket, drawing his attention away from thoughts of engaging the last of the gunmen in hot pursuit. He pulled it out and checked the screen. A collection of images that had been recorded by Metit and Holt had been transmitted to his PDA as a means of mapping out the route into the Spear of Destiny underground compound.

It was an impressive view, a large entrance hall that was camouflaged by overhanging rock. While there were indications of ancient-Egyptian hieroglyphs along the walls, it was the modern additions that concerned the Executioner. On the floor of the hall were several long-range missile launchers mounted on tracked vehicles. While Holt had called them SUDs, Bolan knew that they were an upgraded artillery missile system that had been developed by the Syrians and North Koreans. They were a refinement of the old Soviet-era OTR-21 Tochka missiles, known in NATO parlance as the Scarab. The most recent of Soviet military variants, the Scarab-C had a maximum range of 120 miles, and had a payload that could carry a nuclear warhead, 1000 pounds of high explosive or equal amounts of chemical weaponry. A dozen of the big, ugly weapons were locked into their squat, rectangular, eight-wheeled motorized launchers and ready to unleash doom on their targets. Support trucks carried reloads for the dozen launch systems.

Israel was within easy reach of these blockbuster missiles, as was Cairo and the rest of inhabited Egypt. The twelve six-wheel-drive artillery trucks would be capable of firing in both directions. During the civil war in Grozny, Chechnya, six of those mobile launchers had killed hundreds in one coordinated salvo, smashing hospital infrastructure and marketplaces, even while using only conventional 1000-pound explosive payloads. With Syrian chemical weaponry filling the warheads, the death toll would be massive. The return fire between Egypt and Israel would cause even more tragic loss of life.

The last image that Metit had transmitted was a flood of crewmen swarming toward the launch vehicles, scores of troops joining the throng.

"Isoba! We need to get to Rashida and Eartha now!" Bolan growled.

In defanging Redjedef's plan to implicate Israel into

a war-inspiring massacre, Bolan had shoved the Eternal
Pharaoh's schedule up dramatically. Missiles would fly,
and the dogs of war would heed the cry of havoc.

CHAPTER TWENTY

Only the barest of luck and the swiftness of his own reactions had carried Khaldun out of the massacre staged
and executed by Bolan and Kamau. The site of the mass
murder he'd committed as part of the plan to bring the
Middle East to flashpoint had suddenly turned into a resounding military defeat at the hands of a smaller force.
Certainly, grenade launchers and recoilless rifles had
evened the odds considerably, destroying two aircraft,
disabling the others and overwhelming the infantry on
the ground. Additionally, the two men had the benefit
of uneven terrain, blinding flames and choking smoke
to provide them cover.

It was still two men, one some form of military sorcerer who had engaged in a slaughter against superior
numbers. Khaldun suddenly empathized with the terror
of the lone survivor of his massacre. He had seen dozens
of people he knew and trusted cut down by relentless,
merciless firepower. He'd handpicked them and indoc-
trinated them into the news that the first of kings, the
son of a god, had returned to claim Egypt and bring
her back to her rightful place in the world, free from
the machinations of a prophet of an obscure moon god
and stronger in the face of the Hebrew slaves who once
toiled and battled in the service of the god kings.

The blood of those highly trained soldiers had spilled

as if they were unarmed students and careless terrorists. Just like when Khaldun had first encountered Cooper at the camp as he worked, loading Masozi's conflict diamonds for transport to Syria.

Masozi. That clumsy fool. He couldn't have been more of a failure. The Shabaab commander and a few dozen of his allies and Alexandria's most bloodthirsty gunmen had been left at an abandoned construction site as bait to bring in Cooper. The simple fact that the man had come down like a rain of war hammers hurled by an angry god was proof that Masozi had either failed, or the obvious bait hadn't been taken by the canny, prepared soldier. However, Khaldun suspected that somehow the one-man army had finished off the Somalian murderer and his kill force.

Khaldun grabbed a rock as the ground slid from beneath his boots. He'd almost dropped his gun, a .44 Magnum Desert Eagle, for all the good it had done him. He'd emptied two clips at Cooper, and ended up alone and in flight for his life. The Eternal Pharaoh had counted on him to prevent the unraveling of his master plan, and all Khaldun had done was bring an implacable menace down upon the seat of the Spear of Destiny and Redjedef's throne.

Such failure would mean his execution, even if the son of Khofu managed to throw Egypt into a mad war against Israel. The use of Syrian missile launchers and weaponized ricin would be the kiss of death for the nominally Islamic leadership of Egypt. Redjedef was on the warpath to purge his nation of a cancer that had relegated the country to Third World status.

The Spear of Destiny had been doing more than

preparing biochemical weapons. It had been working at making radical Islamists in the country smear the reputation of the Muslim population. It hadn't been hard. The terrorists of the Muslim Brotherhood had been in need of cash, so they were easy to hire for countless acts of violence in addition to their usual schedule of raising havoc and creating menace. They had been included in dozens of incidents of mayhem that had ruined the image of the religion of peace. Moderate believers started to question themselves. With the breakout of war against Israel, those who doubted the fanatical drive of terrorist fanaticism would revolt under an unworthy leadership.

That would be where Redjedef stepped in.

It was simple. Sell surplus Egyptian military equipment to raise funds, then launder the money into Liberian conflict diamonds. Offer a large cache of historically proved poison to the Syrians to perfect into an artillery distributable vector, and pay them with the conflict diamonds for the equipment they would need. Their prior efforts had also involved the Syrians, a plan to simply purchase their chemical weapons while utilizing American lend-lease surplus weapons to instigate the conflict. Instead, a mysterious stranger had derailed that plan, even as a flight of unmanned drones loaded with city-killing payloads had been launched. Israel and Egypt had unified in an effort to prevent the war at the lone soldier's bidding, and the man had penetrated into the depths of a mountain stronghold and rendered it a tomb for General Idel and his army.

Khaldun paused, out of breath, looking back up to the plateau.

Redjedef waited in the heart of this particular mountain, ready to unleash biotoxic hell upon two nations in order to bring about the conflict that would sweep him into supreme power over Egypt. Did the Eternal Pharaoh have a plan in motion to fend off a one-man army and his allies where his minion had failed?

"He is a god," Khaldun panted. "He is unkillable…"

He tried to fight off the logic that made it so that thirty-five riflemen and five combat helicopter crews would be unkillable by the efforts of only two men. His heart sank as that reality settled in.

Cooper was, if not an immortal, the living embodiment of a force of nature. He had swept through platoons of opposition with little effort. Elite commando teams hadn't been able to give him pause, except for that one night when they had gunships and the element of surprise. Since then, the lone crusader had fought back with unmatched fury.

Khaldun had calculated that he'd covered the ground almost all the way to the cavern entrance to the hidden fortress. The sound of Klaxons sounded softly in his ears, still distant, muffled by rock and his angle in relation to the huge cave. He gulped air in an effort to revitalize his stamina, and lifted one leaden, unwilling leg, then the other, making strides toward the Seat of Redjedef.

That's when the Egyptian heard movement ahead of him. Was it reinforcements?

There were two figures, but they were too small to have been any of the Spear of Destiny base defense cadre. One of them wasn't even armed except for a video camera, as far as he could see their darkened silhouettes in the night. They were women!

Holt and Metit, according to what Parma had told him. He reached for the .44 Magnum pistol in its holster, drawing it as quickly as he could. Unfortunately for him, Eartha Holt caught the sudden glint of metal. She shouldered her rifle reflexively, but held her fire.

Khaldun didn't rest his finger on the trigger of his Desert Eagle, as well. The three people were caught between two forces, and one gunshot would bring a world of trouble down on them, either in an overwhelming assault by either side, or in the form of a brutal cross fire that would slice through both parties. Sweat beaded on Khaldun's forehead, as they didn't have room to pass each other in the narrow passage leading to and from the Seat of Redjedef.

"Standoff," Holt said with cold determination. Khaldun had no doubt that the woman would pull the trigger on him. If she was the same agent who had appeared in the reports he'd received, she was nearly as ferocious as Cooper.

"How do we deal with this?" Khaldun asked.

"You could always stuff that big gun in your mouth and blow off the top of your skull," Holt offered.

Khaldun managed a smirk. "At least you're straightforward about it."

Holt motioned for Metit to get behind her. "Neither of us wants to fire a shot. We'll just draw too much attention."

"So how do you propose we solve this?" Khaldun asked.

"Knives?" Holt offered.

Khaldun and Holt lowered their firearms at the same time, eyeing each other warily. "I'm so much bigger than you are, woman. It almost wouldn't be fair to you."

Holt's eyes narrowed, a cruel grin on her lips. "Keep telling yourself that, errand boy."

"I am the weapon of the pharaoh," Khaldun replied. "I am no mere minion."

"Says the running dog of a Nazi dynasty," Holt prodded.

Khaldun's brow wrinkled. "Nazis?"

"Why do you think a Jew like me worked so hard to track down something as out of the way as your group?" Holt asked. "You sit behind the scenes, jerking around Islamic terrorists, but you're no fans of the Prophet. And I know the men who came to Egypt to work with those who sought to revive the Old Ways."

Khaldun shrugged as he and Holt set their guns down at the same time, gently so as not to unintentionally discharge their weapons. Tossing them aside, while cocked and off safe, would have resulted in a shot being fired. Caution was the order of the moment. "So we have an old German helping us lead the way back to Egypt's glory. Your point?"

Holt backed away from her discarded rifle, stepping sideways as Khaldun did likewise. He flicked a glance toward Metit, but she seemed to cringe against the wall, her dark eyes staring at him. He could almost smell the fear on her. "My point is, your dream has been usurped, not assisted. My grandfather came back from Egypt *after* Erich Abelard massacred the Spear of Destiny's high command."

"Again…so what?" Khaldun asked.

Holt sighed as her hand dropped to the handle of the knife in her belt. Khaldun reached behind his back, feeling the checkered fiberglass grips of his own combat blade. It was a quality Pakistani-made weapon based off the old Fairbairn-Sykes commando knife, his only change to it being the reinforced modern-material handle. Khaldun didn't know what knives the woman had, but in one of her hands, she had a ring with what looked like a hooked talon, while the other was a Bowie-style blade, cast in black, low-reflective metal with a rubber handle. Her green eyes flashed with anger as she sized him up. "It means that he's likely been lying to you for years."

"Either way, I'm sitting at the right hand of the man who will rule a nation," Khaldun countered. "What makes you so intent on finding this man?"

"He's family. Likely a cousin," Holt said. "My family name, my real family name, is Abelard, as well. And Grandfather didn't particularly care for maintaining the memory of the Reich."

Khaldun nodded. "So this is just personal."

"That, and I really think it'd fuck up my day if my country were hit with chemical weapons," Holt added.

"Pardon me if I wouldn't be as torn up about the loss of Israel as you would be," Khaldun answered.

"No, no pardons," a soft voice said from the side. "No reprieves. No mercy for a fucker like you."

"Stay out of this, child," Khaldun growled. "I'll finish with you when I'm done with this one."

He caught the young woman's glare. The fury he noticed gave him pause. While Holt was ferocious, there was a rage he'd spurred in Rashida Metit that chilled the Egyptian to his very core.

EARTHA HOLT GLANCED toward Metit, seeing the anger on the student's face. There was something angry and twisted in it, but she had to return her attention to Khaldun. The Spear of Destiny military commander was too much of a threat, and she couldn't afford the distraction. But there was something, a change in Metit that she could feel, as if it were a sudden change in the temperature, or a great weight that fell on her chest. This fight would have been a straight up-and-down knife duel, but with Metit's anger, there was always the potential of her causing a fatal distraction for Holt.

She clenched the handle of her Ek Bowie, feeling the subtle shift of its handle as the rubberized material compressed slightly. Her finger was through a control hole in a Kerambit-style knife. The shorter blade, shaped like the sharply hooked beak of a predatory bird, was capable of carving long stretches of muscle away from bone and split skin and major blood vessels easily. The stubbiness of the Kerambit also allowed it to produce a thrust that could punch through skull bone. The only drawback to the hooked knife was that it extended only an inch and a half from the knuckle of her grip. She had already given up a lot of reach to Khaldun to rely on it as her primary knife.

Holt's opponent had been distracted by Metit's presence and her reaction to his growled threat. Both had been given pause by the hardness of the young woman's glare. Some switch had been pushed inside her, causing the release of a dam of emotion that had been held in check until he delivered his ultimatum to her.

Holt decided to make the first move, lunging with the clip-point tip of the Bowie. It was a fencer's thrust, and Khaldun had been distracted just enough that his shirt snagged on the point, fabric tearing. The Egyptian had caught the blur of movement enough that he only received a shallow scratch as he jerked out of the way. He grabbed at her wrist, but Holt twisted nimbly to one side, lashing out with her other fist and the Kerambit.

Khaldun grimaced as the hooked edge tore at his knife arm, fabric and skin carved by Holt's blade. He flicked his own knife, and the woman grimaced as her hip felt the sharp sting of his dagger. The tough little Israeli agent swung her Bowie around to snag the Egyptian on his knife wrist, but the other man was just too quick, jerking into retreat.

First blood had been taken on both of them, probative cuts that had been a test of each other's reactions. Holt had been involved in knife fights before, so she knew that there was no way that she could avoid receiving a few nicks and other injuries. It was the nature of blades and close-quarters combat that there would be souvenirs in the form of scars from any such conflict.

Khaldun's reactions showed that he was a man dedicated to the art of the short blade, and Holt knew that when it came to equal levels of skill, she'd come up on the short end in terms of strength, even if she had twice the blades he did. She hoped that she had enough speed and more ability than her bigger, stronger opponent, otherwise this was going to end badly for her.

Khaldun's dark eyes locked on her, his face grim and

concerned. Holt hoped that his reservations were due to the fact that she'd scored twice as many cuts on him as he had on her, that she showed talent with the blade that was superior to his. That was her hope, but she knew better than to put false premises on the facial reactions of any opponent. He could have been faking, acting in order to put her more at ease than she should have been. If she assumed she had the advantage, she wouldn't be able to catch a feint, and be drawn into a lethal trap that ended only with his double-bladed dagger slicing her from crotch to sternum.

Holt studied his hands and feet instead of his expression. Even that wouldn't be a good indicator if he was skilled at footwork. The way Khaldun shuffled showed that he had background experience in boxing, which meant that he was adept at misleading an opponent with a step, transferring that advantage from fisticuffs to knife fighting.

Khaldun made another probative slice, the tip whistling through the air near her ear, narrowly missing her shoulder. Holt brought up her knife to slip in under his thrust, but an iron grasp clamped around her wrist, and suddenly, the fight turned from feint and thrust into a wrestling match. Holt lashed out with the talon-like Kerambit, its hooked edge tearing into Khaldun's shoulder and breaking his grip. The two combatants recoiled from each other, backpedaling from another encounter that had threatened their lives.

Khaldun had been nimble enough to minimize the damage her Kerambit had caused to him, turning to avoid all but the tip of the slice. Blood seeped into his shirtsleeve, but his arm still moved. She hadn't caused any muscle damage with her strike. He reached up, fingertips dipping in the blood, then moving to his tongue.

"My first suggestion's still open to you," Holt prodded. She needed something to get him out of his game plan.

The fierce smile on his face as he tasted his own blood was his own attempt at intimidation, and Holt had to admit that his reaction to his own injury was disturbing. She'd been in plenty of fights, but the sight of a man tasting his own blood and grinning was still a powerful image.

"No thanks, Jewess. I'll take my chances with you," Khaldun replied.

"Can't say I'm disappointed," Holt returned. Still, her cocky confidence was only voice deep. Her wrist was sore where he'd grabbed her, squeezing hard enough to leave bruises and to grind wrist bones against each other. She knew that he may have caused some tendon damage, hurting her chances of maintaining her grasp on her knife. A loosened grip meant that she couldn't hold the Bowie tightly enough to plunge it deep into one of his vital organs.

Khaldun took a step forward, and Holt held her ground, forearms crossed so that she had sharp edges pointing out in both directions, giving her a maximum arc where she could slash and draw blood without hindrance. The feint unanswered, Khaldun withdrew and circled, Holt mirroring his sidesteps.

The two of them looked for openings, seeing dozens, but they faded as quickly as eyes focused on them. It was as much a mental chess game, except in this contest, one didn't lose a simple carved piece, but they lost chunks of flesh on a bad move. Every twist, each turn was preparation for one move that the other moved in reaction to counter. They were fluid in their motions, eyes probing to find the slightest of weaknesses in each other's defense while closing up their own vulnerabilities.

Khaldun took a halting step and Holt tensed, forcing herself not to react to his movement, but after the Egyptian's brief pause, he carried through the move she thought he was only pretending to make. He swung down his knife in an icepick-style stab, the point glancing off Holt's shoulder as she whipped up the Kerambit. Khaldun grimaced as the inch-and-a-half crescent of unyielding steel pierced his forearm, his own knifepoint not quite as deep as her blade in her pectoral muscle. The pain was excruciating for Holt, but she still managed to whip up the Bowie knife, aiming it toward Khaldun's abdominal muscles. Her point scratched skin just before Khaldun's iron grip once more snared around her wrist.

The two combatants were frozen. Holt had stopped Khaldun's stab with her blade stuck in his arm, but Khaldun had more than enough strength to hold her knife at bay. Muscles flexed, and this was where Holt knew she was outmatched. Their swiftness had been nearly equal, and their timing had been sharp enough for them to make this a standoff. But when it came to muscle, Khaldun simply had her beat. It would be minutes before Holt exhausted herself, but she would fail before the Egyptian did. Her back was drenched with blood, and it felt as if her forearm bones were breaking under the pressure of his steely fingers.

"Rashida! Run!" Holt rasped.

"How noble," Khaldun snarled.

"Eat shit and die," Holt returned.

Her cut hip was draining more of her ability to stand than she had calculated. Khaldun had shifted his bulk forward, making her support him as well as her body. He was stealing her strength with his mass pressing on her. She wasn't going to last minutes as she had calculated. She struggled to push her Bowie harder, but he resisted. She wouldn't be able to gut him and get one last bit of revenge on the man intending to kill her.

A figure loomed in the darkness, gaining Holt's and Khaldun's attention. It was Metit, her face a pained, motionless mask.

"She told you to run, gi—" he began.

A dull thump sounded, and Khaldun stopped. A second thud, and Holt felt a relaxation on her enemy's part. Blood trickled over his lower lip.

"You couldn't risk a shot," Metit whispered, leaning in close to Khaldun's ear. "But I'm a scientist. I figured out that a gun won't make a sound if you contain all that pressure making contact with the air."

Khaldun's mouth frothed as he tried to speak.

"Stuck in your ribs, my gun is silenced," Metit concluded. "That's for my classmates and my teachers, you son of a bitch!"

Another pop sounded, and Khaldun collapsed into a boneless heap, Holt scurrying out from under him.

"Rashida?" Holt asked.

The young woman backed away, Beretta locked in her fist. She didn't tremble with shock. Emotion had bled from her. She was numb, days of anger and impotence washed away with just a few actions of her index finger. Metit remained quiet, her dark eyes unfocused.

Holt wrapped her arm around the younger woman's shoulders, and Metit leaned her head to rest against hers. "It's okay. It's over."

"That's the problem," Metit answered. "It's not done yet. We've got too much to do."

A Black Hawk sliced through the night sky over their heads, the whine of its engines resounding. The helicopter paused, and Holt could see the outline of a man standing in the open side door. It was Matt Cooper. He was watching them through night-vision goggles.

Her arm aching from the wound in her shoulder, she still managed the strength to give Bolan a thumbs-up. He returned the gesture, then turned to speak to the pilot.

"We're done. Matt and Isoba are going to take the last of this," Holt promised her.

The Executioner sped toward the Seat of Redjedef on wings of night.

CHAPTER TWENTY-ONE

Mack Bolan and Isoba Kamau looked at the screen of the Executioner's PDA, fixing the images in their minds to form a quick map of the mountainside fortress. It was something to do while they waited for Nakti to bring the Black Hawk around to pick them up. Running along mountain paths in the dark in an effort to beat the Tochka missiles and their launchers would be too dangerous, especially with at least some of Khaldun's soldiers alive and possibly on the loose. Combat would delay them, and a slip or fall would cause an injury, which even if it wasn't fatal, would slow either of the men around.

Besides, using the Black Hawk would give the two men a vantage point where they had the high ground to slow Redjedef's deployment of his Tochkas. The Carl Gustav 84 mm launcher was still where Bolan had left it behind, and Kamau scooped it up as Nakti zeroed in on the landing zone.

"We're going to have to be damn careful," Kamau said. "We pop one of those missiles by accident…" He gave Nakti a brief salute as he and Bolan jumped into the helicopter.

"Gahiji is going to need hazmat suits to clear out the fortress," Bolan concluded. "If the missiles look as if they're ready to launch, we're going to have to make a few sacrifices."

"Without asking Eartha or Rashida?" Kamau asked.

Bolan nodded, feeding an HEDP round into the breech of his rifle/grenade launcher combination. "Which is why we're going to need to lay down a lot of firepower to get them to retreat."

Kamau glanced at the belt-fed Helwan 920 that was mounted on a pintle at the side of the helicopter. The Helwan was a license-produced variant of the Fabrique Nationale MAG machine gun, a reliable weapon that could trace its heritage back to World War I, where its fire mechanism was first blooded in the trenches of Europe as the BAR. The Helwan was able to throw out its brutal 7.62 mm x 51 mm NATO payload at a blistering rate anywhere from 650 to 1000 rounds per minute. It was a bullet hose, and when mounted on the side of a helicopter, it was perfectly capable of dropping hell on opponents.

"It still could puncture one of those Tochkas," Kamau noted.

"But less likely, and a .3-inch hole doesn't disperse a large cloud of weaponized ricin," Bolan returned. He checked his hands-free radio system to see about Holt and Metit. It was possible that the women could have escaped to a minimum safe distance in the event of a catastrophic toxic release. He couldn't raise them, which was sensible. They had gone to radio silence right after the high-speed information dump that had ended up on his PDA. He was concerned for the women. They were brave, but bravery only went so far when it came to dealing with a hostile force.

Bolan remembered the last image that Metit had transmitted. The throng of military men racing to the eight-wheeled launch trucks and their support vehicles. Redjedef had command of an army of fanatics, and the crews of the Tochka missile launchers were supported by infantrymen, a group bristling with assault rifles, grenade launchers and light machine guns. They appeared to be equipped with M-1043 Reconnaissance Scout vehicles, the Egyptian supply of HUMMVs lent by the U.S. armed forces. The heavy-duty off-road trucks had heavy machine guns mounted. He couldn't tell from the blurred image, but knowing the resources of the Egyptian military, he could count on anything from the legendary Browning M2 .50-caliber all the way up to the Soviet-era ZPU-1 14.5 mm machine guns. Be it a mere 12.7 mm bullet or a 14.5 mm, it would be a moot point as to the exact caliber they would face, as each slug carried tons of force with it, capable of tearing through a Black Hawk helicopter as if it were made of tissue paper.

Compared to the truck-mounted guns, the Helwan 920 might as well be throwing spitballs.

"Cooper! I've got a visual on a mountain path!" Nakti called over his headset.

Bolan moved to the side door, adjusting the night-vision goggles on his helmet. He saw a rapidly cooling corpse, the body of a man. Standing over him were two women, each leaning on the other for support. The pilot slowed the Black Hawk to give the soldier a moment to check on the two. They were twenty yards down, but communication would be difficult, even if Holt were willing to break radio silence.

He saw Holt lift her fist, thumb jutting up. She seemed to have been weakened by her recent conflict, but she still appeared to have enough strength to convey to him that she and Metit would be all right. Bolan returned the gesture.

"All right, Nakti. Time to get to work," Bolan said. He glanced back toward Holt as the Black Hawk rose, pulling away from the pair.

He hated to abandon them, but there was work to be done. Kamau wiped his mouth as he looked up from the Helwan. "They'll be fine?"

"They're not going to be getting any better if we occupy our minds with them instead of what we have to do," Bolan replied.

Kamau frowned, looking back toward the woman he'd fallen in love with. "That is cold…"

"I don't care too much for it either, but they're alive right now. Thousands die if we're distracted. Hunker down. We've got business to attend to."

Kamau nodded, his jaw set firmly. He rested his finger on the trigger guard of the Helwan.

Bolan was satisfied he'd cleared his mind of doubts and fears. The warrior wanted his ally mentally focused.

The Black Hawk turned sideways, slipping horizontally so that Nakti could give Bolan and Kamau the proper facing to unleash their broadside. Gripping a strap, Bolan held on as the helicopter decelerated quickly. Kamau had the mounting of his machine gun to grasp in order to maintain his balance. They were looking out over the cave hewn into the side of the mountain, floodlights illuminating the first vehicles out onto the carved road. Two of the Egyptian Hummers lead the way, cupolas installed in their roofs so that heavy machine guns with shields could be installed.

Bolan leveled his M-203 grenade launcher and punched out the high-explosive, dual-purpose shell toward the lead Hummer. With a grimace, he realized that the 40 mm shell probably lacked the stopping power of the much larger warhead of the 72 mm RPG-7 that had taken such a savage toll on U.S. Hummers in Iraq and Afghanistan. The fat, football-shaped RPG shells could cut through the light armor of the utility vehicles, and nominally, so should the grenade Bolan had fired.

The shell struck the front hood of the Hummer and detonated on impact. The engine cover crumpled and flew away like a chunk of tinfoil, and the Hummer ground to a halt as shrapnel ripped out the guts of its engine. Unfortunately, the gunner who was situated in the cupola was protected by quarter-inch-thick steel wings around the sides of his M-2 Browning machine gun. The concussion apparently had scrambled the Egyptian's senses, as he didn't immediately open fire, but he was still alive, and hunkered down behind bulletproof armor.

Kamau raked the stunned machine gunner with a taste of his Helwan's dragon breath. Sparks flew as 7.62 mm slugs rang off the armor plating, Bolan swinging the aim of his M-16 toward the second vehicle in line. The two men cut loose on full-auto, but the second Hummer swerved around its crippled partner, the gunner in the back cranking the muzzle of his cannon upward.

"Nakti! Evasive!" Bolan bellowed into his helmet's headset.

The Egyptian pilot reacted with lightning reflexes, sending the Black Hawk into a power ascent that carried the bird above a line of sizzling .50-caliber slugs that would have cut it in two. Bolan continued to pump short bursts down toward the Hummer, hoping that the higher angle would allow him to nail the gunner, but the rapid movement of the helicopter threw the warrior's aim off. Precision fire on a helicopter taking evasive action was a near impossibility, especially from an unstabilized rifle.

Kamau cursed as the sudden ascent kept him from angling his machine gun toward the enemy vehicles. The big Ethiopian turned and scooped up the recoilless rifle. "Clear shot?"

"Do it!" Bolan returned, feeding a new grenade into his M-203. From the cave's entrance, rifles crackled in response to the helicopter's presence. So far, none of the eight-wheeled launch vehicles had been exposed to their fire, and presumably the detonation and autofire had convinced their crews to remain under the protective canopy of stone.

Kamau swung the Carl Gustav M-86 as if it were a toy, leveling the gaping 84 mm barrel toward the undamaged Hummer. He pulled the trigger, causing Bolan to flinch as the hot gases from the launcher's back tube scattered, some of it deflecting into the cabin of the chopper. Luckily, Bolan wore a helmet with protective lenses, and both men were clad in heavy BDUs, jackets made of blended ripstop material and Nomex. Kamau grimaced as an exposed sliver of neck was stung by superheated air, but his missile flew true—sort of.

The powerful recoilless rifle shell struck one of the Hummers, but it had been the one that Bolan had taken out of commission. It clipped the side of the roof. While the 84 mm rocket had only twice the diameter of Bolan's grenade, it was several times more massive, much longer, with room to pack an explosive charge that tore the enemy vehicle apart. Body parts flew, mixed with mangled metal and fire from the detonation. The other Hummer raced to get to a position where its gunner could get a better firing angle against the Black Hawk.

"Cooper?" Nakti asked as Bolan released his strap and somersaulted to the opposite side of the helicopter. The military pilot kept the helicopter still as the warrior changed sides to deal with the Spear of Destiny gunner.

The Executioner snared another loop of webbing, bringing himself to a halt as he stiff-armed the M-203. His hand was wrapped around the magazine of his M-16, making it an ungainly pistol, but his wrist and finger strength were sufficient to grip it firmly. Gritting his teeth, he pulled the heavy trigger on the grenade launcher, forearm muscles screaming as the weapon's recoil tried to wrest it from his hold. Bolan's strength had been sufficient to hold the 40 mm launcher steady, and his familiarity with the arcs of fire from grenade launchers had allowed him to make a spur-of-the-moment, nearly unaimed shot.

Instead of striking the hood of the enemy vehicle, Bolan had aimed slightly upward, planting his explosive charge in the general area of the gunner's protective cupola. While the other machine gun's armored shields had stopped shrapnel and minimized concussive force from an explosion five feet away, the HEDP shell impacted on the left wing. Metal deformed as six ounces of high explosive struck it, hot shrapnel cutting through the Browning's receiver and its shooter. The cupola was reduced to a mangled mess, the gunner blown in two. Bolan knew he'd never be able to make another shot like that in the same night, and his knuckles whitened around the nylon strap he gripped as Nakti guided the Black Hawk out of the line of fire.

Kamau reached out and wrapped his big, sausage-thick fingers around Bolan's wrist, hauling him across the floor of the aircraft. "What now? There's too much antiaircraft fire coming out of there!"

"Nakti, level this bird out for a second!" Bolan called out.

"Let me know when to go back in," the Egyptian answered.

Bolan stuffed his rifle/grenade launcher into a loop to secure it. It was a temporary solution, but now he had a hand free to give Kamau another shell. "As long as they can get Hummers into the entrance with Fifties, we'll be a target."

"So we risk taking a shot into the cave with this thing?" Kamau asked as he closed the breech on the recoilless rifle.

"They're not suicidal down there," Bolan answered. "They'll pull the Tochkas back to keep their warheads from being damaged. With the Hummers up front, there'll be enough to shield things."

"You to take the shot," Kamau suggested. "I'll see if I can keep their heads down with my Helwan."

Bolan accepted the big Carl Gustav, then pointed to his M-16/M-203. "Open your game with the grenade launcher. They'll be waiting for a reload with the first blast. Nakti, you'll need to tilt us a little. Unless you want another set of burns."

"I'll point you wherever you want," Nakti answered.

The Black Hawk pivoted and swooped around as Kamau wrapped the sling of the combo rifle around one shoulder. Perched by the pintle-mounted machine gun as he was, he'd be able to let the M-16 drop and swing out of the way in a heartbeat as he transitioned to the Helwan. Bolan stabilized himself in order to get the most accuracy out of his M-86. He'd been lucky to fire his grenade launcher one-handed and off balance with enough accuracy to strike the large area of a Hummer's roof and shielded machine gun once. He wasn't going to try a second shot on blind luck.

As soon as Kamau could see the entrance of the cave, he pumped the trigger on his grenade launcher. The 40 mm shell spiraled toward the entrance where a squad of riflemen had perched, ready to fire upon the Black Hawk as it had returned. Their rifles barked, muzzle-flashes further illuminating their position in the green haze of Bolan's helmet-mounted night-vision goggles. The Hummers remained farther back behind the gunmen, and for the present, they didn't have the angle to add to their pedestrian allies' fire. Kamau's grenade struck the ground right in front of the knot of

Spear of Destiny shooters, and a powerful shock wave bowled them backward.

Kamau's switch to the Helwan couldn't have been faster as he held down the trigger on the big general-purpose machine gun. Heavy bullets vomited from the muzzle at 800 rounds per minute, the natural vibration of the weapon and the motion of the helicopter creating a cone of devastation. The rain of lead finished off the wounded gunners, and Bolan could see the grilles of the heavy vehicles spark as they were struck. The Hummer's big machine guns started to open up, but drivers tried to back up, disrupting their aim. A line of tracers cut uncomfortably close under the Black Hawk, a near miss that would have unnerved a lesser warrior.

Bolan kept his cool, locked the M-86's scope onto a windshield and triggered his recoilless rifle. This time, the hot gases of the rocket-propelled shell vented out into the night sky through the far side of the cabin. True to his word, Nakti had given Bolan a proper angle to fire, tilting the helicopter just right. Bolan's aim had been slightly off. The fat, explosives-packed missile impacted on the cupola of the Hummer, not the windshield.

The 40 mm shell he'd used on the other vehicle had contained only six ounces of explosive and shrapnel. The Carl Gustav's shell was three and a half kilograms of high-powered shaped charge and copper cone. Whereas the prior Hummer's gun shield deformed and poured concussive backwash through splintered metal, this cupola disappeared in a violent flash. Metal didn't bend, it shredded, explosion-melted copper searing out into a spray of superhot metal that sliced through flesh and vehicle armor alike. The top of the Hummer that had

just been hit had become as much a weapon against
the forces at the mouth of the cave as the shell itself.
The explosive blossom that Bolan had planted reaped
a whirlwind of death as jagged metal and a wave of
high pressure pulverized Spear of Destiny soldiers with
nearly savage abandon.

Kamau continued to lay into the entrance with his
door-mounted machine gun. The Helwan belched out a
foot-long tongue of flame as an indicator of how many
bullets were going through its barrel. Every ninth round
was a tracer, and Bolan could see the line of Kamau's
fire as the tracers' magnesium cores ignited, making it
look as if laser bolts stabbed into the cloud of smoke and
debris thrown up by his rocket shell. The ferocious rate
of fire of the machine gun swept through the entrance.
That gave the Executioner an opportunity to load one
more shell to fully soften up the cavern mouth.

Muzzle-flashes flickered through the cloud, gunmen
having moved up in order to replace fallen comrades in
the defense of the hidden fortress. Some of the gunners
stopped as Kamau focused on them, delivering instant
death. It had taken a moment or two for Bolan to finish
the reload of his recoilless rifle, but he shouldered the
heavy weapon and fired it again. He'd run out of the
HEDP rounds for the big cannon, but he'd been able
to resort to HE shells. The three-kilogram missile was
devoted to delivering an explosive detonation, meaning it carried more of a charge than the armor-piercing
HEDP round, a large amount of space devoted to a cone
of copper that would turn into a superheated knife that
sliced through steel. The HE shell struck the ground
and the mouth of the cave, venting air and smoke upon

detonation. In the enclosed space of the fortress's entrance, the overpressure displaced atmosphere rapidly.

A consequence of that displacement was that soft objects, such as human beings, were crushed by the shock wave. Eyes and ears ruptured, and lungs were squeezed by the force of the concussion. Bones snapped and blood vessels tore while the liquefied froth that used to be brachial tissue was ejected from nostrils and mouths.

Kamau eased up on the trigger as the cloud at the cave entrance cleared. Corpses and twisted machines lined the corridor leading out of the cavern. Whatever was left had very little intention of putting up a fight, though his night vision could make out shadowy movement at the rear of the cave. He remembered from the photos provided by Metit and Holt that the passageway into the hidden fortress was measured to around thirty yards. Bloody bodies lined the floor like crushed insects, and the Hummer that Bolan had struck was a flattened, mangled curve of metal that gave no indication of its prior form. The HE blast had snuffed out flames on other Hummers, though shattered windshields gave the Ethiopian a glimpse of drivers mutilated by the glass that should have protected them. Machine gunners dangled off the roofs of the dead vehicles, their limbs flopped as if they were casually discarded rag dolls.

"Remind me never to piss you off, Cooper," Kamau said. He started to hand Bolan back his M-16, but the warrior shook his head, stripping his grenade launcher and magazine bandoliers to give to his ally.

"You'll need more maneuverable hardware than that RPK in close quarters. I also don't want to give up the firepower of the grenade launcher," Bolan said. He took one of his micro-Uzi machine pistols from his shoulder holster and opened its wire stock. The compact chatterbox would be ideal for the confined spaces he anticipated inside the fortress.

"You think there's going to be that much resistance?" Kamau asked, exchanging his bandolier of RPK mags for the M-16's.

"Let's go for overkill. If we don't need this much, then no loss," Bolan replied. "If we do need it, we'll be glad we brought it along."

Nakti's voice cut over their headsets. "You're going in?"

"Once you drop us off, look for the others," Bolan said. "They might need assistance, and if they don't, I'd like to have that Helwan covering me in case we need to make a fast exit."

Nakti took a deep breath. "I'd say just nuke the place. It's the only way to be sure."

"No, the only way to be sure that the Spear of Destiny and Redjedef don't rise again is to confirm the kill," Bolan replied. "I'm not leaving anything to chance."

"Godspeed, gentlemen," Nakti said as he swung the Black Hawk over a stretch of road just in front of the cavern.

Bolan grabbed the winch rope, rappelling gloves in place, and slid down into the darkness, Uzi hanging around his neck. Kamau followed him.

There was no turning back.

CHAPTER TWENTY-TWO

Hagan Abelard, the man who'd inherited the title of Eternal Pharaoh, watched from the command center's cameras as his soldiers were hammered by grenades, rockets and machine-gun fire. He had spent some time since his last effort at inciting a war making certain his plot wouldn't be interrupted, and now, it was gone.

One screen showed the Crescent channel, a pan-Arabian news network, displaying footage from an Egyptian news conference. It had been breaking news, interrupting all other programming, occurring almost exactly at the time that Khaldun had landed with his strike force. Rather than displaying the slaughtered corpses of students and teachers, laying the blame on their deaths at the feet of the Israelis, the men at the podium spoke of a conspiracy that had been tormenting Egypt for years.

When Abelard heard the name Redjedef, his stomach twisted. Decades of secrecy had been trashed in the space of a few moments. He knew it was something to do with that professor née spy Holt who had shown up at the university, but the primary cause of this nightmare of failure was the American, Cooper. Abelard rested his hand on his grandfather's old P-38K. He had prepared to unleash a storm of violence between Egypt, Israel and Syria. The three-way battle would have been the start of regime changes that he and allies around the Mediterranean had calculated would begin. Abelard was Egyptian by virtue of being born there. Both his grandfather and father had married Egyptian women.

Abelard still had piercing blue eyes, but his hair was brown, and his skin was olive. He wouldn't have fit in as the president of a new Egypt, but any such person would merely be a figurehead, easily replaced at whim. Abelard was too comfortable in the role of puppeteer to consider making himself a target for political assassination.

All of that disappeared with his "outing" on international television.

"Sir?" one of his men asked. "They've stopped firing on our position."

Abelard glared at the man, then frowned. "How many have we lost?"

"Thirty men and six vehicles," the lieutenant replied.

"Including the two caught in the open?"

"Forty men and eight vehicles," the man amended.

Abelard closed his eyes, pinching a knot between his brows. "Can we get the launchers out of the cavern?"

"There is too much wreckage in the way. We'd need tow trucks," the Spear of Destiny officer told him.

Abelard sighed. "Eighty men, five helicopters and eight Hummers gone in less than half an hour. Did Colonel Gahiji send an army?"

"As far as we could tell, a lone pilot ferrying one man," the Egyptian replied. "A scout party could have infiltrated the dig site without our patrols noticing, though."

"Which explains why our war bait disappeared,"

Abelard grumbled. "What do we have covering that entrance?"

"Three Hummers with mounted machine guns, and everyone with a rifle that we could spare."

"Numbers?" Abelard asked.

"Fifty or so," the lieutenant replied.

Abelard sighed. "You see my concern, don't you?"

The lieutenant nodded. "But we do what we have to."

Abelard clapped the man on his shoulder. "We're not defeated yet."

"Sir! We have a vehicle backing into the motor pool!" a technician manning a monitor announced.

Abelard felt his heart skip. A shred of hope dangled. If there was a Hummer crew still in action, then they could have been at work holding off Cooper. "Are there any sounds of gunfire?"

"Nothing yet," the tech confessed. "We lost our cameras in the corridor when they hammered it, and the microphones are dead, too."

"Even so," the lieutenant commented, "there were blind spots in the entrance we couldn't cover."

Abelard took a deep breath, his fingers tightening around the grips of his Walther. "No gunfire. Give the order to blast anything that shows up, even our own vehicles!"

The lieutenant whirled to a microphone to convey the order, but on the monitors, Abelard could see a battered Hummer with flat tires limp into the open, backward, with its rear bumper and wedge-shaped roof most visible. There was a machine-gun cupola on the top.

Abelard sneered as the enemy vehicle was the first to

open fire, a 14.5 mm KPV cannon flaring to life. Abelard watched as one of his remaining Hummers was torn apart under the assault by 990-grain armor-piercing incendiary slugs. The vehicle burst into flames as the high-powered slugs smashed through steel and ignited oil and fuel in the lines. The crew of the Hummer was no more lucky, since even an engine block was little protection against the heavy machine gun, designed to blast low-flying airplanes out of the sky.

"Fuck!" Abelard cursed. The other two Hummer gunners cut loose, managing to jar themselves out of their stunned state. A barrage of .50-caliber rounds slammed into the armored back of the commandeered vehicle, but the sloped rear of the vehicle and its armor allowed for deflection. The rear independent axles were shattered by return fire, but the fuel tank was still behind cover. The attackers had positioned themselves to make certain they could survive this initial conflict.

Abelard scowled and he pulled the Walther from its holster. "They're going to make it in here. All men, fall back! Fall back!"

"They can't hear me in there!" the lieutenant countered. "It's a war—"

Abelard pulled the trigger on his Walther, blowing the Egyptian's brains out. "Useless idiot."

The command center emptied as the Spear of Destiny force sought to escape their leader's rage. They were caught between a furious commander and an invading enemy.

Dying with a fighting chance was their preference, as Hagan Abelard snarled at the monitors showing the one man who had brought devastation to his front door.

BOLAN WAS GLAD that they were able to get the battered Hummer moving, its tires flattened by the tremendous pressure of explosions and the puncturing force of shrapnel. He and Kamau had dragged the corpses of the driver and the gunner out of their positions. Though the gun shield around the KPV heavy machine gun had been pockmarked and gore smeared, the inner sides of the armored wings, the mechanism and belt were in fine condition. It had taken only a few moments to ensure that the barrel was undamaged.

Bolan didn't want to be on the weapon when one of its massive 14.5 mm bullets hit an imperfection in the barrel, especially since he saw that it was loaded with armor-piercing incendiary ammunition. The lumbering, wheezing Hummer had lurched to a halt right where Bolan told Kamau to stop it, at a perfect spot where they still had plenty of rock to protect the vitals of the battered vehicle.

As always when it came to surprise attacks, Bolan had bought himself a few seconds' worth of free kills the moment he opened up with the monster machine gun. The unchallenged salvo soon ended though. The two remaining vehicles and their mounted machine guns thundered, and Bolan was thrown off balance as both independent rear axles were destroyed by incoming .50-caliber slugs. One of the armored wings began to deform under a stream of relentless autofire, and only the sheer luck of Bolan's being thrown off balance had saved him from catching a 750-grain bullet.

"Get down here, Cooper!" Kamau shouted.

The Executioner disregarded his ally's plea to retreat, knowing that he would end up even more vulnerable as he struggled through the gunner's hatch. What he could do, however, was remain semiprone behind his armored shields and pivot the KPV toward the remaining enemy gunners. The air around him was filled with rock dust and the racket of powerful bullets hammering on thick steel plate. Bolan triggered his KPV, but without being in position to use the sights, all he could do was spray and pray.

Holes began to appear in Bolan's protection, the massive enemy bullets slicing through the steel after a relentless hammering, but screams and small blasts resounded in the distance. The warrior kept up his pressure on the trigger, swiveling the gun as it belched out its slugs, each one of the massive projectiles carrying twelve tons of kinetic energy, double the horsepower of the enemy's 12.7 mm weapons. Bolan could see a jet of fire and smoke erupt skyward, and the hammering that the rock wall and his shields took suddenly stopped.

"Move!" Bolan snapped as he slithered backward. As he dropped into the Hummer, he noticed that the rear of the vehicle looked like a colander, the floodlights of the fortress's motor pool spilling light through dozens of holes. If it hadn't been for the lip of stone that offered their Hummer protection, Bolan realized that his legs would have been shorn off.

Kamau's big hands wrapped around Bolan's belt and tugged him through the door. The soldier paused, hanging on as he unclipped a hand grenade and dumped it into the back of the vehicle. Then he whirled and pushed Kamau along. The American and his Ethiopian ally ran full tilt for cover, diving behind the wreckage of another smashed car. The last remaining Hummer started its fire again, a few more shots slamming into the battered vehicle before Bolan's grenade erupted.

"What was that for?" Kamau whispered.

"Making them think they solved the problem we represent," Bolan answered. He unhooked another hand grenade, but left the pin in place.

Kamau checked the breech of his M-203, satisfied he had it loaded. He didn't need to be told that he'd have to pump out a 40 mm packet of hell on the Executioner's mark.

Bolan saw the shadows of riflemen advancing and popped the pin on his hand grenade. Kamau popped up and triggered his M-203 at the same time, both bombs hurtling toward the enemy. Kamau aimed low, just behind the wreckage of their old Hummer, while Bolan's weapon sailed farther and deeper into the entrance. Bracketed by explosions and shrapnel, the group that had ventured into the open was devastated.

After so much violence, the silence in the cavern was deafening. It took a moment for Bolan's ears to adjust. The post-detonation ringing faded thanks to the equalization of the pressure in his auditory canals. He heard the clatter of metal on the ground, an unmistakable sound of rifles being thrown down. Men began to call out in Arabic.

"They've given up," the Ethiopian translated.

"Reload and cover me," Bolan told him. He stood up and drew the second of his micro-Uzi machine pistols so that he had one in each hand. He was going for menace, and both fists bristling with weaponry. But he doubted that he'd need to fire a shot.

The Executioner stepped into the open, his face a

grim mask as he looked on the shell-shocked survivors. Many were waving white kerchiefs in surrender while others kneeled, empty hands in the air. Rifles, handguns and grenades had been piled away from the group of surrendering troops. Bolan was clad in black, wearing a vest festooned with spare ammunition, grenades and pistols, his hands full of stubby Uzi chatterboxes. His face was striped with black greasepaint supplemented with smeared dirt and gunpowder.

From the looks on the faces of his enemies, he had to have seemed like the wrathful god of war.

"Who speaks English?" Bolan growled, looking over the survivors.

One man lifted his hand higher.

"Where is Redjedef?" he asked.

The man pointed, his throat too constricted to speak. Bolan looked to see a hallway leading deeper into the mountain. Ancient pillars, pockmarked from the battle, displayed hieroglyphics. The warrior nodded to the Egyptians.

"Isoba! Unarmed noncombatants coming through!" Bolan bellowed.

He stared at the English speaker. "Walk away. Your pharaoh's eternity has ended."

The Egyptian nodded, translating for his allies. The survivors didn't need to be told twice as they scrambled to their feet. They started toward the exit but paused when they saw the massive Kamau step into the open, the M-16/M-203 combo up and ready. Bolan didn't envy the Egyptians as they skirted Kamau, who scowled at them as they continued their run to freedom.

Kamau joined Bolan, who then pointed the path that his prisoner had indicated.

"They're full of terror," Kamau noted.

"Good. That means they won't be interested in causing trouble again," Bolan answered. "We just can't count on that being the last of the resistance we'll face."

"Should I make a special delivery?" Kamau asked, nodding toward a hallway.

Bolan picked up a side mirror that had been torn off a Hummer in the gunfight and used it to look down the corridor without exposing himself to enemy gunfire. Four riflemen were at the far end of the hall, crouched and ready to repel an attack. Kamau, standing next to the Executioner, saw them, as well.

"Say hello to them," Bolan told him.

The big Ethiopian pointed the M-203 around the corner and triggered it. The grenade's detonation obscured the target, but Bolan knew that there wasn't going to be anyone left with the will to fight.

"Stay here in case someone gets past me," Bolan told Kamau.

"In other words, they fight their way past you, I put a grenade into their chest?" Kamau asked.

Bolan nodded. "And get on the horn to Eartha and Gahiji. We'll need a cleanup crew to take care of the Tochkas and their payloads."

"I've had my fun, so now I'm stuck with the paperwork," Kamau replied.

Bolan looked at his partner. "This isn't my idea of fun."

"I know," the Ethiopian replied. "Be careful."

Bolan walked down the corridor as the dust settled.

Silence surrounded him once again, only his footsteps accompanying him as he walked deeper into Redjedef's hidden fortress. Hundreds had died over the past few days. Fortunately, the Executioner had ensured that the vast majority had been enemies of humankind, pirates and terrorists who left nothing but fear and mayhem in their wake. He'd unleashed violence upon them before they could harm others, but there were still innocent victims who had been sacrificed by the madman who'd wielded the Spear of Destiny.

There was a survivor among the riflemen who'd been dug in at the end of the hall. One arm had been shorn off, and the right side of his face was a red smear. He rasped, trying to speak. Bolan could tell that he was in agony, and the warrior locked eyes with the mortally wounded man. He could make out the Arabic word for *please*. The man was suffering, and he wouldn't die easily.

Bolan pressed the muzzle of his Uzi under the agonized man's chin, then pulled the trigger. Mercifully, the light went out of his eyes forever. One more death due to a madman's plans.

"Touching," a voice echoed down the hall. Bolan made out the Arabic accent flavoring his words, though his English was perfect.

"Redjedef? Or should I just call you Abelard?" Bolan asked.

"I presume Holt told you our family name," came the reply, angry and defiant.

"She did. Now she won't have to worry about any black sheep haunting her clan anymore," Bolan replied, standing up.

"So you assume, Cooper," Abelard said. "Why not make this a fair match, like in those cowboy movies?"

Bolan looked at the micro-Uzi in his fist. Flecks of the wounded man's blood slowly dried on its barrel. Though the Egyptian was far from innocent, he was still another victim, a pawn of a greedy man who didn't care who died in pursuit of his desires.

"You think I've come all this way to satisfy your delusion that you deserve a fair fight?"

"I thought that you Americans—"

"You don't think about anything, Abelard," Bolan cut him off. "You act on a whim. Sure, you may meticulously plan and conspire, but it's all in service to your knee-jerk urges for power and self-gratification."

Bolan heard the metallic clack of a magazine entering its weapon's feed well. The heavy clunk of a bolt retracting preceded the snap of the top round stripped off the magazine. It was the unmistakable noise of an AK-47 being loaded.

"Self-righteous and never afraid to judge others," Abelard said with a sigh. "All right, if you're so interested in gunning me down like a dog, just remember that this could have been an even fight. That little popgun of yours doesn't have anywhere near the power—"

Bolan had pulled a fragmentation grenade from his harness. The pin clinked on the floor as Abelard yammered on about a "fair" fight, and the moment he got to the word *power,* the Executioner lobbed his deadly bomb down the hall toward the man.

"You fucker!" Abelard growled, triggering his rifle as the fragger bounced on the floor toward him. The

Executioner had gauged the distance to the madman thanks to the measurable metallic sounds created by the AK-47. A volley of 7.62 mm rounds sparked on the wall, but Bolan had already stepped out of the line of fire. The fragmentation grenade exploded with a force that shook the floor, and Bolan whipped back around the corner, the Uzi shouldered, with sights trained on the curling smoke left over from its detonation.

Cautiously, the soldier advanced, fully aware that Abelard had plenty of room to retreat from the hand grenade. He saw a twisted rifle on the ground as he closed in on the grenade's impact point. There was a trail of blood in the shape of a boot print, informing Bolan that his quarry still lived but was wounded.

The bloody footprints tracked around a corner, and the soldier paused. He leaned his head forward, listening for the slightest noise. The click of a hammer drawn back reached him. For a conspirator who had engaged in multiple long-term plots, he showed too much impatience when it came down to real combat.

Bolan bent and picked up the AK carefully, making no noise. He hefted the rifle, judging the distance that his opponent had traveled and the weight of the weapon. He then lobbed the weapon underhanded, throwing it through the air.

Surprised, Abelard acted on instinct, triggering his Walther, blazing away with four shots before he realized that he was shooting at a distraction. He poked his head out, and the Executioner locked onto him with the micro-Uzi. The stubby SMG cut loose on full-auto at 1250 rounds per minute, a rattling burst that homed in on Hagan Abelard's skull. A burst of 9 mm full-metal-jacket rounds pierced through the Eternal Pharaoh's skull.

There was no way that the madman was going to survive his wounds. At such an extreme rate of fire, the warrior's marksmanship and strength had combined to control the stream of death so that it excavated the man's brains from his skull.

Nearly decapitated, Abelard tumbled forward, flopping on the floor in a lifeless heap. Blue eyes, an unmistakable symbol of the German's heritage, stared lifelessly from a deformed face.

The hidden fortress was quiet now. Bolan dumped his partially emptied magazine, reloaded the Uzi, then turned to join Kamau and the others.

Egypt could sleep safely. The would-be king was dead.